"No one knows."

His tone was bleak, the words tripping over each other.

"No one will," she whispered, though that wasn't her place to promise. "I'll keep it a secret."

His laugh was a harsh bark. "What am I supposed to do? Just trust you?"

"Yes." The adrenaline in her blood spiked, and she leaned in closer, driven to comfort and consume him. "I'm very good at secrets."

He shook his head. "You don't—"

She had no idea what he was going to say, because she settled her lips over his. It was a ridiculous urge, born of panic and desperation and a deep-seated drive to calm him. Their lips fit together perfectly, and she moved them over his, tasting the faint hint of mint in his mouth.

Finally. Finally. Now she knew what kissing him felt like.

It was perfection.

He froze for a second, but then a growl came from deep in his chest. He tightened his hold on her, crushed her close, and kissed her back.

By Alisha Rai

The Forbidden Hearts Series

HATE TO WANT YOU
WRONG TO NEED YOU
HURTS TO LOVE YOU

The Pleasure Series

GLUTTON FOR PLEASURE
SERVING PLEASURE

The Campbell Siblings Series

A GENTLEMAN IN THE STREET
THE RIGHT MAN FOR THE JOB

The Bedroom Games Series

PLAY WITH ME
RISK & REWARD
BET ON ME

The Karimi Siblings

FALLING FOR HIM
WAITING FOR HER

The Fantasy Series

BE MY FANTASY
STAY MY FANTASY

Single Titles

HOT AS HADES
CABIN FEVER
NIGHT WHISPERS
NEVER HAVE I EVER

Hurts to LOVE You

Forbidden Hearts

ALISHA RAI

AVONBOOKS

An Imprint of HarperCollins*Publishers*

HURTS TO LOVE YOU. Copyright © 2018 by Alisha Rai. All rights reserved. Printed in the United States of America. No part of this book may be used or reproduced in any manner whatsoever without written permission except in the case of brief quotations embodied in critical articles and reviews. For information, address HarperCollins Publishers, 195 Broadway, New York, NY 10007.

First Avon Book mass market printing: April 2018

Print Edition ISBN: 978-0-06-256676-8
Digital Edition ISBN: 978-0-06-256677-5

Cover design by Nadine Badalaty
Cover photography by Michael Frost Photography (couple), ©Kasa_s/
Shutterstock (tattoo)

Avon, Avon & logo, and Avon Books & logo are registered trademarks of HarperCollins Publishers in the United States of America and other countries.

HarperCollins is a registered trademark of HarperCollins Publishers in the United States of America and other countries.

FIRST EDITION

18 19 20 21 22   QGM   10 9 8 7 6 5 4 3 2 1

For my family by blood, my family by chance, and my family by choice. I love you and I'm thankful to have so many places I can call home.

Acknowledgments

THE LAST book in a series always feels a little bittersweet, especially when so many people have helped, supported, and cheered me through writing every single word. I'd like to thank my agent Steven Axelrod and editor Erika Tsang, as well as the entire Avon team, for their enthusiasm for each Forbidden Hearts title. Sasha, Bree, Alyssa, Courtney, Beks, Leah, Bea, Sarah W., Aly, Corey, Allie, Rose, and Zainab, thank you for getting me through this year and helping me craft the stories I wanted to tell. Finally, Aai, Tai, Pinky and Ash, thank you for being my light in the dark.

The theme of this series was meant to be hope: hope that maturity and wisdom can conquer the most seemingly insurmountable obstacles, hope that love can triumph, and hope that we can be imperfect and accepted and adored as we are. My wish is that you enjoy these families as much as I loved writing them, and if you need it, that the Kanes and Chandlers refill your well of hope.

Chapter 1

GABRIEL HUNTER understood women's bodies. He'd studied them, touched them, decorated them with art, delighted in them, lusted over them. He viewed breasts and asses and thighs on a daily basis.

He shouldn't be fazed by a single inch of flesh. The human body should hold no mystery for him any longer.

And yet, here he was, salivating over a woman's bare arms.

Gabe rested his hand on the pristine linen of the tablecloth, his fingers itching. Her skin was so pure and luminous. What color was it? Not pale, not brown, not tan. Some people might call it olive, but he'd never been able to visualize that as a color properly.

"The dulce-de-leche cake is one of our bestsellers, with ribbons of golden-brown caramel threaded through the—"

Golden-brown, yes, that was a good description. Creamy, lit from underneath with a golden-brown light. There was a scar on her upper arm, disrupting the smoothness, but a good artist didn't expect any work of art to be flawless. Imperfections were what made a piece unique. Impossible to replicate.

Fuck me.

Gabe hid his grimace. Barely a foot separated them, but she might as well be on Mars for all he could touch her.

She was Evangeline Chandler. Roughly a dozen years younger than him, the sister of a man he called friend. Sweet and shy and innocent. Oh, and the daughter of one of the richest families in the country.

Him? He was a tattoo artist. The son of a housekeeper. A guardian of a secret that made any union between them complicated as fuck. Too friendly and respectful of women to be a player, but definitely not any kind of good long-term bet.

Mars, son.

Eve raised her gaze to his, and he snapped to attention, ensuring she only saw bland interest. She cocked her head, her straight, expensively cut dark hair slipping over her shoulder. The overhead light reflected on the strands, bringing out shades of mahogany, cherry, burnt umber.

"What do you think of this one?"

"It's perfect," he said without thinking.

Her brow furrowed. "It doesn't look like you've even tried it."

Oh. He looked down at the row of cake slices assembled in front of him. Cake. She was talking about cake.

Dutifully, he took a bite of the presented confection and swallowed. He had to fight not to screw his face up in distaste at the overly sweet explosion of flavor on his tongue. He took a giant sip of water. "It's . . . fine."

The man standing next to their table released a small sniff. Gabe had been around rich people enough to know exactly what that sniff meant. *Get the fuck out of here, you uncultured swine.*

Eve, being a rich person, could also undoubtedly read the waiter's sniff, but she didn't acknowledge it. "Livvy, neither of us like it very much."

"Oh, that was my first choice," came the feminine voice from the speaker of the phone set on the table. Only, with the speaker's cold, the words came out more like *Doh dat was by first choice.*

"It's very sweet."

"Ugh. I wish I was there."

Jacques linked his hands in front of his waist. "Once again, Ms. Kane, we would be happy to have the tasting at your home."

"She can't really taste anything right now," Eve explained.

"It's the saddest." Livvy sniffed.

"And the groom?" Jacques asked delicately.

Gabe suppressed an eye roll. The guy was digging for gossip, which was pretty standard amongst town people. Kane and Chandler drama was a favorite topic.

"My brother is busy today." Eve cast the waiter an inquiring look. "What's the next flavor, Jacques?"

Jacques placed a dish with a slice of light yellow

cake in front of each of them. The small, exclusive restaurant was closed to the public for this tasting. A tasting Gabe was sure had been granted due to the Chandler name. "A delicate lemon-thyme, Ms. Chandler. You'll find alternating layers of lemon curd and a rich vanilla buttercream, garnished with sprigs of thyme and candied lemons."

That sounded disgusting to Gabe's decidedly simple tastes. "Aren't most wedding cakes like chocolate and vanilla?"

Livvy made a derisive, nasally snort. "Nothing about this wedding is traditional. Why start with cake?"

True. Most people in Rockville were accustomed to the unexpected when it came from the Kanes and Chandlers.

Once upon a time, the Chandlers and Kanes had been best friends and business partners, each family owning half of a grocery store company, the C&O. Then, ten years ago, a series of tragedies had befallen the two families, starting with Robert Kane and Maria Chandler dying in a tragic car accident on a late winter night.

A minute later, and widower Brendan Chandler, Nicholas and Eve's father, had swindled Livvy's grieving mother, Tani, out of her half of the company. Two minutes later, and Livvy's twin brother, Jackson, was under suspicion of burning down the flagship C&O store in revenge.

At some point during that mess, Nicholas and Livvy had broken up, their childhood love destroyed. But they'd reconciled last fall, and had seemed destined for the happy ending they'd been cheated out of. They'd decided to get married on Livvy's birthday, which meant they'd only had a month to prepare a wedding following their engagement.

It might have still gone okay, but it felt like every possible calamity had befallen the bride and groom over the course of the last three weeks. The original venue had sustained damage in a storm. Nicholas had injured his back playing basketball. Livvy's dress had been mysteriously lost. The florist had burned down. The baker hired for the cake had canceled due to a family emergency. Multiple invitations had gotten lost in the mail.

When Livvy, upset, had come into the tattoo shop he owned and she worked at, Gabe had consoled her. Of course her mother was wrong and this wasn't a curse, he assured her. It was all going to be fine. He'd cracked a joke, she'd laughed. They'd all pitch in. It would come together. And things *had* started to gel.

Until Nicholas's and Eve's beloved grandfather, John, who wasn't in the best of health to begin with, had come down with the flu. Livvy's mother and aunt had been the next ones down. Everyone had held their breath, but John had recovered, and Tani and Maile's sickness had subsided to some sniffles. Then yesterday, Livvy had gotten sick.

There were no such things as curses or bad omens. But the bride getting sick a week before the wedding was awfully bad timing on the universe's part.

The waiter raised his voice to speak to Livvy. "It's not the usual sort of cake, but your reception will certainly stand out, Ms. Kane."

"Goo—" A sneeze interrupted Livvy's word. "Ah, fuck."

Gabe leaned forward. "Liv, why don't you go rest? We can handle this."

"No, no." A loud sneeze. "I want to participate. This is my wedding cake, damn it."

Gabe dug into the lemon cake. The taste surprised him enough he forgot to swallow fast. The sour from the lemon tempered the sugar, making it edible. He glanced at Eve and promptly forgot his own name.

Her eyes were closed, her lashes long fans on her upper cheeks. The fork slipped out of her mouth, the tines leaving indentations on her bottom lip. She didn't wear much makeup, but her pink lips didn't need adornment. "Mmm," she moaned, and a tiny part of him died.

He didn't like the cake that much, but he took another bite, if only to taste what she was tasting and enjoying.

This was pathetic.

She opened her eyes, and he wanted her to eat more cake. Hell, he wanted to buy her a whole cake and feed it to her, have her lick lemon and cream from his fingers.

And then have her lick whatever she liked on other parts of his body too.

"What do you think?" Livvy asked.

"I really love it," he said huskily.

Eve raised an eyebrow. Her eyebrows were the most dramatic thing about her, thick and arched. "Really? You haven't seemed to like the others at all."

He didn't like sweets, period, but he couldn't tell her that. Otherwise she'd wonder why he'd agreed to accompany her to this cake tasting. "They were okay." He tried to remember what the pretentious waiter had said about some of the other flavors. "But this cake, I was really captured by the ribbons of lemon threaded through the moist . . . sponge." Okay, that probably wasn't exactly right.

He could ignore Jacques's sniff because her lips twitched, and he wanted to pump his fist. Eve rarely smiled, and laughed even less often, he'd discovered.

Eve adjusted the phone. "We both like this lemon one, Livvy."

"Hmm." Paper rustled on the other end. "That one was pretty high on my list. Let's do it." A series of sneezes followed.

Eve nodded at Jacques, taking charge. "We'll do the lemon. You have the photos I sent over, yes?"

"We do, ma'am."

"Excellent. And please tell the chef how grateful we are he can accommodate us on such short notice like this."

"Oh no, ma'am. The chef is delighted to assist you. He conveys his deepest well-wishes." The man's eyes softened. "Your families have done so much for this town."

Both Eve and Livvy murmured their thanks. Gabe kept silent. He'd grown up in the Kane household, but as the housekeeper's kid, albeit a well-treated one, he'd always been on the outside looking into this world.

Eve picked up her phone. "Livvy, I'll call you later to talk about those other items."

"Gotcha. Bye, guys. Gabe, I can't thank you enough for pitching in."

Gabe placed his napkin on the table, relieved he wouldn't have to choke down any more sweets. Give him bags of potato chips any day. "No thanks necessary, kiddo."

"No one's given you grief over my canceling to-day's appointments, have they?"

One girl had yelled at him this morning. Gabe didn't blame her—Livvy's specialty was watercolor tattoos, and people traveled from all over to see her. But he wasn't about to tell the overwhelmed bride that now. "Nope. We have it handled. Feel better."

Gabe and Eve gathered their belongings, Eve shrugging on a light jacket that blessedly covered her lush arms.

Gabe squinted at the spring sunshine when they came outside. The last frost had passed, and the days were growing longer. The perfect weather for a hike, Paul would have said.

Gabe shoved the pang of grief aside. After al-most two years, Paul Kane's death shouldn't still feel so sharp, but reminders of his old friend often came when he least expected it. They'd grown especially strong since Livvy and Jackson had moved back home. Paul's younger siblings were nothing like him, but occasionally Livvy would smile or Jackson would roll his eyes, and Gabe would feel a need to excuse himself for a minute or so.

Eve finished typing something on her phone. "I can't believe we managed to get Chef José on such short notice."

"Is Jackson peeved he doesn't get to make the cake?" Jackson had a strong aversion to crowds, which was why Gabe was taking his place at Livvy's side in the wedding party. One of her bridespeople, as Livvy called them. A world-renowned chef, Jackson was instead handling the food for the event.

"I think between taking care of his café and his mother and making sure Sadia doesn't wear herself out with wedding planning, Jackson has his hands more than full. He was the one who asked me if we could outsource this. He'd prefer to concentrate on the wedding dinner menu." Eve tucked her phone into her purse. "Thanks for coming with. I know this task isn't in your wheelhouse."

"Is picking cake in your wheelhouse?" It was a genuine question. Prying details out of Eve about her life was like chipping away at a stone tablet. Time-consuming and a little hypnotic.

He might have been raised on the estate that neighbored the Chandlers', had even been best friends with Nicholas, but he'd been so much older than Eve she'd barely registered on his consciousness when they'd been young.

And then the split between the two rich families had happened. Though they'd lived in the same town, his interactions with the Chandlers had been sporadic at best. He'd seen Eve twice over the years—once when she'd come into his shop with a friend, and a second time when she'd been a drunken coed in a bar. He hadn't viewed her as anything more than a kid either of those times. A lost, shy, vaguely lonely-looking kid.

When grown-up Eve had been reintroduced into his life a month ago, at a lunch Livvy and Nicholas had hosted, that kid was long gone. Her body was curvy, her face innocent yet erotic, with full lips and sharp eyes. She was buttoned up inside and out, not a single emotion or spare inch of skin visible.

Lust and desire had hit him instantly, but he was a grown-ass man, and he'd tamped it down. Slowly, over the past few weeks, that desire had grown. And now here he was, salivating at the sight of her bare arms.

Good thing you can't see her ankles. You might straight up die on the spot from lust.

"I do eat a lot of cake."

He looked down at Eve. She was so sweetly rounded but so much smaller than him. He'd never been particularly attracted to short women, but he imagined she would fit perfectly under his arm.

Imagine is all you'll ever do. He made his tone deliberately light. "I eat a lot of burgers. Is there a wedding burger that needs to be chosen?"

Another twitch of her lips. "Please don't give

Livvy any ideas. We're at capacity on what we can whip together in the next week or so." Her voice was low and throaty. It skimmed over all of his nerves and senses, promising rough and lusty delights.

"I'll try not to."

They stopped at her car, a nicely maintained Acura. It was bland and personality-less. As were her clothes, a brown silk shirt and wine pants. She was like a painting framed with the most mundane of wood, but she'd shine no matter what she wore.

You sound like a smitten fool. You're too old for this.

Was he? No, probably not. But he was definitely too smart for this.

A strand of mahogany hair flew in her eyes and she pushed it away. Her wrist was surprisingly delicate for such a sturdy woman. "Well, thank you for coming with me today. I know you're probably busy making sure your shop will survive without you for the week."

"Nah, it'll be fine. Business has been on the slow side this month. Junie and Rod can handle anyone that turns up." His business wasn't a huge moneymaker, given the size of the town, but he was good at what he did and hired good artists. With social media and word of mouth, they did pretty well. Enough that he could afford to leave the place for a week when he needed to.

"Good." She hesitated, and something moved behind her eyes. Unable to help himself, he took a step closer.

"We're still on for meeting up at the house to-morrow, right?" After their first choice venue had fallen through, Nicholas and Livvy had opted to have their wedding at a large estate they'd rented a few hours away. They'd planned on the wedding party—him, Eve, Jackson, Livvy's best friend Sadia, and Sadia's son, Kareem—going up a week early to relax and unwind before the festivities.

Of course, that was before everyone had gotten sick. Since they were paying for the place, Livvy and Nicholas had insisted the rest of them go up, and they would join once Livvy felt better.

"Yes." Her smile was faint. "A little unconventional, a bridal party celebrating without the bride and groom."

As Livvy had said, the whole wedding was unconventional. "It'll only be for a few days. I'm looking forward to it." A week with Eve within easy reach.

Surrounded by others, though, including her big brother eventually.

Yes, it was safe. He would be able to control himself. Even if he did happen to catch a glimpse of something as scandalous and sexy as, like, her knees.

"Me too," she said. "There's an indoor pool."

It took a gargantuan force of will not to think of her in a swimsuit. He rubbed the back of his neck. "Is there anything else you need me for?"

"Um, no. I'm . . . I guess I should get going."

"Got a hot date tonight?" His tone was light, but the emotion that drove him to fish for info wasn't.

Mars.

"No. I have to attend the annual foundation gala." She lifted a shoulder. "I planned it before I left my job."

"Ah." Eve had worked for the Maria Chandler Foundation, a nonprofit established by her late mother, until she'd quit in the fall.

She hit the unlock button on her keys, and her car chirped. "What about you?"

Was she asking if he had a hot date? *Calm yourself. She's being polite.* "Might go to O'Killians. Have a beer or two." He forced himself to smile. Not too long ago, smiling had been easy for him, especially in front of pretty women. Maybe, if he drank enough tonight, he could recapture the cheerful veneer that had always masked every other emotion. Masked them so well he barely had to think about them. "Have a good time at the gala."

"You as well. I mean, not at the gala, but . . ." She cleared her throat. "Have a good night."

He reached past her to open the door for her, and his palm brushed her arm. Even though it was covered in fabric, an electric thrill ran through him. He jerked away, unable to temper the motion. She didn't appear to notice, thank God, slipping into the car and waving goodbye.

His hand lifted belatedly, after she had already driven out of the parking lot. He looked at his palm, which still tingled. Soft. Warm. Like the sunlight inside her skin had touched him.

He got inside his car and pulled his tablet and a digital pen out of his bag. Some tattoo artists carried sketchbooks, but he'd grown tired of having multiple scraps of paper cluttering up his life.

He was known for his fine line designs, and this one was no different. A sun interlocked with the moon took shape under his fingers, deceptively simple but so detailed and intricate it would jump off luminous skin.

When he glanced up, he realized he'd been sitting in the empty parking lot for almost an hour, lost in his own head. He shook out his fingers and put the tablet back in his bag.

It was fine—better he channel his desire for Eve into other things, like drawing. Maintaining a happy facade would be difficult enough next week, without adding in his desire for a woman who was way out of his league. No more bad omens could befall this wedding, and definitely not from his corner.

He started his car. Tonight, he'd go to the bar. Maybe he'd find some pretty girl. Someone actually attainable for him who wanted a good time.

He couldn't prevent the surge of distaste the thought of fucking someone else brought. He made a face. Okay, he wouldn't do that. But he could drink his desire away.

He just had to keep reminding himself, Eve was a fairy tale. And right now? He needed to deal in reality.

Chapter 2

THE CLOCK was about to strike midnight and Evangeline Chandler was wearing far too many clothes.

Or rather, the wrong clothes. Silk and satin and gold and diamonds were fine for the heiress to an empire, but they weren't right for her night job.

In a move practiced from years of wearing ball gowns, Eve discreetly lifted the hem of her skirt as she walked. Not too much, lest people think her gown wasn't couture and tailored to her body, but enough so she could take more than mincing steps. Ladies didn't run, though, especially in a ballroom.

In the nonprofit world, the more a charity gala looked like a party where a supervillain might take the guests hostage, the more of a success it was. This would be considered one of the finest parties in the county tomorrow, and she felt a spurt of satisfaction, though she'd never much enjoyed her position as event director at the foundation.

These were her peers, people who had grown

up as wealthy as her, with powerful families and trust funds. They had more vacation homes than they could count, and more modes of transportation than they needed.

They didn't know her at all, and that was fine with Eve.

"Eve!"

She lifted her lips in an approximation of a smile for the older woman bearing down on her. Braces had fixed the worst of her crooked overbite when she was a teen, but she'd never quite shed her self-consciousness over her two front teeth. "Bernice." She returned the woman's air kisses. Bernice was her parents' contemporary, but her skin was as smooth as Eve's. In another decade or two, Eve would have to make some inquiries as to where Bernice got her Botox from, because her dermatologist was excellent.

The woman's expensively colored and cut silver hair swung forward. "Everything is lovely. You organized a wonderful gala."

She started to demur the compliment. Party planning wasn't really a viable life skill, but—

Be proud of your accomplishments. No one will be proud of them for you.

Livvy's admonishment had been looping in Eve's head for months. Eve straightened her shoulders, as if her future sister-in-law had poked her with a prod. "We raised a lot of money."

Bernice grasped her hand and squeezed it. "Your mother would be so proud of you."

Eve gave no outward reaction, other than a

slight incline of her head. Bernice wasn't a malicious woman, but Maria Chandler's death had been a salacious topic for gossip for the decade she'd been gone. Eve had learned as a child not to feed the talk more with displays of emotion. Joy, sadness, hurt, anger. All of those things could be powerful tools in a vindictive person's hands. Better to hide them all.

Still, it was nice to hear about her laughing, vivacious mother from a woman who had been Maria's contemporary, so her "Thank you" was sincere.

Bernice fiddled with her pearl necklace. "Is your brother here?"

Aaaand here was the reason she'd stopped Eve. "No, he unfortunately couldn't make it. He sends his regrets." The Maria Chandler Foundation and the Chandler Corporation were independent entities, but the future CEO and current president of Chandler's would normally have been in attendance. However, even if Livvy wasn't sick, Nicholas wouldn't have come. Her big brother had sharply limited his public appearances lately. He didn't like to go many places without his fiancée, and a Kane and a Chandler showing up anywhere caused a minor stir neither Livvy nor Nicholas particularly enjoyed.

For their sakes, Eve hoped everyone got used to seeing the two of them together. It was going to get really tiring if the couple couldn't so much as get dinner without people marveling over the decade-long family feud finally being put to rest.

Bernice looked disappointed. Normally Eve would stay and smooth things over, but she couldn't right now. She glanced at her diamond-encrusted watch. Two minutes to midnight. A thrill ran through her. Yes, she was wearing far too many clothes. Her skin tingled. "I'm sorry, Bernice, I have to head out. A previous engagement."

People in this circle understood previous engagements. The words could mean anything: an assignation, a meeting, another party. The phrase was rarely questioned, and Bernice reacted no differently. "Of course, of course." They exchanged air kisses again, and then Eve was free.

Well, sort of.

She still had to walk sedately through the crowd, nodding and fake smiling at people. She started walking faster as she neared the exit, no one stopping her. The hallway was empty, and she picked up speed, jogging by the time she reached the hotel's main doors. She smiled distractedly at the valet and handed him her ticket.

It felt like forever for her car to be brought around, but it was, in reality, probably no more than a few minutes. She slid into the Audi and headed off, wincing when her tires squealed. She did love to drive fast, but not when anyone was watching.

She didn't go home, but to the storage unit she'd rented to store her cars. She pulled her sedate sedan into one bay. The 1960s powder-blue convertible next to her was covered, lest its pristine finish be scratched. The Range Rover on the other side of it was her larger car, meant for when she had to ferry friends around.

The five-year-old Camry to her left was a little more out of place.

It was a well-maintained car, but there was nothing remarkable about it. She'd bought it over the Internet, paid cash. The owner had been delighted she'd only given it a cursory inspection and hadn't quibbled at all over the price. Nor had he looked twice at the oversized hooded coat and sunglasses she'd worn to disguise herself. It had been in the next county over, but the Chandlers were fairly recognizable in most of the Northeast.

Eve unzipped the duffel bag in the back seat. By the light of the overhead fixture, she wrestled off her gown and heels and Spanx, and slid into the ripped jeans, comfortable white shirt she'd stolen from her brother's closet, and a hoodie. She donned a baseball cap, and then pulled the hood up over it, hiding her face and the elaborate updo she didn't have time to take apart, pin by pokey pin.

She checked her reflection in the window and tugged the hat lower to hide her face. It was a silly disguise, but it had worked for her so far.

She glanced at her watch with a frown and then rolled her eyes before snapping off the Rolex and tossing it in the bag. Eve bundled her couture gown and shoes into the duffel as well and threw it into the trunk. Then she got into the Camry and backed out.

Her nerve endings felt alive in a way they never had, and she couldn't tell if it was because of her super-secret-agent-style quick change, her undercover job, or the man she might see soon.

Of course it's the man.

A Gabe sighting twice in one day? It was like Christmas.

She zoomed through the street, going faster than she'd ever dared in her own car, but still no more than five miles over the speed limit. She wasn't a complete celebrity, but odds were good any cop who pulled her over would recognize her as the heiress to the Chandler fortune, and that would lead to too many questions. She went to great pains on nights like this to not be Evangeline Chandler.

She zipped from her upper-class neighborhood into the slightly seedier end of town. She had to dodge a few college students and various revelers as she made her way to the alley behind O'Killians. She couldn't park in front of the bar. It would be too obvious. But she still needed to be in close proximity so she would be the first person who got pinged when Gabe called for a lift.

She opened her Ryde app on her phone, clocked in, and placed the device in her dock. Then she sat back and waited.

A contract driver didn't seem like a natural job transition for a director at a nonprofit, probably because it wasn't. She'd left her job at the foundation in a spurt of independence and a desire to spread her wings, but then she'd run into a big problem.

Her name. Anyone and everyone was ready to

employ her. No matter how competent or incompetent she might be.

It was a princess problem, but it was a problem. She'd spent two months after she'd quit adrift, half-tempted to take her big brother's well-meaning job offers even though she'd rather stab herself in the eye with a banana than work for the family's corporation.

Then, over the holidays, when she was feeling especially lost and depressed by the lack of direction in her life, her roommate had urged her to at least get out.

"Go volunteer somewhere," Madison had said.

Eve had picked at her pajamas. It was noon, and putting on pants was far too much work. "People will recognize me." She was a Chandler. The youngest, the girl, the baby. The afterthought. The useless one.

Despair had pressed down hard, but she'd kept her face expressionless, because that was what she did, even around her best friend.

Above all, she wanted to hide from her name. The name she didn't really feel like she deserved to have.

Madison had tapped her foot. "So don't be you."

She'd huffed. "How am I supposed to do that?"

"I don't know. But hell, Eve. You gotta get out of the house. You're moping. Become a waitress. Or a Ryde driver, even. A position where no one looks too closely at you."

The idea had seemed absurd at first, but that night she'd opened her laptop and researched how difficult it was to be a driver for the most popular ride-sharing service. Frighteningly easy, she was startled to find.

And even more startling . . . she liked it. It had been exhilarating to drive people around, chat with them without the baggage of them knowing who she was. Sometimes she simply sat silent and listened to their conversation, on the phone or with each other. Couples feuding, or people on their way to a hookup. Mothers exasperated with their sons. Senior citizens eager to talk with anyone.

Her mother had liked to call her a sneak, and that was exactly what she was. She liked to fade into the woodwork and listen to people. Gather information, whether she ever used it or not.

At some point, what had started as a way to get out of the house and keep herself busy had transformed into something else. She'd started talking to the customers some more, memorizing their grievances. She'd scoured over her payments from Ryde, calculating taxes and expenses. Night after night, she'd come home and researched and read, trying to figure out where she would change things.

Obviously, she had no ability to change Ryde. But she could absolutely use it all as market research. If she set up a competitor service.

She'd grown up surrounded by entrepreneurs and businesspeople, and she'd assumed her disinterest in the family business and nonprofit meant she was an oddball. But in hiding from her name, she'd discovered she was more Chandler than not.

Eve made sure her doors were locked and rubbed her hands together, staring at the app as if she could will it to ping. She'd stopped taking fares as she drew up her business plans, but Gabe was the exception. Gabe was *always* the exception.

A couple of months ago, on a cold and blustery February night, she'd been driving around this area when her app had sounded. She'd taken a look at his name and photo and almost declined the fare.

When she'd been a kid, Gabe had seemed like a larger-than-life god. She'd felt the first stirrings of a crush for him as puberty hit, but then the tragedy had happened, and he'd essentially left her, like everyone else. She'd seen him a few times over the years, though, and one drunken night at a bar she'd even worked up her courage to approach him. He'd rejected her, which hurt, of course.

She'd surprised herself by accepting the fare. He'd come stumbling out of this very bar and gotten into her back seat. She'd pulled her hat down lower to hide her face, but he hadn't recognized her.

Most tipsy guys she picked up that late were content to either play on their phone or doze. He'd folded his long body into her back seat and said in his low, deep voice, "Evening, Anne."

It wasn't her name, but it didn't matter. She'd fallen quickly under his spell. They'd talked about something so mundane she couldn't even recall it—she'd been too focused on regulating her heartbeat and trying her best to disguise her voice—but the topic wasn't important.

The way he'd made her feel. Special. Aroused. Attracted to someone for the first time in a long time. That had been important.

She hadn't known at the time he'd be in a wedding party with her, or maybe she might have rethought this double-life nonsense.

Liar. You wouldn't have turned down more time in his presence, no matter what name he called you.

So here she was. Waiting for a man who knew her as Eve, the organized glorified trust fund princess party planner by day, and Anne, his trusty Ryde driver by night.

And he had no idea both women had a crush on him. Fuck her life.

Her app pinged and she jumped, almost dropping the phone when she grabbed at it. She wasn't a religious person, but she said a little prayer as she accessed the ride request. It could easily be someone else. He might not be out tonight. He could have gone to a different bar, and not this dive he seemed to prefer.

She clicked on the passenger.

Yes!

Gabe. Pickup location, the bar she was currently sitting behind. User rating 5.0, which made her perfectionist heart happy. She was also a 5.0.

She accepted the request and went to tidy her hair before she realized it was stuck under her hood and hat. It didn't matter what she looked like. She was careful not to let him see. Anyway, lately, he'd been more and more inebriated when she picked him up, which meant he was even less likely to recognize her.

She pulled out of the alley and eased up to the entrance of the bar. A huge figure stumbled out of the door.

She'd seen him less than seven hours ago, but the length of time didn't matter. Her breath caught.

Even drunk, Gabe Hunter was beautiful. He was huge and muscular, his face broad and usually creased in a grin. He was thirty-five now, and lines were carved deep around his lips, though she assumed they came more from smiles than age or frowns. The light from the neon sign of the door caught on the red in his too-long dark auburn hair, and when he came close, she knew his green eyes would be clear and dancing.

He wore snug jeans that encased his thick thighs, his T-shirt clinging to his flat stomach. What she'd do to lift that shirt and see his ridged abs. She'd glimpsed them, once, but she tried not to think about that mortifying experience too much.

She swiveled and faced straight ahead when he came close enough to see into the window. He knew her car now. Her back door opened and he slid inside, the car rocking a bit with his massive weight.

He could break her, and she didn't think she'd mind being broken. Her thighs clenched.

"Anne," came his boisterous voice. It was deep and slightly thick, his tongue rolling over her alias. "Fancy meeting you here again."

"Good evening, Gabe." She kicked herself as soon as she uttered the frosty greeting. It was what Evangeline would say, not Anne. She cleared her throat and put the car into drive. "Hey." She felt a little ridiculous deepening her voice, but since he'd been talking to Eve less than seven hours ago, she wasn't taking any chances.

"It's funny how you're always the one taking me home, isn't it?"

Not that funny. She'd figured out the app's algorithm worked purely off of distance on her second day. If she hovered around the bar when he was coming out, odds were she would be able to intercept his ride request.

If she wasn't a totally harmless stalker, she'd be concerned with how easy it was to game the system. When she got into the business, that would be the first thing she changed. There were weirdos out there! Clearly Ryde didn't have enough paranoid women working for them. "Yes. So funny."

"Favorite movie."

Her shoulders relaxed. He'd started this on their first night, and she adored it. Everyone thought they knew everything about her. No one ever took the time to ask her silly questions. Despite her subterfuge, she always answered honestly. It wasn't like he'd pause in a cake tasting to ask Eve her favorite movie. *The Sound of Music.*

"Classic. But don't you think it's weird the answer to how do you solve a problem like Maria is to marry her to a widower with ten kids?"

She swallowed her smile. "He has seven kids, I believe."

"Still a lot of kids."

"It may not be the most feminist message, no. But I watched it with my mother every year." Her mother had shared her name with Maria, and it had tickled young Evangeline to no end.

He stretched his legs out so far his knee bumped her elbow on the armrest. She didn't move away, and neither did he. "Aren't you going to ask me for my favorite movie?"

She edged her elbow back a hair, the contact thrilling her. "I know it."

"That right? What is it?"

"*Die Hard.*"

He guffawed. "I do like *Die Hard* a lot, but it's not my fave."

"What is?"

"*Star Wars.*"

"No."

"Why are you surprised?"

She peeked in her rearview mirror. "You don't seem like a geek."

He folded his big arms over his chest. "We come in all shapes."

"I suppose so."

He yawned, showing off his teeth. "I do like being driven around by you, Anne."

Her heart picked up, though she cautioned it not to. Twice now she'd picked him up and witnessed women hanging off of him. He was a ladies' man. Flirtation was as natural to him as breathing.

They went over a pothole, and he groaned. "Sorry," she murmured.

"Don't apologize. I'm sorry. I must have drank too much tonight."

She could sympathize. Her inability to process alcohol was legendary, though she assumed he'd drank more than her standard single glass of wine.

"Don't worry. I won't make a mess in your car, I promise."

"I'm not worried."

She split her attention between him in her rearview mirror and the road in front of her. When he rolled his neck, she cleared her throat. "Rough week?"

His laugh was without humor. "I've had better."

Since he'd spent at least two days during the week with her, she was a little insulted. She made sure to keep her voice deepened an octave. "Do you want to talk about it?"

He was silent for a moment. "Have you ever wanted something you couldn't have?"

Her heart thudded. It was like he'd peeked inside her soul and found the one sentence that described her life.

She had the money to buy everything, but the things she wanted couldn't be bought. Sometimes she felt like she was starving, even when she was eating four-course meals.

The ease with which she could buy four-course

meals was why she didn't complain. She didn't face the challenges a lot of people faced. But yes. There were many things she'd wanted, craved, even, and she couldn't have. "Yes," she whispered, then said it louder. "Yes. I have."

"I guess we all have."

She'd picked out chairs and cake and discussed flowers with this man over the past month. In the light of day, Eve would have never asked an intrusive follow-up question. Ladies didn't intrude.

But it was dark now. She wasn't Eve. She could ask. "What is it you want?"

He was silent.

She overtook another car, though she resisted the urge to speed easily. Speeding now meant she'd get him home quicker. "The thing you want—what's stopping you from getting it? Is it you, or is it someone else?"

"Both, I suppose."

She tried to think of what her therapist or her friend Madison would say. "You can change your behavior. You can't change someone else's."

"Hmm."

She glanced in the rearview mirror. His eyes were closed, head back. She thought he might be asleep, but instead he spoke. "I'm going on a trip tomorrow."

Her fingers clenched around the steering wheel. "That's nice." Her heart stopped, then started up again at the reminder of how dangerous this was. In a week, she was going to be standing opposite this man at an altar. Hell, starting tomorrow, she was going to be spending the week with him in a not-nearly-large-enough estate four hours away from Rockville. The home they'd rented wasn't far from where they'd all used to vacation growing up. She knew exactly how remote it was.

If Gabe recognized her as his friendly neighborhood Ryde driver . . .

"Maybe I'll find what I'm looking for there."

If what you're looking for is a girl you treat like a little sister who has had a massive crush on you forever, then you can find her right here, right now, sir.

Only that was foolish, because he obviously wasn't looking for any of that. "Is the trip for pleasure or for work?" She should stop poking at the hornet's nest and stay quiet. Any second he could realize who she was.

"A little of both. I'm in a wedding party."

She swallowed. "Exciting."

"Yeah. She's—the bride—she's like my sister."

Evangeline couldn't help but soften. Livvy and Gabe did seem to have a tighter bond than most employers and employees, but that was what happened when you grew up together. "I'm sure it'll be romantic." Personally, she'd been working like mad for the last three weeks to make her brother and Livvy's day as special and romantic as possible.

It hadn't been easy, especially with the curse . . . that is, the not-curse trying to screw everything up.

"You a romantic?"

She wished she could deny it, or rather, she wished it weren't true. She loved romantic love.

She dreamt of a man swinging her around in his arms and kissing her on her forehead and looking at her like he adored her.

She couldn't say any of that, though, because strong women didn't confess to being foolish romantics, right? And more than her love-starved heart, she wanted to be strong. So she shrugged. "I suppose. Are you not a romantic?" He was a flirt, for sure.

"No," he said shortly.

Oh. She rolled her lips in to stop herself from bombarding him with a million questions about that flat denial.

He shifted, his knee bumping her again. "Wake me when we get home, will you?"

His home. Not theirs. "Certainly."

"I like the way you talk sometimes," he murmured, half asleep, and totally unaware of the way her heart exploded into confetti at that confession.

He didn't like her. He liked things about her, and that wasn't the same. And he didn't really even like things about her, because he didn't even know her.

She didn't speak the rest of the way, taking comfort in the way he breathed even and deep in the back seat of her car.

This is mildly creepy.

Well, no shit, it was. She'd been obsessed with Gabe for years, especially after their run-in a few years ago, but she'd managed to limit her obsession to peeking in on his social media and scouring his website—activities that were slightly less weird than this.

Maybe just a different level of weird.

For sure, deliberately manipulating an app so she could get to know him was a whole new level of obsession.

But since he was asleep and because she was a creep, she took the long way to his house, through winding roads and a rural stretch where gardens were starting to peek up through the frozen ground. All too soon, she pulled up in front of his tidy little brick home.

She turned slightly, making sure nothing but her profile was in view. Not that it mattered. He was dead asleep. She cleared her throat. "Gabe?" Ugh, she loved the way his name sounded on her lips.

He didn't move. In the light coming in from outside, she could see his long lashes resting on his high cheekbones. His chest moved up and down in a deep, steady rhythm.

Now is when you kidnap him, said the devil on her shoulder. *Take him to your lair and do with him what you will.*

Such a creep. "Gabe?" she said a little louder.

His only response was a snore.

She couldn't let him stay in her car all night. He'd recognize her in the morning for sure. "Gabe!"

He snuffled and rolled his head one way, then the other. His shirt tugged at the buttons, revealing a tiny glimpse of a white ribbed fabric.

She stared at that little slice of cotton for far too long. An undershirt shouldn't be sexy.

Except . . . what if it was a tank? And what if he took his shirt off and then he was just in that white ribbed tank, and maybe a little sweaty and there was a smear of dirt on his face and he was working on her car? And what if his muscles bulged when he leaned over and picked up a wrench?

You don't even know if he likes to work on cars.

She shook her head and tugged her cap lower, making sure her face was as obscured as possible. Then she got out and trudged around to open his door.

Her hand hovered over his shoulder. It was one thing to borderline stalk him. Another to make physical contact.

No, all of those things are terrible.

With one finger, she tapped his shoulder lightly. "Gabe?"

Nothing. She dared to grasp his shoulder, trying not to notice how hot and solid it felt under her touch. "Gabe? We're home." She shook him, and his head rolled back.

His eyes blinked open and he stared up at her. "Anne," he slurred. "You have the prettiest lips."

Chapter 3

GABE WAS usually great at telling women exactly what they wanted and needed to hear, generally because he sincerely meant whatever he was telling them. But he knew immediately he'd said the wrong thing.

It was just that Anne was standing with her back to the streetlight, and that silly hoodie cast most of her face in shadow, but he could see her lips. They were pink.

And familiar.

He searched through his alcohol-soaked brain for why they were familiar. He came up empty. But he wasn't so drunk he couldn't identify how her lips tightened.

"Thank you," she said.

"You don't mean that."

"Excuse me?"

"You're annoyed. If you want to tell me to fuck off, tell me to fuck off. I shouldn't be commenting on your lips." He hiccuped. Thank God it wasn't a belch. "It's ina-inapprop—it's not right."

"It's not?"

"I mean, no. Right?" Wasn't it inapprop—not right? She was in his service, albeit only for the length of his drive.

Those lips pursed again while she thought. There was something familiar in that too, in her hesitation before uttering words. "I'm not annoyed. I was surprised."

Her hand on his shoulder registered. The heat of it penetrated through his shirt, right through to his skin. It was nice. "I don't want to surprise you." What did he want? He wasn't even sure anymore.

Her fingers curled in, the tiniest bit, and then her hand was sliding away. "We're home. Uh, you're home."

"We are?" He looked past her, at his small house. The lawn was starting to grow, a sure sign of spring. He'd be mowing it soon, a chore he enjoyed. "Why is the sidewalk so crooked?"

"It's not."

"Looks crooked." She skittered back when he moved, and he felt bad. He tried to make his body smaller as he stood, hunching his shoulders so as not to overwhelm her small frame, but that made him overbalance. He grasped the door when he staggered. "Whoa."

She hovered, twisting her hands together. Her baggy hoodie barely left her fingers uncovered. He'd never seen her in anything else, had no idea what her body actually looked like under those huge clothes.

Whoa. Why was he thinking of his driver's body?

He liked Anne, was always happy when they matched up. He liked talking to her. He didn't *like* her. He was a flirt, but he was careful of who he flirted with. Women at bars, yeah. Waitresses, bartenders, drivers? Women he was paying for a service? No.

But those lips.

"Are you okay?"

"Sure. I'm always okay." He cautiously let go of the door and shut it, a thud that made him wince. He took one step, then another, and then he grew cocky, because he looked at her instead of his feet on the third.

He stumbled, but before he could fall, she was at his side, her body propped up under his. "I can help you."

"I'm okay."

"No, you're not."

Yes, he was. He was a man. A manly man! He could work a grill and chop firewood.

He straightened, but then he realized he wasn't actually straightening, just leaning on her harder.

He deflated. No, he was not okay. But he didn't know if he wasn't okay because he was drunk or because his brain was firing up with even more not-right thoughts, like how good she smelled, like some sort of expensive perfume. She was smaller than he'd thought before, barely coming up to his breastbone. *As small as Eve.*

He shied away from that thought. He'd done a pretty good job all night of not thinking about Eve. He wasn't about to fuck up now, after he'd invested so much time into pickling his brain so that weird tension choking him would go away. "I'm so sorry," he muttered, and the remaining sober part of his brain cringed at how slurred his speech was.

Fuck, she was going to one-star him, and then he'd have boring, impersonal drivers forever. He'd grown fond of their chats.

He deserved it. Carrying his drunk ass into his house definitely wasn't her job. Shame shot through him. He adjusted his grip around her shoulders so she wouldn't be forced to bear as much of his weight. "Thanks for helping."

"No problem," she said, and he peered down at her. Her voice sounded different, but the alcohol was making it really difficult to pin down why.

Maybe it was the breathlessness. He tried to lessen his weight on her more, but he almost overcorrected backward, and she had to haul him close. For a second, he felt every round, soft inch of her against him.

No, no, no. "Ugh, just leave me here."

"We're at your door." A tiny hand extended in front of him. "Keys?"

He stared at that hand for a second. "Huh?"

"Your keys?"

"Oh yeah." He propped himself up against the wooden frame. He'd never been so delighted as the day he was able to afford this house. His big sister had offered to buy him the mansion of his choice, anywhere in the world, when she'd struck it rich in the tech world, but he'd wanted something he'd bought and paid for himself.

Something that would prove to the town and to the world he was more than an abandoned, unwanted charity case.

He shook the dark thoughts away and dug in his pocket. He pulled out his keys, handing them to her. There was no way he'd ever be able to fit a key into a lock in this current state.

Or anything into anything, for that matter.

Yikes, way too inapp—not right, these thoughts.

"Gabe!" Her voice sounded like it was coming from so far away, and there came that body, pressing up against his side again. His arm automatically went around her shoulders. Her sweatshirt was old and cheap, the cotton catching on the calluses of his hands.

She should be out getting more fares, not caring for him. He'd send her off, but Jesus, had he almost fallen asleep standing up? He started to tell her he was fine now that he was a foot away from crossing the threshold, but truth be told, he wasn't sure if he was. The floor lurched with every step he took into his home, his head ringing when she closed the door behind them.

"You shouldn't come inside passengers' houses," he had the strength of mind to scold. "Especially when they're in this condition."

"Are you going to hurt me?"

He looked down at her head, hating the hoodie. He wanted to see her hair. He wanted to see her face properly, here, where he could catalog her features by the faint moonlight. "No. Never."

"Then I think we're okay. Where's your bedroom?"

He nodded at the stairs. A small beam of light bounced on the wall, and he frowned before realizing she'd turned her phone's flashlight on. On their way up the stairs, they knocked into one wall, then the other, and he had to take a deep breath and use every ounce of sobriety left in him to focus. "A serial killer would say the same thing."

"Huh?"

What had he been saying? Oh yeah. "A serial killer would tell you he's harmless, and then by the time you wind up with your head in a freezer, it's too late."

"Your Ryde rating wouldn't be a perfect five if you were stuffing all your drivers' heads in freezers."

He had to untangle that to find the flaw in the logic. "But they'd be headless and therefore unable to rate me."

She wheezed out a laugh and he tucked it close into his sandbox of perfect sounds he'd heard.

"I don't understand whether you're trying to convince me or you that you're going to behead me."

He narrowed his eyes at her joking, but that made the floor difficult to see in the dark. "You don't know me," he insisted. He didn't know why he was so determined to chase her out, when she was the only reliable thing in his life right now.

Right now in general, because she always came when he called, and right now in particular, because she was the only thing keeping him from face-planting.

And wasn't that so sad, on both accounts?

He didn't trust reliability, not really. If you got used to someone, it would hurt a billion times more when they left.

"I know you're a decent man. You wouldn't hurt any woman."

He opened his mouth, then closed it again. Truth. He adored women, for all that he was incapable of committing to one.

They stumbled through the dark hallway, her phone's flashlight guiding them. He could turn on one of the overhead lights, but it would only make his eyes hurt, and she seemed fine with this.

They made it into his bedroom, and he toed his shoes off while she held his arm, and then it seemed like whatever had been powering his body abruptly shut off. He could no longer control his arms and legs fully. He looked down at his bed, knowing the sequence of events that had to follow. Remove his arm from around her, get on the bed, under the covers.

Instead, he simply . . . toppled. Without grace or ease or anything that would lend itself to a remotely not-silly-looking fall.

He didn't realize he hadn't taken his arm off her first until he found himself on top of her, their bodies pressed together, hips, legs, and chest.

Oh no.

The bill of her cap jammed into his forehead and he nudged it up, but his nose was smushed against hers, so it was hard. He tried to hoist himself up, but his biceps felt like they'd been carved from jelly.

Fuck. He'd wondered now and then what his driver looked like. Finally, he was in a position to see her whole face, not in puzzle pieces but as a perfect picture, but it was too dark to properly see anything. Except her eyes. They were dark and wide, the whites around her pupils brilliant in the room lit by moonlight.

"This seems to be a weird way to start the beheading process."

Oh my God. "I'd never . . . So, so sorry," he said. Or he thought he said that. He wasn't sure anymore. "I didn't mean . . . Let me . . ." He tried to lift himself off her again, but this time it was her hands that stopped him.

They were small and cool, moving over his heated face, around to the back of his neck. "It's okay," she whispered. "Stay here for a minute."

"You . . . sure?" he confirmed. He was the drunk one. She was not.

She relaxed underneath him, yielding to his larger body. Her legs shifted, and his pelvis slipped easily into the cradle of hers. "I like it. You're heavy."

"Too heavy."

"No. Perfect."

He wanted to argue with her. He was not perfect, and she should not be here, and yes, he could totally still be a murderer intent on decapitating her.

But her body was so soft, and he could feel every inch of it. The only good thing about his alcohol-soaked brain was he was too drunk to have an erection, thank God. How embarrassing would this be if he was poking her belly?

Her breasts were plump and round under his chest, smushed against him. Eve. She felt like what he imagined Eve might feel like.

Jesus Christ. How could he suddenly be interested in one woman because she reminded him, in the vaguest of ways, of another?

Except . . . he was. And she was here, and real, and not the fantasy Eve was. "Go out with me."

Her hands faltered on his shoulders, but then they resumed that calming, stroking motion. "Go to sleep."

It was like she'd said the magic words. His eyes closed, his body relaxing. With his last conscious thought, he turned his head, his lips brushing her hood aside so they could scrape over her ear. Her curvy body shivered, and he filed that reaction away as best he could. When he was sober, when he was capable of thought again, he was going to do that to her while they sat on his couch. He'd peel every layer of her clothes away and kiss his way down her chest and stomach too, but he'd be sure to pay some attention to Eve's ears.

Anne's. Anne's ears.

He nuzzled her neck. "Don't give me a bad rating, 'kay?"

EVE HAD never found herself in this predicament—namely, how to get out from under a massive wall of muscle and man.

Eve stared up at the ceiling. Her phone had fallen when he'd dragged her onto the bed, and her flashlight cast a circle of light above her. She wriggled a little. Her legs had fallen asleep, squished by his, and her boobs were hurting, sandwiched by his chest. Discomfort aside, though, this was nice. He smelled a bit like bourbon. She sniffed. And the outdoors.

Okay. You've gone past the point of helping him. Now she was straight up perving on an unconscious man.

Go out with me.

She bit her lip. He hadn't meant it, or if he had, it had been directed at Anne, not Eve. He'd reject her if she was Eve. She knew, because they'd already played that scenario out in real life once.

Rejection wasn't something she was well equipped to handle. Not because she always got her way, but because when rejection did come it felt fierce and cruel no matter how it was delivered. Even a gentle "no, thank you" or chastisement left her craving a dark spot to lick her wounds and obsess over all the things she'd done wrong.

Have you ever wanted something you couldn't have?
So many times. So many, she'd found it easier

to shove her desires down, far away. Because if she didn't try to satisfy those desires, then she wouldn't have to deal with the pain of being rejected.

As she'd been told so many times, she could only change her behavior. She couldn't change others'. So she'd changed her behavior to make sure others couldn't hurt her with their behavior.

She licked her upper lip, grimacing at the salt of her sweat. Between his body, the room temperature, and her sweatshirt, she was far too overdressed.

She inhaled one last time, savoring the hint of Old Spice and the forest. He didn't just look like a lumberjack! He smelled like one too.

Heart eyes.

Time to stop smelling him.

Easing out from under him was no easy trick, especially when she had to be extra careful not to wake him. He snorted and snuffled a bit, but either he was a deep sleeper or the alcohol had made him that way. She got one leg on the floor, and squeezed her torso out gracelessly.

Her left arm was still stuck under him and she pulled as gently as she could. She froze when he groaned and rolled away, onto his back, catching her arm further under him. The faint light from her phone made his roughly hewn features vaguely sinister. In that sexy way.

This is not better than smelling him.

She yanked at her arm, finally freeing herself. She waited a beat, but his breathing remained steady and regular. She leaned down and scooped up the fallen phone. The narrow beam of light bounced around the room. The place was small, but tidy, no clothes lying around or excess clutter. If she were still sniffing around like a perv, she'd say his room smelled like him too.

She made her way out of his room, closing his door as quietly as she could, and then crept down the stairs, shoving back her hood and ripping off her hat so she could fan her overheated face with it. She got to the bottom step and her flashlight happened to angle to the left, to the living room, sweeping over a gray leather couch and a fireplace. There were a surprising number of bookshelves ringing the room. She'd never have pinned him as a reader.

She cast a guilty look over her shoulder, up the stairs. She was not going to creep around his house, compounding her weirdness. For one, every second she stayed here, she was at risk of being found out. So far, the darkness, her silly disguise, and his intoxication had all worked in her favor, but that wouldn't last forever.

Second, this was all morally questionable.

Gah.

She crept into the living room and toward a shelf. In a second she would leave, but since she was already here, she could glance at his books, right? That wasn't intimate. She wasn't sniffing his underwear. Or him. Anymore.

She scanned her light over the spines on the shelf closest to her. Art history mostly, which shouldn't surprise her. The man owned a tattoo parlor. What were tattoos but pieces of art? Livvy had showed her pictures of designs she'd done, and they could easily have been in any museum.

Eve had scrolled through Gabe's social media more than once, taking note of every photo he'd posted. He seemed to favor tiny, intricate designs and delicate script. So odd, paired with his big body and frame.

She took a few more steps, and her light dipped over a cluster of frames. She couldn't help but smile at the first one. It was a family photo that must have been taken not long after Gabe was adopted. He was in his mother's deceptively fragile arms, his ginger head resting on her shoulder, a green blanket clutched in his fist. He was pudgy, his tan face round and sweet and serious. Sonya Hunter was smiling at the camera proudly, one dark brown hand resting on Gabe's bottom. A tall, handsome black man stood at her side with his arm tight around his wife, holding a little girl a year older than Gabe, her hair braided and tied with pink ribbons.

Gabe's sister, Rhiannon. Though Eve hadn't known her well, she was infamous in Rockville. She'd gotten into every single Ivy League college, and then ditched Harvard midway through her sophomore year to run a tech start-up in Silicon Valley.

Eve touched Sonya's face. She had fond memories of Gabe's mother. Eve had been so much younger than the Kane children and Nicholas that she'd always felt left out of all the fun, but Sonya had always taken an extra second to pull her in for a hug when she was roaming the Kane household alone, hunting for someone to play with.

She shifted over to the next photograph. This one was of Tani Oka-Kane, surrounded by her children, and Gabe and Rhiannon. Tani wasn't smiling—even now, the woman wasn't a fan of smiling—but there was a light in her eyes that didn't really exist anymore.

Sorrow moved through Eve. After her mother had died, Eve had missed out on a lot of things, but one of those things had been having a second and even third family at the Kanes' home. There had been nowhere to escape her father.

She moved down the shelf, and then stopped. *Speaking of fathers.*

She hadn't seen a picture of a young Robert Kane in a long time. In her brain, he was forever memorialized as the man who had died in a car wreck on the icy road leading to the Chandler family cabin, her mother in the passenger seat.

Rumors had swirled after the accident that Robert and Maria had been carrying on a longtime affair. There had been no good reason for the two of them to be on that road together that night— Robert should have been in Pennsylvania, Maria in Manhattan on foundation business.

For a while, Eve had wondered if those rumors were true and dreamt about Robert Kane being her biological father. But that dream had vanished when she was fifteen and stuck in the hospital, getting blood drawn left and right. Brendan was definitely her biological father, unfortunately.

Eve eyed the picture wistfully. Robert had always positively beamed at his three children, and he looked similarly delighted in this photo. She peered closer at the photo, trying to suss out when this had been taken. Was it Paul or Livvy or Jackson he was holding?

The floorboards above her creaked and she startled, turning the flashlight off on her phone, plunging herself into darkness. Heavy footsteps sounded and she flattened herself against the shelf, holding her breath.

Oh no. Oh no.

The plumbing clanged and she jumped, but then a flushing noise came. She counted the heavy footsteps, and released her breath when all was quiet again. Time to go.

She engaged the lock on his front door before she closed it. In the interests of caution, she usually went to the storage unit and switched cars, but she was too exhausted for that tonight. She drove home on autopilot.

Go out with me.

Her body tingled, both from his touch and the words. It was so weird to have gotten what she'd thought she wanted and to also feel like someone else had gotten that something. Was it possible to be jealous of herself?

Her lips twisted, and she repeated the words designed to keep her excitement at bay. He hadn't meant it.

She pulled into her garage and glanced down at her hands, opening and closing them to still the slight tremor in her fingers.

That was when she noticed her bare wrist.

Oh no.

She checked her car, including the duffel. Her bracelet was nowhere to be found. It had been her mother's, before she'd become Maria Chandler and had simply been a pretty young girl named Maria Kritikos. A plain gold bangle, it looked cheap and out of place with all Eve's other jewelry, but it meant more to her than the rubies and diamonds and platinum. It was like her touchstone when she became overwhelmed or frightened, something that could calm and ground her instantly to the present.

Shit.

She thought of how she'd yanked her arm out from under Gabe and slapped her forehead. Oh no. Her hand was bigger than her slender mother's had ever been, but she'd probably exerted enough force to pull it right off. She could have easily left that bracelet in his bed.

She breathed in and out slowly, trying to still the panic rising inside her. There was no need to fear recognition. He'd really only known Eve as an adult for the past month, right? He definitely hadn't noticed she wore this bracelet quite a bit. Her mother's initials were inscribed on the inside, but it would be even more unlikely he'd connect *M.K.* with her.

Sorrow moved through her, loss hitting her as

the panic subsided a bit. It was such a tiny piece, but it was a piece of her mother.

Go ask him for it.

She shoved her hand through her hair, the impossibility of that course of action hitting home. *Have you ever wanted something you couldn't have?*

Always, it seemed.

Chapter 4

Eve CRAVED a hot bath and a cold drink, but the instant she saw the light on in the living room of her condo, she knew she wasn't going to get to escape.

"Eve?" Madison called out. "Is that you?"

It wasn't that she didn't love her roommate. She just didn't want to talk to her right now. She felt too raw and vulnerable to talk to anyone, and Madison saw too much.

No choice, though. If she jetted off to her room, her friend would definitely realize something was up. Eve unzipped her hoodie and gave up on being quiet, walking to the entrance of the living room, trying to seem casual, even if she was scraped up inside. "Hey."

Madison glanced up from the cross-stitch she was working on. A *Golden Girls* rerun blared on the television screen. She had a scarf tied around her hair, and wore one of her boyfriend's oversized graphic comic T-shirts. Her friend's gaze dipped over her. "Interesting look for the gala."

Eve's lips twisted. "Haha."

Madison studied her. "What's wrong?"

"Nothing." She shrugged off the sweatshirt and draped it over the armchair. After much argument, Eve had been the one to buy all of the furniture for their place, but only after she'd sat Madison down and showed her friend the statements from her trust fund. Furnishing a condo was nothing to Eve. It would be far more expensive for Madison, who was just starting her career, with little financial help from her family.

"Something's wrong."

Eve lifted her shoulder. "I lost my mother's bracelet." It wasn't a lie. It wasn't the only thing wrong, but she was upset about it.

Madison made a sympathetic face. If anyone knew what that bracelet meant to her, it was Madison. "Can I help you find it?"

"No, it's . . . it's gone." Because life wasn't a fairy tale, and sometimes you didn't get everything you wanted. She walked over to the kitchen and opened the fridge, grabbing a can of sparkling water.

Madison raised her voice slightly. "Are you sure there's nothing that can be done?"

There was, if she wasn't so weird and inept at life. She popped the tab of her drink and made her way back to the living room. "No."

"You seem really upset. Want to talk about it?"

Madison was a clinical psychologist by profession, and Eve tried not to let their friendship get so imbalanced that the other girl felt like she was Eve's therapist. Eve had a therapist. She'd had a string of them since her mother had died and Nicholas had demanded she see someone.

She could have quit once she became an adult, but her visits had become a habit, like tennis lessons. Over the past year, she was glad she hadn't quit. The woman she saw now was a little stodgy, but out of desperation, Eve had opened up more to her than anyone else. In return, the older woman had listened well and given her a number of helpful coping strategies to manage her emotions.

Like using her mother's bracelet as an item to ground her. She took a sip of her drink, letting the cold bubbles tickle her throat. "Annoyed I lost this bracelet, is all."

"Hmm." Madison stuck her needle between her teeth and looked through her bag, pulling out blue floss.

She dropped into the armchair. "How's Reese?" she asked brightly. "You still need me to pick him up from the airport tomorrow, right?" Madison's boyfriend was a budding filmmaker and traveled often for work. Madison had to take her grandmother to an appointment tomorrow, so Eve had happily volunteered to fetch him.

"Nah. Like I said, he can order a Ryde, and I don't want to make you late to leave for the wedding retreat or whatever Livvy's calling it."

"Livvy's calling it a prewedding retreat and bad-omen cleanse. I'm going to go with 'party.'"

Madison grinned. She'd fallen in love with Livvy at first meeting, which was pretty easy to do. Eve adored Livvy herself. Until the split had happened between the two families, Livvy had been the best surrogate sister a girl could hope for.

Eve wanted this wedding to be perfect for her brother, but she also couldn't deny there was an element of selfishness in her encouraging this union. She wanted Livvy back as her sister. When she'd lost her mother, she'd lost everything except her brother. And even he had changed. He'd stopped putting her in headlocks and had started ensuring she was eating properly and going to bed on time—all the things her mother had done.

She'd felt very alone for a long time, until she'd learned how to make friends into family. Which was why she was careful to give Madison as much as Madison gave her. "I am a Ryde, and I can absolutely pick Reese up. I'll be at the estate all week anyway, so whether I get there late or early doesn't really matter. Besides, it's just going to be Sadia and Kareem and Jackson for the first couple days. Livvy's still sick."

Her friend started stitching again. "And Gabe, right?"

Damn it. It wasn't like she could keep her crush a secret from Madison, though. The woman had been there for her most mortifying seduction attempt. "Yeah."

"You're going to great lengths to see Gabe as much as you can lately, so you're probably looking forward to seeing him for the whole week, huh?"

Eve pressed her lips tight, recognizing the gentle doggedness in her friend's tone. Whether she wanted it or not, she was going to get some kind and probably on-the-nose advice. "Yes. Of course."

Her friend put her stitching down in her lap and took a sip of water. "Eve, do you remember what we talked about a few months ago?"

"About how I needed to get a job?"

Madison snorted. "Before that."

Eve tightened her arms around her middle. "About how I'm in an emotional straitjacket."

"Your words, yes. But remember how we talked about some things that could help you break out of it? Because you wanted to break out of it?"

She looked down at the floor and dug her toes into the carpet. When Livvy had first come back to town months ago, Eve had . . . She didn't like the word *snapped*, but it was like someone had snipped the cord that held her tight to her own self-control. She'd almost felt disassociated, like she was a bystander to her own actions. To her eternal shame, she'd cornered Livvy, demanded the other woman leave town, had even told her she would buy her off to get her away from Nicholas.

Afterward, when the full impact of what she'd done hit her, she'd been horrified and sobbed in her roommate's arms. *I don't know how I could have done this.*

Madison had stroked her hair. *Expressing emotions has never been easy for you, and that's not your fault. It's not uncommon to have it all explode like this. Livvy seems fine. No harm done.*

One feeling. That had been Madison's advice,

and one her therapist had approved of when she'd related the episode to her. Feel something, anything. Express it. Embrace the full expression of it. One feeling at a time, if need be. Combined with other coping mechanisms, she could maybe start to learn how to identify and articulate her emotions.

Eve had tried it. It had worked, a little, to varying degrees. She'd figured out where her seeming anger toward Livvy had stemmed from. She'd quit the job she hated. She'd acknowledged her father was a thoroughly toxic individual and confronted her sorrow and regret and desperate desire for love.

Feeling was hard. Maybe not for most people, but for her, it was like standing on a cliff, sharp winds buffeting her from every single direction. Staying steady in the face of that storm, with no one to rely on but herself—it was terrifying.

Madison started sewing again, the rhythmic up-and-down motion capturing Eve's gaze, calming her.

"How do you think that's worked for you?"

"Fine. I . . . I'm in a better place than I was then."

"Are you happy?"

"I don't know," she answered honestly. She didn't entirely know what pure happiness felt like.

"I think you're in a better place too." Madison's gaze was warm when it rested on her face. "Abuse isn't a quick or easy thing to recover from, Eve."

Eve bit back her instantaneous response to that, the one she'd given Madison for years, since they'd met in college—her father had never raised a hand to her or her brother. She had no physical scars. She'd had every financial resource and advantage a woman could have.

They were excuses Madison had always been quick to frown at, though it had taken Eve years to understand why. Emotional abuse was abuse.

Poor little rich girl.

She squared her shoulders. A distant father wasn't something that was unusual in their social circles. Most women worked through it with therapy or ever-aging romantic partners. Eve was already in the former, and wasn't interested in the latter.

But Brendan wasn't only distant to her. As a child, her older brother had come up with a million reasons why their father had treated her with disdain. She looked so much like her mother, and he was grieving. He was busy. He was preoccupied. If Brendan wasn't one of those things, of course he would love her. Of course he wouldn't ridicule her. Of course he wouldn't mock her. Of course he wouldn't hurt her.

Her brother had meant well. Eve had shut herself down like a computer in power-saving mode, waiting for her father to love her. Trying not to give him any more reasons to hate her, or even look at her.

In the process, she'd shut herself down with regard to the rest of the world too. "I'm trying," she said with some difficulty. "It's not easy. Sometimes I feel like a . . . a turtle."

Madison didn't stop that soothing needle motion, though she wasn't even looking at her canvas. "How's that?"

"I stick my head out, and then I get scared, and I draw back into my shell." She clasped and unclasped her hands. "I rejected my father but I never fully confronted him. I quit my job and I hid. I got a business idea and never told my brother. And Gabe. Oh my God, Gabe."

"What about him?"

She leaned forward and dropped her head. "I saw him this afternoon. We went to a cake tasting. He said he was going drinking tonight, so I . . ." Basically stalked him. "I made sure I would be in a position where I could accept his call if he called for a Ryde."

"And what did you hope to get out of that?"

She wrapped her arms around herself, feeling silly and childish. "I—I don't know."

Madison's tone gentled. "It's okay not to know. It's okay to just want to see someone."

"No . . . I'm so *weird*, Mad."

"You're not weird."

"I am. I wish I could straight up tell him I liked him." *Go out with me.* He'd been drunk, yes, but how had it been so easy for him? It was never easy for her. "Or even tell him I'm Anne, his friendly neighborhood Ryde driver, and get my bracelet back."

"Ah. He has it?"

Impossible to explain how she'd wound up in

his bedroom, without Madison realizing she really was weird, so she didn't bother. "Yeah."

"Do you want it back badly?"

"Yeah."

"What's the worst that could happen, if you told him you liked him?"

"He'd reject me." He already had once. How to explain the soul-crushing terror she felt at the thought of someone even gently denying her?

Her sense of self-worth was like spun sugar. She feared it cracking more than anything.

"What's the worst that could happen if you tell him you're Anne?"

"He'll think I'm strange. Or an object of pity."

"Possibly. That's not fun, I know."

"It's scary."

"Fear is natural. It's hard not to be afraid. I was in bed with Reese about three hours after we first met, and I was terrified for, like, two hours and forty-five minutes that he didn't like me," Madison said.

"How did you stick your neck out long enough to get into bed with him?"

"I jumped." Madison shifted. "And you know, some people like the Band-Aid approach, but you don't have to rip that shell off completely. If you feel like you're stuck in a rut, how about, instead, you keep your head out for a while longer each time? Feel two emotions, or three. Try something low-risk that scares you a little, but nothing that could really hurt you."

Eve nodded. No wonder her friend had pushed her to get out of the house during the winter. Becoming a Ryde driver had been intimidating, but low-risk.

"You don't have to jump in and seduce Gabe this week. Spend some time with him. Enjoy his company. See if you even like him beyond his hot body. No expectations. No stress on either of you for more." Madison put her project aside and smiled faintly. "I know you like costs and benefits, and the cost to you on that is fairly low. And the benefit . . . hey, you may end up smooching him or you may just stay friends or you may get your bracelet back. Any way you look at it, you come out on top."

Eve ran the cost-benefit analysis on that proposal. It was extremely low-risk to her. "What if I do something that makes him think I'm weird?"

"First, you're not weird. And second, if he does think you're weird, the literal worst thing is he thinks you're weird. It's an opinion. Not a fact."

She chewed on her lip. It was good advice, for most people. Most people who hadn't lived their lives for fear of other people's opinions. *Which you vowed to stop doing.*

It was sticking her neck out a little more. A little longer. It was safe. "I'm—"

Her phone rang, making them both jump. She pulled it out of her pocket. "It's Sadia." She answered. "Hello?"

"Hey, Eve." A loud clanging noise came from the background and Eve raised an eyebrow. "I'm sorry to call so late."

"Don't worry about it, I was awake."

"Listen, we're having an issue with the new oven at the café," came Sadia's grim reply.

Eve frowned. Sadia had inherited Kane's Café from her late husband, Paul, but Jackson had bought it from her recently.

Eve and Sadia had an odd relationship. While Sadia had been Livvy and Jackson's best friend growing up, she and Eve had barely interacted. And then she'd married Paul Kane, making her firmly off-limits to any Chandler. Paul, once Nicholas's best friend, had been the one most enraged by Brendan buying Tani out of the Kane's share of C&O.

Sadia was dating Jackson now, but since the feud was old news, she and Eve could be friends. The two of them were still feeling each other out, though. Eve was pretty sure Sadia knew about the time she'd tried to bribe Livvy to get out of town, and slights against best friends were hard to forgive. After all, Eve was still holding a grudge against Malcolm Caldwell for breaking Madison's heart their sophomore year of college. "I'm sorry to hear about the oven."

"Yeah, it's, like, falling apart, and Jackson isn't ready to leave it until it's fixed. The repairman can't come until Monday, so it might be Tuesday before we can get up to the lake house."

Her brain never took long to make connections from A to B. She froze and looked up at Madison, who was watching with curiosity. "Uh. Thanks for the heads-up."

"You're welcome." Another loud clanging came, and Sadia cursed. "I'll see you later, Eve. Gotta go."

Eve hung up slowly.

"What now?"

"Sadia and Jackson and Kareem aren't going to be able to come up to the house until Tuesday."

"And Livvy and Nicholas are also going to be delayed," Madison said shrewdly.

"Right."

Madison's lips slowly curled up. "Girl, someone is looking out for you."

"I should tell Gabe, right?"

"Wellllll." Madison smiled. "I think you should do whatever you think is best. But since the two of you were planning on going up tomorrow anyway? And now you're going to have days alone with him in a rural area to charm, possibly, the literal pants off him? I would say it's okay to . . . um. Go."

Eve flushed. "He did say he was prepared to go tomorrow."

"Mmm-hmm."

She continued to work this moral dilemma out loud. "If he didn't want to go, he could always cancel."

"That's right."

She hesitated, then quickly opened her messages and sent a text.

"Are you telling him?"

"No." She looked up, taking a deep breath. "I told the butler to move my bedroom so it's next to his." She wasn't going to rip her shell or her clothes off and attack the man. However, it might be nice to be closer to him.

It was maybe silly to feel . . . empowered by the decision to simply make friends with the man, but she did. It was an action, however small. Madison was right. She'd spent her life having things done to her and for her. Doing anything for herself was going to take practice. She'd have to make conscious, repeated attempts to stick her neck out.

A slow smile spread across Madison's face. "Good girl."

Chapter 5

GABE TURNED the ignition off and stared up at the massive mansion. He wasn't surprised by the size of the place or its grandeur. The Kanes and Chandlers had had "lake houses" not too far from here when he was young that had been equally large and grand.

It had been a long time since he'd been around this kind of display of wealth, though. His sister was rich, but that was fairly recent—and as far as he could tell, she mostly spent her money on gaming systems and takeout, with the occasional splurge for trips to Comic-Con.

The evening was starting to take hold of the day, darkening the sky to a lavender hue. He fiddled with his keys. Leaned over to the passenger seat to make sure he'd packed his precious tablet. Pulled his hair out of the stubby bun and tied it back up. He'd meant to get a haircut before the wedding, but he hadn't had time. Maybe he could go now?

Stalling.

He grimaced. Maybe he should have waited a day to come up. His mood might have been improved if he wasn't suffering a low-key headache from his overindulgence last night.

He didn't remember every second of how he'd gotten home, but he vividly recalled what an ass he'd been to Anne. Poor Anne, who had probably told everyone she knew today about the dick she'd had to drag inside.

And who had tripped into bed with her. Who had gracelessly asked her out.

Some of his friends called him a ladies' man, and that wasn't wrong. So how had he been such a mess with this one lady? He could only recall snatches of the night, had a vague impression of her voice and body and absolutely none of her face.

So. Stupid.

You are not allowed to drink any more alcohol for the rest of the week. For the rest of his life, maybe, but definitely for the rest of the week. There was no way he would have done any of that shit if he'd been sober.

He wouldn't say he had a problem, but the fear he might be on his way to one was enough to have him vowing to dial back. He'd never drunk so much before Paul had died, and it had ramped up over the past few months. He'd always liked to go to clubs and bars, but not like this. He hadn't *needed* the social lubrication alcohol gave him before.

He reached into his pocket, his fingers brushing

the bangle he'd found in his bed, and he pulled it out to look at it again. The gold was scuffed and worn down. He lifted it against his own wrist. The wearer was so much smaller than him. There was an inscription inside, an *M* and a *K*.

When it had tumbled out of his comforter, he'd been ecstatic. He hadn't had any other woman in his bed for a while, which meant Anne must have dropped it, which meant he had a non-creepy reason to track her down. The app provided a number for them to contact each other, but only for the length of the ride, so he'd shot a message to Ryde. **Hey, I think my driver dropped her bracelet last night. If she did, she can contact me and we can arrange a pickup. Or I can mail it to her.**

Casual and friendly and not at all stalker-like. He'd signed off with his name and number, and a barely repressed hope he'd get back in touch with Anne. He could apologize and maybe assuage some of his guilt.

The low tones of *Star Wars*'s Imperial March sounded, and he glanced down at his phone, though the ring identified the caller before the display could.

He debated not picking up, but there was no one more tenacious than his mother. She seemed to have a sixth sense when either of her children were struggling with something. "Hey, Ma."

"Please don't tell me you were sleeping," his mom said disapprovingly. He could imagine her sitting at her kitchen table, a worried frown creasing her otherwise-still-smooth forehead, black hair braided on top of her head.

He hated worrying Sonya Hunter. "Of course not."

His mother scoffed. "I know the sound of my son when he's hungover."

Was she psychic? Orange juice and a greasy breakfast and lunch had killed most of his headache, but he was indeed hungover. "You've been living in too many big cities. How wild do you think Rockville gets?"

Sonya snorted. "I know how wild you can get."

His smile was reluctant, but genuine. "I'm a choirboy."

"Let's not risk the Lord striking you down right now."

"How's Chuck?" he said, changing the subject. Chuck was his mother's new . . . he wasn't sure what the word was. *Boyfriend* seemed odd, given the fact that this was his mom, and he wasn't about to call the man her lover. They'd been together for a couple of years now, both eager to go explore the world.

Her tone softened. "Chuck's fine. We had a lovely night out last night."

"That's good."

"I'm excited to see you next weekend."

"I'm excited to see you too." He tried to inject extra enthusiasm into his voice, but he didn't think he succeeded. He *was* excited to see his mom, as well as his sister, who he barely got to hang out with anymore with her living all the way across the country in California.

His mother's voice lowered. "Are you at the house yet?"

"Yes. Just got here."

"I think this week will be good for you," Sonya said gently.

He shifted. Psychic, indeed. "So you've said."

"I know Livvy and Jackson aren't Paul, but you should forge a relationship with them anyway. They're—"

"Ma." He ran his hand over his face, feeling every inch of his thirty-five years, the scrape of pain at Paul's name far too raw. Every day he missed his best friend. Missed and cursed him for dying so young, alone on that hiking trail. Why the man hadn't asked him for company, he'd never know. "I'm trying. I'm here," he said

His mother was silent for a beat. "You could maybe tell them—"

His eyelid twitched. "I should go."

"Okay, okay. I won't say anything more. Don't run."

"I'm not running."

"I know you, Gabe. You run when anyone gets too close."

His stomach tensed. What an unflattering view of him. "No, I don't."

"Other than me and Rhi, who are you close to?"

He opened his mouth, then closed it again. "Lots of people," he said.

"No. You only reached that level of closeness

with Paul." She dropped her voice even lower. "And even he didn't know everything about you."

"He couldn't," he said harshly. "You know why he couldn't."

"He could, baby." His mother's tone was soothing, like she was speaking to a child. "That secret doesn't need to be kept any longer."

It did. His mother didn't understand.

"I don't want you to be lonely."

"I'm not." He had lots of friends. Plenty of people to hang out with. A never-ending stream of drinking buddies, and he never lacked for female companionship. "I'm never alone."

"There's a difference between being alone and not being surrounded by people."

His hands were shaking, a slight tremor. He would chalk that up to a hangover, not fear. Men who looked like him were never scared.

He tightened his fingers around Anne's bracelet, the cool gold absorbing his heat. "I'm fine."

You're not, though. Why do you think you've been drinking so much?

Because . . . because . . .

He closed his eyes. He didn't know.

His mother didn't speak for a beat, and when she did, her tone was soft and soothing. "Okay, love. Go on, go have fun with your little friends. I will see you on Friday."

He exhaled, grateful his mother was dropping the issue. "Yes, ma'am."

"If Tani gets there before me . . . if she says anything to you, tell me."

He gave a rueful smile, imagining his mother and Livvy's mother scrapping. Sonya and Tani had always had an odd, guarded relationship. His mother took her duty to protect her children pretty intensely.

But Tani had never been anything but distant and polite to him. He'd crossed paths with her multiple times since Robert Kane had died, and each time, they'd sidestepped around each other so carefully they'd barely brushed. "Yes, ma'am."

"Okay. I love you."

"I love you more, Ma."

"If you talk to Rhi, tell her I'm bringing a nice dress for her for the wedding."

Gabe winced. He definitely would not be telling his sister that. Rhi and their mother had battled more than once over clothes growing up, but since she'd become rich, Rhi had solidified her reputation for never dressing up any fancier than a fitted hoodie. If she owned a dress, he'd eat Anne's bracelet. "Uh, sure. Bye." He hung up and tucked his phone and the jewelry into his pocket.

He got out of his car and retrieved his suitcase and garment bag from his trunk before walking up the ramp to the massive double doors. He rang the bell, then glanced around, taking in the eight tall pillars that framed the front of the house.

The door opened quickly, and Gabe found himself face-to-face with a butler who looked like he'd stepped out of the pages of central casting. The older man looked down at him—how, Gabe wasn't sure, because he was taller than the guy. "Mr. Hunter, I presume? We've been expecting you. My name is Alistair."

"Ah, yeah. Hi." He walked inside, wheeling his suitcase, a little nonplussed when the butler plucked his tux and the suitcase out of his hands. "I can get—"

"Not a problem, sir." The butler turned away and thrust Gabe's things at a young man who appeared seemingly out of nowhere. "Take this to Mr. Hunter's room. Come, sir, let me show you around."

He knew better than to tell the man to call him by his first name. His mother hadn't run the Kane household like this, but he knew this level of formality wasn't uncommon amongst the super rich. "Is anyone else here yet?"

"No, sir. I understand the bride and groom have been delayed a few days. However, Ms. Chandler called ahead and said she'd be here late tonight."

Eve. He couldn't think about her when he was already so discomfited. "And Jackson and Sadia?"

"Mr. Kane and Ms. Ahmed have been delayed a few days as well."

So it was just him and Eve for a few *days*?

Oh no.

He halted, and Alistair stopped with him. "Is something wrong, sir?"

Yes. Yes, everything was wrong. He was wildly attracted to a young woman he couldn't have and he was a lie and a fraud and . . .

He needed to leave.

You can't. How are you going to explain that to Eve? The butler will tell her you got here and bolted.

He would . . . make up an emergency.

And then Livvy will get stressed out, thinking some other bad omen is befalling her wedding.

Fuck.

He could control himself. He could definitely be around a woman he desired and not jump on her. He'd play it cool. Keep his mask in rigid place. Smile. Look pretty. Charm people. He wouldn't let her know who he truly was.

"Sir?"

He looked at the butler and deliberately relaxed his shoulders and smiled. "I'm fine, thank you."

He barely paid attention during the tour of the massive estate, though he made a mental note to inspect the priceless art that decorated the walls later.

He was shaken out of his preoccupation with Eve when he stepped out onto the deck at the back of the house. "This is where the wedding will take place at the end of the week," Alistair said.

Gabe walked to the railing. Now he understood why Livvy and Nicholas had picked this place. The deck was large enough to easily accommodate their wedding party and guests. Perched high above the lake, the water was spread out below in bejeweled beauty, a mix of cerulean and emerald, small boats riding the placid surface. A small forest stretched out around the house, dots of forest green and budding wildflowers. He absorbed the colors and breathed deep, some of the tension unraveling inside of him. "This is beautiful."

"The view is exquisite. We have a fire pit below, should you and your companions wish to spend the evenings there."

His brain conjured up the image of him and Eve, bundled in a blanket next to a fire pit, and he turned away from the breathtaking view. One thing to have lustful thoughts about her. Quite another to have domestic thoughts about her. Domesticity, like wedding cakes, was far out of his wheelhouse.

"We have a stable filled with horses, should you wish to ride." Alistair droned on about the trails in the surrounding area as Gabe followed him up the stairs. The butler stopped in front of a door upstairs and opened it. "This is your room. Your possessions are in the closet."

Gabe took in the all-white decor and delicate furnishings. It was a distinctly feminine-looking room, but his manhood could handle a little antique furniture. "Thanks."

"Would you like dinner downstairs in the dining room or up here?"

"I'm not really hungry, thanks. I'll, uh, explore the house a little."

The older man inclined his head. "Very well, sir. Mr. Chandler asked us to provide some refreshments in your room, and the kitchen is available for your use at any time. Please use the intercoms if you require anything. Mr. Chandler and Ms. Kane requested a small, discreet staff this week, so your privacy is assured. However, I am always at hand, should you require something."

Once Gabe was alone, he prowled around the room. There was a small gleaming silver tray on the table, with fruit and cookies under the lid. Nice of Nicholas. Gabe had lied to the butler; he was always hungry.

He grabbed an apple and bit into it, walking to the window to look out. There was a view of the lake from here as well, which was good. The sight of the water calmed him.

He should be happy. This place was swanky, he had a full week off of work, and he was about to spend it in the midst of his beloved nature.

He was supposed to be happy.

He realized he was caressing the bracelet in his pocket, and he stopped himself. He had to . . . go do something. Silence had never been his friend.

There's a difference between being alone and not being surrounded by people.

His lips tightened and he polished off the apple and tossed it into the trash, then strode to the closet. He'd get changed and go for a run, and then maybe he'd go swimming.

He'd keep himself busy until someone else showed up, even if that person was Eve. It was harder to lose himself in his role around her, but he could do it. That man—the laughing, fun, cheerful guy—was who he wanted to be. The guy without a worry in the world.

The guy who was never lonely. By the time Eve showed up, that mask would be firmly in place, and he'd be more than ready to face her without a single inexplicable vulnerability on display.

Chapter 6

Eve quietly made her way up the dark staircase of the mansion. Traffic had been horrendous, and she'd texted the butler on staff earlier to tell him she didn't require anyone to wait up for her. She'd visited this place with Nicholas and Livvy last week to make sure everything was set up properly for the week and the wedding, so she had a key and knew which room was hers.

She came to the top of the stairs and paused. The place was massive, more than large enough to accommodate a dozen people. Nicholas and Livvy were all the way at one end of the hall, with Jackson and Sadia at the other. Kareem had a little room adjoining theirs. When the older generation and Gabe's family arrived, they'd be housed in the first-floor suites, to accommodate her grandfather's power chair and Tani's lack of mobility after her broken hip last year.

Gabe had originally been on the first floor, too, but after her impulsive decision last night, now he'd be in the room adjoining hers. No one would raise an eyebrow. They both had to open a door in order for either of them to enter the other person's room, so they were assured of privacy.

Her romantic brain had spent most of last night spinning fantasies of him scratching at her door. She'd open it and discover him standing there, roses in hand. Hair down. Butt naked.

Self-torture. That was what she was into, clearly.

Just sticking her neck out. That was all. Sticking her neck out wouldn't necessarily lead to butt nakedness.

She crept down the hallway, her shoes in her hand. No light shone from under Gabe's door. A stab of disappointment ran through her. While a part of her had been relieved to be stuck in traffic, another part had been hoping to start practicing sticking her neck out tonight. Just a normal, twenty-something woman who could interact with a man she liked.

Not being weird.

She opened the door to her room and hit the light switch, the lamp on the nightstand bathing the pristine white bedding with a golden glow. The little-girl decor made her itch, but she only had to bear it for a week.

She placed her suitcase next to the dresser and tucked her shoulder bag on the floor next to it. A large tray on the writing desk had her prowling closer. She lifted the domed lid and smiled at the spread of fruit and cookies underneath. A little envelope was tucked under an orange.

Eat something. I made sure the pool is heated. I'll see you in a few days.

N

Her face softened. Her brother was always looking out for her, even when he wasn't in her immediate vicinity.

She chose an apple and bit into it as she opened her bag and sorted through it for her swimsuit. Her brother knew her too well. The indoor pool and Jacuzzi underground had been one of the reasons she'd brought this estate to her brother and Livvy's attention.

Half-mermaid. That was what their mother used to call her. When she'd been very young, they'd had a lake house not far from here, and she'd grown up splashing in every body of water she could find.

At home, she belonged to a twenty-four-hour gym solely so she could go swimming at night. She had enough money to buy her own house with an indoor pool, but places like that were usually huge, like this. Even if she could convince Madison to move in with her, it would be too much space. From her experience growing up, big houses tended to be impersonal. She didn't want to feel more alone.

She slipped into a cover-up and sandals and made her way through the quiet, dark hallway. The elevator took her to the lower level, where the pool was.

She stepped out of the lift and immediately stopped.

There was a man in her sanctuary. *The* man.

Gabe leaned back on his hands. He was sitting on the concrete, legs dangling into the hot tub. Steam rose from the surface of the water, but nothing could obscure the fact that he wasn't wearing clothes.

No, that wasn't true. He was wearing clothes. They were swim trunks, damp and red. Bright. Fire engine. Red. Probably like her face.

"Well, well. Look who finally decided to show up."

Light, playful words, but her first instinct was to run away, her guilty conscience convinced he somehow knew everything—that she was Anne, that her phone still held the Ryde notification about him having her bracelet, that she had a crush on him, that she'd told the butler to move his room next to hers—but she forced herself to walk toward him instead. "I apologize you were here alone all afternoon. Traffic." Her voice echoed over the cavernous, dimly lit room, bouncing off the Olympic-sized pool. How was she supposed to ignore his body? She'd felt that chest yesterday, but this was the first time she was seeing it naked. His pecs were a delight, his belly a perfect washboard. Bright, colorful tattoo sleeves covered his arms from shoulder to wrist, highlighting his muscles. She wanted to grab both arms and inspect them thoroughly.

"It wasn't easy, but I somehow managed to stay entertained in the lap of luxury." He moved his legs back and forth slightly through the water. She tore her gaze away from his thick thighs to focus on his face. Was it her imagination, or was his smile less bright than usual?

You're looking for reasons to run away now. "I—I was going to—" She was about to say, *Go for a swim,* but she recalibrated. "Soak in the hot tub."

"You're in the right place." His smile widened, and this time, it seemed more like his usual friendly grin. "Be warned, it's hot."

"I like it hot." It was an unintentional double entendre, but she refused to get all flustered. Instead, she dropped her towel on the nearest lounge chair and, facing away from him, grabbed the hem of her cover-up. "Have you been here for long?"

SHE'D ASKED him a question, and Gabe was going to answer it, as soon as he could rip his gaze off her body.

Eve was wearing some gauzy white thing that barely skimmed her mid-thighs. It lifted up, revealing round thighs and wide hips, the slowest striptease he'd ever been treated to.

If someone had asked him before tonight what Eve's swimwear might look like, he would have guessed a one-piece in a neutral shade. That would have been sexy enough for him.

But this? This was enchanting. She wore a two-piece, and it was white, with tiny whimsical red cherries dotted all over it. The bottom was high-waisted, accentuating her nipped-in waist and the round curves of her thighs. There was a cute little squeeze of flesh on her back, under the strap of her bra.

He wanted to kiss it, lick it. Nip it with his teeth.

He'd spent a month telling himself she was too young for him, but this was the body of a full-grown woman. When had this happened?

She tossed the cover-up on the lounge chair. Before she could turn around, he slipped inside the hot tub, desperate to hide her effect on his body. "Not long," he said belatedly.

He thanked God he'd gotten inside when she walked toward him. Her heavy breasts were secured, but as well constructed as her swimsuit was, there was no way to still all the jiggle that was going on. He looked while pretending not to look, every tremble searing itself into his brain.

Her hair was in its usual soft waves, but a little tousled, like she'd run her hands through it. Her breasts lifted as she tied her hair up into a ponytail. Even with the modern hair and swimsuit, she looked like one of those angels from an old master's painting, her cheeks plump, lips full, the top one slightly larger than the bottom.

She slipped into the hot tub opposite him, and finally, thankfully, she was buried in the water, the bubbles from the jets hiding both of their bodies from view.

Which was good, because he was definitely more than a little erect. He grimaced internally. He'd been right. Seeing more than her bare arms was far too much for him.

Pervert. It wasn't like she'd stripped to entice him. She was living her life. He had to get himself under control.

She gave a deep groan, which didn't help. "This is heaven."

"For an old man like me, it's necessary." Yes, he would remind them both of his age. Old. Fun. Relaxed. Friendly.

She peered at him. The steam had already curled the tendrils of hair at her temples. "I suppose you know by now Sadia and Jackson have been delayed as well."

He nodded. "Everyone's dropping like flies. I half-expected to be rattling around this big house by myself for the full week."

"They should be here soon. The new oven at the café is acting up, Sadia said."

"You talked to her? I didn't know until I showed up."

Eve shifted. "She called me last night."

"Oh."

"I'm sorry. Should I have texted you . . . ?"

"No. Wouldn't have changed things for me." Wouldn't it have? Maybe he would have thought twice about coming here if he'd known it would be the object of his lust and him, all alone. "I guess bad omens can be oven shaped, too."

"It's not a bad omen. I mean, none of them are bad omens. Just . . . unfortunate timing."

He hummed. "Right. Anyway, you can't expect Jackson to leave his baby. I've never seen someone treat their appliances like children."

Eve's eyes warmed. She might not be given to grinning, this girl, but he'd gotten good at reading her eyes and lips. "Jackson does love his kitchen."

"He does." Jackson was so different from Paul, despite physical similarities. Paul's extroversion had matched Gabe's. It had been easy to be friends with him.

It wasn't easy to be friends with Jackson. The man didn't trust easily, and he was wary of everyone except for his immediate family.

You should tell him.

He stretched his legs out, part of him hoping she'd do the same. "I'm sure we can find things to occupy us while we're up here. I had to tune out the butler's list of activities, there were so many."

"Yes, there—excuse me, this jet is bugging me." She got up, and he pretended to get something in his eye, scrubbing them so he wouldn't watch the water cascade off her breasts.

When she sat down again, it was closer to him. The temperature felt hotter, but he knew that was his imagination. She was sitting on her knees now, so the tops of her breasts cleared the water.

Fuck. When had *that* all happened? Why did she have to have the most enticing breasts he'd ever seen?

He swiped his hand over his face. He was sweating. "Better?" he asked. The view was better for him, for sure.

"Very much so."

Scrambling out of the hot tub and running back to the room would be suspicious, right? "So you ran into traffic, huh?" His voice came out harsher than he'd intended.

"Yes. I might have been able to get ahead of it but I had to pick someone up from the airport. His plane was delayed."

His. Gabe rolled his shoulders. "I only brave the airport for my best friends." *And you, sir, are fishing for information.*

"It was my roommate's boyfriend. She couldn't make it."

"Ah." He cleared his throat, trying to ignore the burst of pleasure at learning this wasn't a boy-friend. "Late to be driving up here, though. Might have been better off waiting until tomorrow."

"I'm an okay driver."

"I'm not saying you're not. It's so dark, is all. Hard to see. Easy to get tired."

"Nah. It's still kind of early for me." Was it his imagination or was her voice overly breathy? It was probably the steam in the room.

"Oh yeah?" She didn't strike him as a night owl like him.

"Getting up in the morning is harder than stay-ing up late. College was a challenge."

"You couldn't schedule your classes later in the day?"

She trailed her fingers through the water. "I overloaded on classes so I could knock a year off."

He raised an eyebrow. "Wow. Impressive."

"It's no big—" She cut herself off and lifted her chin. "Thanks."

"You must have been super studious."

"I had fun sometimes." She licked her lips. "I think I saw you once. While I was having fun."

He tensed. Was she talking about . . . ? No.

It had been at O'Killians, which had once had a solid reputation for not checking I.D.s too closely. He'd recognized Eve instantly, despite the fact that he'd kept his distance from the Chandlers for years. He'd had no choice but to choose Paul in that feud, and Paul wouldn't have tolerated him fraternizing with the enemy.

Gabe had assumed she hadn't known who he was when she'd stumbled up to him and locked her arms around his neck, pressing her body against his, or when she'd tried to drag his shirt up over his stomach. It had only been around five years ago, but she'd seemed way younger then, and he hadn't been stirred at all. He'd gently righted her and helped her to her seat, making sure a waiter got her a glass of water.

He wasn't about to bring that up now, though. He didn't want to embarrass her. She must be referring to the other time he'd seen her. "You came into my shop with your friend, right? I remember that."

She stilled. "Yes. My roommate, Madison. I was there for moral support."

He squinted. "She got a bird, on her stomach." He could see a trio of tiny birds on Eve. On her shoulder, maybe. His fingers itched for his pen.

"Uh-huh. You have a good memory."

The temperature didn't seem so warm anymore. She was looking away from him, her lips pressed tight.

Had he offended her? He focused in on those pursed lips, something niggling in his brain. The moment of recognition flitted away, though.

They'd both had a long day. Maybe it was time to cut this meeting short. He rose to his feet, hoping his wet trunks weren't sticking too close to . . . things. "I'm going to head upstairs. I'll see you tomorrow?"

"Yes." She nodded. "Good night."

"Good night."

He was preoccupied as he took the stairs to the top floor, so preoccupied he barely registered the oddity of the light being on in his bedroom, though he was normally a fanatic about turning lights off.

He didn't bother to go into the bathroom, just tossed his towel on the bed and shoved his swim trunks down his legs. That was when he heard the door open behind him.

Startled, he looked over his shoulder, finding Eve standing inside the door. Her gaze was dark and wide, and fixed firmly on his butt.

Her head lifted and the blood in his brain went straight to his cock. For once he had no trouble reading her. Her eyes were startled, shocked . . . and aroused.

Interest was written all over her, from the flush on her cheeks to the pulse beating at her neck to the lust stamped on her face. "Oh," she whispered. Her hand fluttered over her chest and the clinging fabric covering her damp bathing suit. The white cotton had become see-through in a couple spots, giving him peeks of blurry cherries. "Oh."

His cock thickened, his pulse beating a steady thump. He could have her. They could destroy the purity of the white bedding with all the filthy, needy acts he could think of. No one else was in the house . . . no one who knew them at least. This would simply be two people from opposite sides of a bridal party engaging in the time-honored tradition of pre-ceremony fucking.

Her pink tongue touched the corner of her mouth, and he snapped out of the lust-filled spell he'd fallen under. Fuck.

They weren't the usual sort of bridal party.

He leaned down and grabbed his shorts to yank them back up, his cock protesting at being strangled and tucked away. He pivoted to face her, but not before picking up the towel to hold in front of his lower body. "This is my room," he said, his voice so harsh it surprised even him.

"No, it . . . it's supposed to be mine?" It came out as a question, and then she blinked. "Oh. Oh, there may have been a mix-up. I'm . . . You know what, I'll grab the room next door." Her cover-up fluttered as she almost ran to the suitcase tucked into the corner, lending support to the claim that she'd genuinely thought this was her room.

Next door? Next door wasn't much better. At least she'd be out of immediate proximity to his bed there, though.

"I'm so sorry," she babbled, and he knew he should put her at ease, but all he could think about was that all-too-clear heat in her eyes.

He could have her. Only he couldn't. Goddamn it.

"It's fine."

She paused at the door, and her aroused, curious gaze licked over his bare chest. Christ, she was killing him.

"I'm—"

"Go to bed, Eve." Before he put her in his bed.

It was like his rough command flipped a switch. Her face went totally blank, cold. If he hadn't seen that naked lust, he might have wondered if he'd imagined it.

"Yes," she said, and her tone was as smooth and cool as glass. "Apologies. Good night."

The door closed behind her and he sank down on his bed, burying his face into his hands, feeling like an ass. Better she be miffed at him, though, than under his body.

He gave a mirthless laugh. Or at least he would keep telling himself that.

Chapter 7

GO TO bed, Eve.

The words had looped in her head all night, on repeat, until she'd finally fallen asleep, exhausted. She'd examined them from every angle, for intonation, aggression, anger, annoyance.

Four words had ruined any pleasure she might have taken from finally getting a glimpse of Gabe's naked butt.

Okay, that wasn't totally true. His butt had given her plenty of pleasure, had featured prominently in her dreams, once she was asleep. It was an amazing butt. Very bubble-y. If she hadn't known it was wildly immature, she would have texted Madison its exact dimensions and roundness and muscularity so they could squeal over said butt together.

Eve sat in front of the vanity and fiddled with her hair. She'd been fully dressed for hours, but she didn't want to go downstairs, where she would probably face Gabe.

So much for sticking her neck out. Four words

in an angry tone, and she was diving right back into her shell.

Most women wouldn't be so timid. Be braver.

Her shoulders slumped. Easy to say. Harder to do.

She'd been disheartened when she'd followed after Gabe last night. He didn't even remember the night she'd drunkenly thrown herself into his arms all those years ago when she'd been a coed. It had taken every ounce of courage Young Eve had possessed, as well as a hefty amount of alcohol she could barely tolerate, to try to kiss him in that bar.

She twisted her fingers together. Such a huge deal for her, and nothing for him. He probably had women crawling all over him when he was out.

Spotting his butt in the wild had temporarily alleviated her dismay over being one of many. But then it had come crashing back with his rebuke.

A perfunctory knock came at the door, and she jumped. Her heart soared for a second before she realized there was no reason for Gabe to be at her door at all.

Sure enough, it was Alistair standing outside the threshold, a garment bag in his arms. She'd met the butler when she'd toured the estate, and appreciated his formality, though the bow he gave her now was a little much. "Ms. Chandler."

"Hello, Alistair."

"Mr. Hunter informed me there was a possible mix-up with the rooms. I do apologize." A slight flush colored his cheeks. The man wasn't comfortable with apologies. "When we received your text to change the room assignments, there must have been a miscommunication. I take full responsibility—"

"Did you tell him about the text?" she interrupted Alistair. She didn't want to compound her embarrassment by Gabe knowing she'd asked to have their rooms moved to be close to each other.

Alistair didn't blink an eye. "No, ma'am."

Because the man knew his salary was being paid by a Chandler, not Gabe, but Eve was fine with his discretion having been bought. "It's fine. We sorted things out. Is Gabe . . . is he downstairs?"

"He is currently in the breakfast room, yes."

"Good, um. Good."

Alistair lifted the garment bag in his hand. "This arrived a few minutes ago for you as well."

Her dress for the wedding. She accepted it. "Thank you."

"Would you like me to have a plate sent up?"

Saying yes felt like acknowledging her weakness. Plus, she'd grazed on the tray of snacks in her room. She wasn't hungry for more. "No, thank you."

She closed the door and paced to her bed to lay the garment bag down. A flash of unfamiliar pink at the opening of the bag had her frowning. She unzipped the thing.

Five minutes and a phone call later, Eve had almost forgotten her obsession with Gabe in favor of a new crisis.

A bad omen.

Or, more accurately, a pain in the ass.

"I am so sorry, Ms. Chandler." The woman on the other end of the line sounded both apologetic and terrified.

Eve stared at the flamingo-pink dress on the bed. It was the style she'd chosen and had altered, but definitely not the right color. Both she and Sadia had agreed on pale pink. "Explain to me how this occurred." She cringed at the cold, rich-bitch tone of her voice, but she was so shocked she couldn't help herself.

"It appears there was a mix-up with the notes for your dress and another customer's dress. Hers was supposed to be dyed to a darker color."

Oh. There was another dress. Saved. "Then that's an easy fix, yes? We can swap dresses."

"Hers has already been altered in a way that will make it impossible to fit you, ma'am." Real tears entered the woman's voice. "I am so sorry."

So what she was hearing was that the other woman's friend's wedding was going to go off without a hitch, while she had to somehow explain this to Livvy. One more thing to add to the bride's worry. She groaned. "There's no way you can get another dress in for me in a week?"

"No. If we had two weeks, perhaps."

"No, that won't work. The wedding is this weekend."

"I do apologize, Ms. Chandler. If there is anything at all we can do for you, we would."

It was a long shot, but . . . "Do you have anything

in stock in my size? Anything at all? Something that could be altered quickly enough for me?"

"Only wedding gowns."

And she could hardly wear a white dress to a wedding, even if Livvy had opted for a blush gown. She grimaced and quickly made her good-byes.

She hated calling Livvy with this, but she didn't see how she had any choice. Reluctantly, she dialed her soon-to-be sister-in-law.

"Hello," Livvy croaked.

"Hey. How are you feeling?"

"A little better than yesterday. I'm hoping we can make it up there in a couple of days. How's the house?"

Fantastic. I saw Gabe's butt. "Amazing. Thanks. Um, so listen . . ."

"Oh no. I knew you were calling for a reason. What tragedy has befallen us now? Is the house on fire? Ugh. Is there a freak spring snowstorm?"

"What is it?" Nicholas's voice boomed from the other end of the line and Eve winced. She did not want to talk to her brother, not at all. She had, in fact, been avoiding him at every possible turn lately.

It wasn't that she didn't love her brother. It was just that every conversation lately invariably turned to how she hadn't found a new job yet. He'd been super supportive of her quitting the foundation. He wasn't supportive of what he called Eve "finding herself."

"It's no big deal," she said hurriedly. "No need to bother Nicholas."

"Go away, I can handle this," Livvy said.

There was a whispered argument, and then Nicholas got on the line. "Eve, I told you to call me with any problems. I want Livvy to rest."

"I haven't left bed in, like, a week," Livvy squawked. "I'm resting. Go to work."

"This is a wardrobe issue, Nicholas. I thought Livvy might have more insight than you."

Another scuffle, and Livvy was back, Nicholas sputtering in the background now. "I said I could handle this. Go run an empire. Stop upsetting me, it's not good for my health."

Eve figured it was probably the last thing that had Nicholas walking away. He was as careful and protective with Livvy as he was with Eve. Maybe more so. Eve was pretty sure he still worried Livvy might disappear on him again.

"Okay, lay it on me."

"It's not the worst thing that could happen," Eve hastened to reassure Livvy.

"Literally if I break a nail now my mom's going to start on me about a curse. Is it worse than that?"

Eve looked at her dress, wincing at the garish color. "There was a mix-up in my bridesmaid dress and they dyed it indigestion-medicine pink."

There was a moment of silence on the other end, and then Livvy gave a congested cough-laugh. "Oh my God. Okay, you're right, that's not the worst thing."

Well, Livvy wasn't the one who would have to wear this monstrosity.

"You and Sadia don't have to match, if that's what you were worried about."

Her instinctive response was to say it didn't matter, that she'd wear the damn dress and not make any waves, but she cringed at the thought of how she would look. This was selfish, maybe, but if there was some way out of this, that would be good. "It's, um . . . really not attractive. I can send you a picture."

"You don't have to do that." Livvy sobered. "I trust you, if you think it's unwearable. We'll go to plan B."

"Was there a plan B?"

"Thanks to Sadia, there was. I never cared what anyone wore to this thing. You're on the groom's side. Go buy a black dress. You'll look great."

Eve exhaled, relieved Livvy was so chill. "I think there's a little boutique in the village." She used to go to the village when she was young. Their first lake house had been barely a few miles from here. Her parents had bought a second, more ostentatious one about a year before her mother had died, closer to Rockville. The car crash taking Maria's life had occurred on the road leading up to it.

Eve hadn't mourned when her father had sold the second house, but she'd mourned for the first. Mostly because she'd loved the little bustling village that supported the wealthy vacationers.

"Yeah. Go there. Buy whatever you want."

Livvy coughed. "How's everything else going? You and Gabe settling in okay?"

"Fine." *I saw his butt.* "Really fine. How's your mom and Maile?"

"Doing better than me. I'm gonna go lie down before Nicholas nags me to death. Stay out of trouble until we get there."

Eve smiled faintly. "As someone who has been sick around Nicholas, I can assure you he won't nag you to death. To annoyance, perhaps."

Livvy made a growling noise. "How do you stand him when he gets like this?"

"I . . . don't?" she ventured. "I'm really good at hiding from him."

"Well, I'm not hiding." She sighed. "But I am kind of tired, so I'll go rest. Give Gabe a hug for me. I'll see you two in a couple of days, hopefully."

Eve would definitely not be giving Gabe a hug, but she only murmured her goodbye and hung up.

She waffled for a couple minutes, but then pushed to her feet, grabbing her purse on the way out the door. She slowed as she approached the breakfast room, remembered mortification tingling through her as she recalled Gabe's words.

Go to bed, Eve.

But then another voice edged that aside, and she came to a slow stop outside the wood-paneled doors. *I'm not hiding.*

Of course Livvy didn't hide from anything. She was tough. Smart. Capable.

Normal.

Eve's hands curled into fists. She didn't have to hide in her shell right now. She could set a tone for the whole week and walk in there right now.

What's the worst that could happen?

Well, he could be mean to her. But that wouldn't kill her. She'd survived mean men before in her lifetime.

She straightened her shoulders. Adjusted her hair. Adjusted it again. Tugged on her shirt. Finally, she pushed the door open. Gabe glanced up, and she nearly retreated, but instead, she forced herself to enter. "Good morning," she said, her gaze directed slightly over his shoulder. It was a trick she'd learned when she was a kid when her father would demand her attention.

A Chandler doesn't stare shyly at the ground. You're not a scared mouse. You look at a person when they're talking to you.

Thankfully, he hadn't talked to her much.

Gabe came to his feet in a surprising show of manners. "Eve. I wondered if you were awake yet."

She suppressed the gallop of her heart. He'd wondered if she was awake yet. That didn't mean he was thinking of her, per se. Just if she was awake. "Oh yes. I, um, was going to—" There went her bravery. She cursed herself, hating how flustered she sounded, and she momentarily forgot her trick and looked at him.

He wore snug jeans and one of his endless supply of plaid shirts, this one a faded and comfortable blue-gray. She bet it was soft. She bet it would feel good against her cheek if she curled up in his lap and snuggled close.

"Do you want some breakfast? They asked if I wanted the buffet, but I thought that would be a little too much for the two of us. There's a bell right over there, though, so if you want something, I can call . . ."

Eve cocked her head. Gabe's body language was strange, the way he avoided her gaze, the rushed words, his hands tucked into the backs of his pockets.

She forgot her own embarrassment and dismay. Hell, she almost forgot his butt. She was too awash in realization.

He was embarrassed and ill-at-ease.

Amazed relief swamped her. She wasn't the only one who felt weird. And somehow, knowing she wasn't alone in this situation allowed her to take a step closer to the table. "Would you like to come with me? To the village?"

He stopped rambling. "What?"

"My groomsperson dress was delivered. There was a mix-up, and, long story short, I need a new dress for the wedding, so . . . would you like to come to town with me?" She almost added, *Unless you're too busy* or *But you don't need to I'm fine on my own*, in case he needed a way out, but then she stopped herself. He could figure his own way out, if he needed it.

"Yes," he said slowly. "I don't have anything else to do."

In that case, sir, please do me.

Without a doubt, a very unseemly thought for a lady to have. She clutched her purse. "Follow me, then."

Chapter 8

GABE PROBABLY shouldn't have agreed to come on this ride, but every second he'd sat at that breakfast table and contemplated how Eve's face had looked when he'd sent her away from his room—and his naked ass—he'd felt more like the aforementioned ass.

It might have been morning, but he'd started to crave a shot or a beer—more evidence, perhaps, that he needed to take a break from alcohol. It was hard to sit sober in that big room with only his thoughts for company.

His relief when she'd finally come downstairs had been cut short by the way she'd avoided his gaze. He never wanted any woman to be embarrassed around him. So he'd slapped on his most cheerful persona and went to work. And when she'd asked him to come to the village, he'd agreed.

He glanced at her in the driver's seat. They'd opted to take her car, mostly because he'd been excited to get in the well-maintained antique powder-blue convertible. It had seemed like an odd choice for her, even odder when he realized she drove it like a grandma, top up.

He wasn't about to tell Eve how to drive her own car. Still, it seemed a shame she didn't open it up on the curving mountain for the full sexy convertible experience.

Not that he needed to find her any sexier than she was. She wore tall brown boots and jeans and a button-down shirt today, her hair neatly contained in a complicated knot at her nape. They didn't speak much on the drive down, which was good, because he had to concentrate hard on many things. Like stuffing down the memory of the sexy expanse of her back in her bikini. And all that jiggling. So much jiggling.

And the lust in her gaze.

It was much harder to forget his desire for her ass when he knew she desired his ass. But after a sleepless night, he'd decided to do just that. Besides, it was entirely possible he'd imagined it. Saw what he wanted to see. Made her arousal up out of thin air.

He wouldn't bring up ButtGate. He'd make sure everything was cool by, well, playing it cool.

She pulled into the stretch of civilization that consisted of the village that served the locals and the rich people who owned land in this area. She easily found a spot in front of the post office, and turned off the engine. "If I remember right, there's a small boutique down that way."

"It always had a bunch of mannequins in the window," he mused.

He glanced her way when she was silent. Her face was unreadable. "You've been here before?"

"Yeah. Of course." But then he realized she may very well not know. The Kanes and Chandlers had had matching side-by-side lake houses, until Brendan had sold his and bought a more ostentatious one closer to Rockville. Gabe assumed Tani had sold hers when everything had been liquidated, but who knew. "I used to come here with the Kanes. You were probably too young to remember." And Jesus, that made him feel old, but the reminder was good—that his ass was an old ass.

She didn't respond to that, merely got out of the car, and he followed suit.

The village hadn't changed much at all. It was still picturesque and quaint, a light dusting of snow away from being a Hallmark movie.

He took note of the hesitation in her step when they passed the ice cream parlor. "Do you want to get some food? You didn't eat, right?"

She checked her watch. "I can't get ice cream now. It's not even noon."

"You're an adult. One of the great things about being an adult is being able to eat ice cream at all hours."

She tucked her fingers into the front pockets of her jeans. "I'm good, thank you."

He fell into step beside her as she walked down the picturesque main street. He nodded at the few locals who were out and about. Well used to vacationers and strangers, they regarded the two of them with distant curiosity. "How long has it been since you've been here?"

"Years."

Longer for him. He'd stopped coming on the Kanes' vacations when he'd hit eighteen. It would have been odd for him to accompany the family after that.

They slowed as they approached the end of the street and took in the empty storefront. "Huh," Gabe said. "Looks like the shop went out of business."

"Well, this is a problem."

"We can drive farther away."

She pulled out her phone. "I'm pretty sure the nearest mall is almost an hour away."

"That's not too bad." He'd be okay spending an hour in her company, enclosed in that tight little convertible.

"I wish I could order something online and have it delivered, but nothing ever fits me—" She stopped midsentence as she turned and he followed her gaze to a little shop across the street.

"Is that a tailor?"

"Yes. He's a designer too." She didn't bother to check traffic as she drifted across the street. No need—the road was nearly deserted, the summer vacationers still far away.

"A designer, here? In the middle of nowhere?"

"Don't let the location fool you. He used to live in Manhattan. His partner loved it out here, so they moved, but the people who know, know how to find him."

They stopped in front of the window and Gabe glanced between her and the black dress that had caught her attention. The skirt was made up of lace flounces and rosettes, the belt a diamond buckle. The neckline was a sweetheart, coming low over the mannequin's chest.

"That's pretty."

"It's beautiful," she breathed.

He looked at the dress again and nodded, though he didn't understand enough about women's fashion to make that call without seeing it on. "Did you want to look at it?"

She shook her head. "I . . . it's a little too ostentatious for the wedding. I have no need of it."

No need of it? Since when did rich people ever care whether they had need of something if they wanted it? Granted, beyond Eve's convertible, she didn't live that luxuriously. Her clothes and jewelry might be expensive but they were understated and elegant.

She might have said she didn't have need of it, but she didn't say she didn't want it. Those were two different things. "Let's go inside," he said, and unlike with the ice cream shop, he didn't wait for her to protest, merely charged inside.

The old man behind the counter looked up when they walked in. "Hello. How can I help—" He craned his neck so he could look around Gabe, squinted, and then laughed. "My God, is that Evie Chandler?"

Gabe glanced over his shoulder, surprised. Eve hadn't said anything about knowing the proprietor personally.

His question halted, though, at the expression on her face. A smile spread over her lips, and Gabe finally realized something.

She'd smiled at him closemouthed, reserved. She was showing her teeth here, and her eyes were crinkled up. She was thrilled to see this man.

He ignored the stab of jealousy he had no right to feel and focused on her happiness.

She drifted past him. "Mr. Perez. Hello."

The man hobbled out from behind the counter. "Come here, come here."

They embraced while Gabe stood awkwardly behind them in the little shop. The older man pulled away and held her hands. "You're the spitting image of your mother," he breathed. He looked around her and gave Gabe a friendly smile. "And who's this, your husband?"

"Ah, no." A delicate flush touched her cheeks and she stepped aside. "This is Tony Perez. He designed some of my mother's most cherished dresses. Mr. Perez, this is Gabe. He's a . . ."

"Family friend," he said automatically.

Mr. Perez's dark eyes narrowed. His skin was a medium brown, and lines had been carved deep around his lips. "You look familiar."

Gabe nodded. "I get that a lot."

The older man snapped his fingers. "Did you used to vacation here with the Kanes?"

Unease slithered down his spine. "When I was very young, yes, sir."

"I remember now. You used to come to the village with Robert! My cousin ran the ice cream parlor. I remember seeing you in there. Always drinking a milk shake. You were much smaller then, of course."

His smile felt tight. "Yes, sir."

"Good to see you again. You grew up big and strong. The Kane size rubbed off on you, eh?" The wizened little man shook his hand, then thankfully turned to Eve. "Well, what can I do for you, Eve? You need a dress? It's been so long. It would be an honor to make a dress for Maria's daughter."

"Oh no. I'm—"

"You liked the dress in the window," Gabe interjected. He wasn't here to butt in, but he had no idea why Eve was being so shy about admitting she liked that gown. Especially when they'd come to town to buy a dress.

Mr. Perez brightened. "That one's a little too big for you, but I could have it fit to your measurements in a couple of days. Business is slow."

"But—"

Gabe tucked his fingers into his jeans pockets. "What luck. She needs a replacement gown for her brother's wedding this weekend."

"For Nicholas's wedding?" Mr. Perez looked utterly delighted. "I would be honored if you wore one of my creations to such an important event. I will give it to you on the house—"

"No," she said quickly. "I don't take things for exposure. If I buy a dress from you, I'll pay."

Mr. Perez pursed his lips, but he didn't argue. "If," he scoffed, and moved away, to the front window. "As if I would let Maria's daughter wear anything but my own creation."

"Why do you want me to get that dress?" she whispered, once Mr. Perez was out of earshot.

"Why don't you want to get it?" Gabe countered. "It's pretty, you like it, and we won't have to drive all over the county to get something that's not as good."

She opened her mouth, then closed it. "It's a lot of money," she said.

"Do you not spend money on clothes?" He shoved his thumb over his shoulder. "You didn't skimp on the car out there."

"Why do you care?"

It wasn't an antagonistic question. She truly was confused as to why he cared.

So was he, to be honest. Except he'd liked seeing the smile on her face and the look of pleasure in her eyes, and he wanted to keep them there.

Before he could answer, Mr. Perez was back. The older man gestured at a seat for him, and led Eve to a small, curtain-enclosed area. She cast him one last searching look before the dressmaker whisked the curtain shut.

SHE FELT like a princess.

"Come out, Evie. Let me see what I need to do to fix this."

Eve closed her eyes, thinking of all the times she'd accompanied her mother to this shop and heard Mr. Perez call out the same thing, while she sat outside, sipping her root beer float.

Her chest tightened, with fear and grief. It had been a mistake to come here with Gabe, but there was no hope for it now.

She walked out from behind the curtain. Gabe lounged on the sofa, tapping something into his phone. He glanced up at her, blinked, and then blinked again. "Wow. You were right. That's beautiful."

Delight warred with wariness. She couldn't have manufactured a better response, or one more boyfriendly.

This was confusing and weird and emotionally fraught.

"Very nice, very nice," Mr. Perez murmured. He led her up to the dais, and she reluctantly stepped onto it, worried the multiple mirrors would show a different reflection than the one in her changing room.

But no. The dress, though slightly large, could have been made for her. The skirt flared with gentle ruffles, the bodice far more low-cut than anything she would have ever chosen for herself.

She swallowed. *Cute* or *attractive* were the words people generally applied to her. In this, she looked downright sexy.

Mr. Perez walked around her, pinching the fabric and muttering to himself. "Tighten it here and here. Won't take me long at all."

She smoothed her hand over the skirt. She'd come too far to back out of this now. Something large and dark loomed on her emotional landscape, the sharp winds prickling against her skin. *What's the worst that can happen?* "Can you have it ready by Saturday for sure?"

"Of course."

She raised her hand to her naked collarbone. "This neckline is low."

"I can add a bit of sheer fabric." Mr. Perez critically eyed her chest. "Yes, trust me." He whipped out his measuring tape and a notebook and started scribbling in it. "Hold still."

She let him do his job. Gabe was out of her line of vision in the mirrors, though she could feel his gaze on her.

He was right. She spent money, though not as much as she probably could. Her clothes were expensive, her cars more so.

She hid the trembling of her fingers in the skirt of her dress. She knew why she was so affected, buying a dress here, but it was irrational to feel this pulse of fear.

She had to be rational. This was not bad or wrong of her. This was okay.

When Mr. Perez wrapped the measuring tape around her waist, he paused and smiled nostalgically. "Do you know what your mother used to say? *Leave me enough room to eat and dance.*"

Oh. Eve breathed out a sharp breath, the prickles of pain clogging up her sinuses. "I remember."

"My mom says the same thing."

She glanced over her shoulder. Gabe's eyes were warm on her, his phone neglected on the couch next to him. "She wears a lot of leggings these days. Says she doesn't want to miss out on something delicious because of buttons."

"Smart lady," Mr. Perez observed.

"Yes." She nodded at Mr. Perez. "Yes, leave me enough room." *To eat and dance.*

Eve held it together while he finished taking measurements, though her fingernails had left indentations in her palms by the time they were finished. She couldn't look into the mirror as she changed, for fear of seeing her mother there instead of her.

She could feel her smile growing more wooden and fake as she chatted with Mr. Perez and determined her bill. After much haggling, she paid what she believed was a fair price for the dress and his labor, though she was sure he was still undercharging her.

Gabe coughed when they agreed on the price, and she glanced over her shoulder, certain she would find him judgmental and glowering. But it wasn't her father standing there. As she watched, Gabe flicked through something on his phone, and coughed again. It was the dust, maybe, then. And not the frivolous, wasteful spending she was engaged in.

She sniffed as they walked out the door, the terrifying trickle of tears clogging her sinuses. She had to hold it together. She couldn't lose it in front of anybody but especially not this man.

She might have made a mistake in bringing him with her. So much for sticking her neck out and not hiding. She wouldn't have broached the memories in this store had he not urged her to enter. She would have merely coveted the dress from outside and walked away, probably driven an hour plus to buy a far inferior dress off the rack. "Are you okay to head home?" She was proud of how well modulated her tone was.

"Sure."

She recalled what Mr. Perez had said about Gabe's childhood. She wanted to ask him a million questions about the life he'd lived before she'd come along, but she didn't know how. "Do you want to get a milk shake before we go?"

"Huh?" He followed her gaze to the ice cream parlor. "No. I'm good."

"I didn't realize you came to the Kane's lake house so often as to be a regular."

"From when I was adopted 'til I graduated high school."

There was something curiously flat and rehearsed about his answer, and she wanted to question him about that, but she'd do it later, when she wasn't dealing with her own memories. "Ah."

They stopped at her car, and she got into the driver's seat. "The weather's nice," he commented. "Want to put the top down?"

That was a good idea. The wind might whisk away any tears that leaked out.

She drove sedately out of town, but as each mile flew behind her, pressure and fear and memories built up inside her, and she pressed her foot down harder on the accelerator. The wind whipped through her hair, burning her face, and she drove faster.

They sped up the road, and around each curve. She let the car become a part of her body, allowing it to take them farther and higher, every sense alert for any other drivers. The road was blessedly empty, though. It was them and pavement.

"Goddamn, you can drive."

She glanced at Gabe, and his grin morphed into horror as his gaze met hers. "Are you okay?"

Fresh fear ran through her and she touched her cheek, disgusted and stunned to find it wet. Oh no. She hadn't been able to keep it in. She hadn't been able to keep the facade of perfect, normal blandness in place.

He'd see the cracks. Now he'd know.

She hit the brakes so hard they squealed and pulled off onto a scenic lookout. Her chest rose and fell as she cut the engine.

"What's wrong?" Gabe asked, and his voice was lower now.

She shook her head and wrestled with her belt before tumbling out of the vehicle. She had to get away.

But there was nowhere to run. She stepped up to the edge of the overlook and looked down at the valley, a knee-high guardrail standing between her and the trees below. The spring breeze was warm and gentle on her wet face.

A car door slammed behind her, and she was

too distraught to even tell him to be careful with her baby. "Hey. Come away from the edge." He grasped her biceps and led her back, away from the drop-off, turning her to face him. His thumb and forefinger caught her chin. His concerned expression was blurry through her veil of tears. "What's wrong? Are you okay? Are you hurt?"

She didn't know if it was the concern bathing her, or her tumultuous feelings, but the truth spilled from her lips. "That wasn't the first dress I got from Mr. Perez. I had one when I was twelve."

He didn't respond, just watched her with that patient green gaze.

"My mother too. They matched." The feelings receded as she spoke, an odd disassociation taking over her body. Her voice was flat, her tears still coming, but she couldn't feel them. A temporary respite, this freedom from feeling. "We came home, and my father saw us. He called me into his office and he made me cut up the dress."

Gabe's mouth tightened, and he cupped her cheek. "What the hell."

She was too distraught to register the intimate touch. The excuses for her father rose up in her throat, the excuses she'd always fallen back on. "He was trying to teach me about fiscal responsibility," she tried to explain, even though a part of her understood how absurd that was. "I was twelve, and it was a fancy gown. I had no place to wear it, really. The money could have been better spent."

Gabe squinted at her. "You don't actually believe that's the best way to teach a twelve-year-old that sort of lesson, do you?"

"No," she whispered.

"Are you feeling guilty about buying that dress today?"

Fear and anxiety twisted up inside her. "Yes. My purchase today was frivolous."

"It was. Do you have the money?"

"Yes."

"Is it your money?"

It was. She hadn't touched much of her salary when she'd been at the foundation. She also had a trust fund from her grandmother she rarely tapped. None of her money came from her father, not since she was eighteen. "Yes."

"Did the dress make you happy?"

"Yes." It had, in between the anxiety.

"Does that happiness hurt anyone, Eve?"

"No."

His lips curved up. "Those are the things I ask my clients sometimes. If something brings you joy and hurts no one else, I don't see the harm in indulging yourself every now and again."

She swallowed. What an utterly simple way of looking at life. She could barely wrap her mind around not cluttering up her every desire with guilt and worry.

"Listen." He stroked his thumb over her cheek. "You're not twelve. No one can scold you for the things you buy with your money."

It wasn't until that moment that she realized

how close they were standing. He was so much bigger than her she had to crane her neck up to look at him.

Please don't go smelling him again.

"I know I don't know you well, but I can assure you, life is short. You should do what makes you happy."

I don't know you well. Her desire to smell him vanished. Well, not completely, but it was definitely dampened.

That was right. She took a step back, swiping her hand over her cheeks and clearing her throat, embarrassment creeping up on her. He didn't know her well, and between this and the butt incident last night, he probably thought she was a strange, overemotional pervert. "I'm sorry I cried all over you."

"Don't be sorry."

"I would—I would like to go for a walk, I think." She glanced up at him, memorizing his red-tipped lashes and his pretty face. He was so beautiful and uncomplicated, and she was a mass of feelings and secrets and longings. "Can you take the car back?" She tossed him the keys before he could agree. He caught them automatically.

He frowned. "Walking? All the way back?"

"It's not far. I know this area. There's a trail."

"I don't think—"

"Please." The word was more plaintive than she might have liked it to be. "Please let me be alone."

He froze, then nodded, his lips compressing.

"Okay. For the record, I don't like this one bit." After another searching look, he walked away. She waited until her car was gone before she let the tears come again.

He wasn't the only one who didn't like this.

Chapter 9

Eve WASN'T purposefully moping in the woods. She was just taking a very roundabout way to get back to the house. By looping the estate three times.

Liar.

Okay, she was moping. But since she had to go back to the house sooner or later and face pretty, perfect Gabe, who was probably eaten up with concern over her well-being, she could be forgiven for a little moping.

Eve kicked a pine cone as she walked and pulled out her phone, opening her messages.

Hey, you. Coming back soon?

Gabe had sent that an hour ago. She'd responded immediately, hating how she must be worrying him. He was so nice. **Yup. I need some air. I'm really fine. Please go enjoy yourself.**

She closed out of her messages, then dialed Madison. Her friend was out of breath when she answered. "Hello."

Eve winced. After years of living with Madison, she could identify that breathlessness. "Oh, you're busy with Reese. I'll call back later."

"How do you know I'm not at the gym?"

Eve glanced up at the sky. The days were getting longer, and the sun was starting to set. "We don't go to the gym, Mad. That's why we make good roommates. I don't guilt you about the gym, you don't guilt me about the pizza I eat four times a week."

"Listen, if I wasn't lactose-intolerant, I'd be right there with you."

She half-laughed. "I'll let you get back to your boyfriend."

"He can wait," Madison said, and ignored her boyfriend's yelped, "Hey!" in the background. "What's up?"

"Can you tell me I'm not weird," Eve blurted out, feeling silly and needy, but unable to stop herself.

"You're not weird," Madison said with so much certainty Eve felt like she'd been wrapped in a blanket of love. "You are absolutely, completely, one hundred percent not strange or abnormal, and nothing is wrong with you. You are fine as you are."

She sat down on a stump and placed her head in her hands. "Okay."

"You don't believe me."

"I was trying so hard."

"With Gabe?"

"Yes. I stuck my neck out. I sat in a hot tub with him, and I talked to him. I saw his butt—"

"Wait, what?"

"That's not the important part."

"Butts are generally important, but I'm going to let you slide a little here, Eve."

"It was an accident. There was a mix-up in our rooms and . . . anyway. He told me to go away, and I felt upset and scared, but then this morning I stuck my neck out again, and I asked him to spend the day with me."

"That all sounds great, Eve. I don't see a problem." Madison thought for a second. "Can we talk about the butt now?"

"No. And I haven't told you the problem yet. I did all of that, and then I blew it."

She quickly gave Madison a rundown of what had happened at the dress shop. Her friend was silent for a beat until she finished, and then she growled, "I hate your father so much."

Eve wished she could hate Brendan. She'd rather hate him than feel this yearning desperation for a father who had always been needlessly cruel to her. "I didn't tell you that story, I don't think."

"No."

"It was only a dress. I overreacted," she fretted.

"No, you didn't."

"I cracked, like I did when Livvy came back to town."

"No. You. Didn't. And you didn't crack then either, or whatever you want to call it. Your reaction isn't the problem here, love. You've done the best you can with the tools you have at your disposal, and every emotion and reaction you have is valid and fine."

The words were simple and Eve knew Madison wouldn't tell her she'd overreacted or anything, but she felt validated nonetheless. "Why is feeling so hard?"

"Well, you're kind of new at it. You've been shoving your feelings down for ages." Madison growled again, "Ugh, have I mentioned how much I hate Brendan? I'm going to dick punch him."

"Don't dick punch him."

"Remember that time you purposefully spilled your coffee on Malcolm's Burberry scarf sophomore year?"

Eve smiled. "Yes."

"That was your version of a dick punch. Best friends get to dick punch men who are awful to their best friends."

She swiped the back of her hand over her nose. "I don't think much of myself, Madison. But I don't think I can be so awful of a person if you can love me."

There was a beat of silence, and then Madison cleared her throat. "You are not an awful person at all," she said, and her voice was husky. "And I do love you, but you don't need anyone's love to validate that you're not an awful person. You're simply a wonderful person."

"Are you guys done yet?" Reese's distant, annoyed voice came through over the line. "You live together! Can't you build each other up when she gets back?"

"Go make us some sandwiches, Reese," Madison shot back.

Eve ran the back of her hand over her eyes and laughed. She never cried much, but today the tears kept coming. "Go hang out with your boyfriend."

"*His* butt can wait."

"Madison!"

"Put mustard on my sandwich!" Madison yelled back.

Eve grinned, her spirits firmly lifted. "I love you."

"Call or text me the second you start to feel like something is wrong with you," Madison said sternly. "I don't care if I have Reese's butt right in my face, I'll shove it aside to tell you there isn't."

Eve smiled. "I will. Bye."

She tucked her phone away. Though it was extremely unladylike, she used her shirt to mop up her tears. A few deep breaths later, and she felt steady enough to return home.

Her roundabout, rambling walk meant she emerged from the woods near the front of the mansion. The setting sun highlighted the beauty of the huge house. The architecture was grand, the pillars in the front making it look even bigger than it was.

For a second it was like someone had put tracing paper over the home, and she could imagine that this was the estate she'd used to frolic in as a child when they'd come up to this very lake.

She had loved that house, though she'd often been alone—her brother, Paul, Livvy, and Jackson all off together. She'd patter along behind her mother as Maria hummed and danced in the kitchen. Her mom had liked cooking.

Maria, we have people who do that for us. Stop acting like you're still poor.

Eve tensed and she placed her hand over her heart, as if that could control the organ better. She rarely ate Greek food anymore. Not because it pained her to be reminded of her mother's cooking. It pained her to be reminded of the fact that her mother had eventually stopped cooking. After a certain point, Maria had stopped humming and dancing too. At least when Brendan was around.

By example, her mother had taught Eve it was better to be ignored than ridiculed or chastised. Let no one see her. No one could hurt her if they couldn't see her.

Out of habit, she touched her wrist, but only her sun-warmed skin greeted her, her bracelet obviously absent. She walked slowly to the entrance, pausing by the small fountain in the middle of the circular driveway. There was no one around to witness her behavior. She dipped her fingers into the water, letting the liquid coast over the digits.

Her refection in the water wavered as she moved her hand back and forth, each second melting away another inch of her dizzying stress.

Gabe had seen her. He hadn't hurt her, though he'd witnessed her breakdown. On the contrary, he'd been kind and thoughtful. Her head just had to transmit that fact to her instincts.

What was the worst that could come from him seeing her?

He'd think poorly of her. And who cared if he'd been left with a bad opinion of her?

You do.

Livvy wouldn't. Madison wouldn't. Sadia— well, Eve didn't know Sadia that well yet, but the woman seemed far too busy with her child and her work to care what anyone thought about her.

So she wouldn't either.

Eve removed her hand from the water, flicked away the droplets, and straightened. Easier said than done, but she could try to do it.

GABE CROSSED his ankle over his knee and took a sip of his iced tea. He knew he shouldn't be as worried as he was. Eve was a grown woman. She'd texted him she was fine.

But he couldn't get her tearstained face out of his head.

He finished the final marks on the sketch he'd made on his tablet, a perfect, elegant dress. It was the dress, of course, the one she'd bought, and it was her body, though he'd left the head off. Bad enough he was drawing inspiration from her. He didn't need to go re-creating her face.

His phone rang and he almost fumbled it, trying to get to it in time. His hope that it was Eve calling him died when he looked at the display. He answered. "Rhi."

"I swear to God, if you don't tell Mom to back down about this dress thing, I'm not coming to the wedding."

Gabe bit off a smile, though Rhiannon couldn't

see him. Or could she? He didn't trust his tech-savvy sister. There was a reason he'd taped over the webcam on his laptop the second they'd started making webcams on laptops. "You know I can't do that."

His sister growled. He imagined her flopped on her hand-me-down sofa in her darkened ware-house apartment, black hoodie pulled over her head, tight black curls peeking out around her face. At some point, he'd ask Rhi what she did with all her cash, because she definitely didn't seem to be spending it on anything tangible. "Mom listens to you," whined the thirty-six-year-old woman who was regularly featured on the cover of tech and financial magazines.

"Mom listens to no one. You know that. And you can't skip the wedding."

Rhi sighed. "I like Livvy. I really do. She is a tolerable human."

That was high praise, coming from Rhi. He noticed she didn't say anything about Nicholas, which wasn't too surprising. Most men were beneath Rhi's notice. "She is more than tolerable. You can't skip the wedding." More than appearances, he wanted her here. "I haven't seen you in forever. Come for me."

"Ughhhhhhh. Fine."

"If you could wear something remotely dressy, Mom would probably get off your back," he suggested.

"Mom won't be happy until I'm wearing an evening gown to every damn place, including the grocery store. She says I need to dress my net worth, whatever that means."

"It means she didn't have much money when she was young, and she wants to make sure no one gives you the hard time they gave her," he said soothingly.

She gave an annoyed growl. "Thanks for making me feel bad, jerk."

"You asked." He scanned the tree line, most of his attention on waiting for Eve to emerge.

"How's your little game of Clue going?"

"Clue?"

"Yeah. You know. House party. Rich people. I'm guessing there's a creepy butler."

"He's not exactly creepy. Just formal. Also, no one's dead yet and most of the actually rich guests haven't even arrived."

"You're there alone?"

"I'm with Eve."

"Eve . . . the little Baby Chandler?"

Funny how he'd stopped thinking of her as young. "Yeah."

"Aw. How old is she now? In college?"

"She's an adult. Twenty-four."

There was a beat of silence and then Rhi spoke. "You like her."

Gabe glanced around, but there was no one on the deck. The door to the home was closed. "Yes, I like Eve. She's a good person. Fun. Sweet." Hot. Mysterious.

"I mean, you liiiiiiike her."

Gabe rolled his eyes, though his sister couldn't see it. "You are the worst."

"I'm the best, and don't you forget it." Rhi dropped her teasing tone. "Far be it for me to interfere in your love life—"

"Then don't. There's nothing going on between me and Eve." Except mutual lust. Maybe mutual lust? Or he'd imagined that interest in her eyes the night before. Anything was possible.

"But a Chandler would be messy."

"You think I don't know that?"

"I mean, any sweet young woman would be messy for you."

He narrowed his eyes. "I'm not a messy guy."

"With the wrong woman? You'd be devastating."

"Hey now."

"No offense, baby brother. You're decent and kind and charming. But you're basically that guy who we in the industry call the several-night stand."

"I don't even know what that means."

"It means a guy who's terrified of intimacy, but also doesn't want the impersonal hassle of a one-night stand. So you sleep with one woman multiple times, which, cool. But it's all shallow. You don't really call her or talk to her outside of bed. You drop her when it gets too close."

Jesus. Now both of the women in his family were harping on his intimacy issues? "That makes me sound like an asshole. I'm never with a woman who doesn't want the same thing as I do."

"You aren't an asshole. Just a man in the modern-love world." Rhi grunted. "Dating isn't what it used to be."

"You made a fortune off a dating app."

"I didn't say I don't take responsibility for my small role in creating this hellscape," Rhi said, sounding mildly offended. "It is what it is."

He opened his mouth to protest, but then closed it again. What could he say, really?

Was she wrong? Not totally, no.

Fuck, that was depressing. "I can't . . ." He stopped. There was no way to end that sentence. It wasn't that he couldn't, it was that he didn't know how to be close to someone else. "You're right. Regardless of what I prefer, getting involved with a Chandler would be messy. Especially with . . . you know."

"Yeah." She was silent for a beat. "Robert."

He dropped his voice to a murmur, because a murmur was all that he could manage. For a secret that had ruled his whole life, for as far back as he could remember.

They hadn't kept it a secret from him. He'd always known. And he'd always known he had to keep it under wraps. "Yeah. Robert makes everything messy." Flat and emotionless. The name tasted vile on his tongue, but not because he hated Robert.

No, he'd loved the man. Resented him. Adored him. Craved his attention. Hate was too simple an emotion to encompass how Gabe felt about Robert Kane.

"You know, little brother . . . Robert is dead, and—"

A scrape from behind him had his head rising, a shot of adrenaline running through his system.

He glanced over his shoulder, but no one was visible through the glass door. "I gotta go," he told his sister.

"Okay, fine, I'll stop talking about this."

"No, it's not that. I just have to go."

"I'm not wearing a dress to this wedding," Rhi reiterated.

"Yeah, yeah."

"I mean it."

"Rhi, we'll talk about this later. Love you, bye." He came to his feet and went to the door, opening it. He took a step over the threshold. "Hello?"

"Sir?"

He startled. Alistair had seemed to melt out of the shadows. Was that who he'd heard? "Uh. Hi. Did you need something?"

"No, sir."

Gabe mentally recapped the things he'd said to his sister, but he couldn't think of anything terribly inculpatory. "I was waiting out here for Eve to get back to the house, but I think I'll go to my room. Can you have dinner sent up?"

"Certainly. And Ms. Chandler arrived back at the estate. I believe I saw her heading toward the library."

"Oh." He glanced right, then left. "And which way is the library again?"

Alistair's faded blue eyes didn't so much as betray a hint of emotion. "To the left. Go down the hall, make a right, a left, and you're there."

"Fantastic. Thanks."

He made it to the library and stopped at the

threshold. Eve stood in front of a bookcase. Her hair had come undone from its braid, and little wisps were all around her face.

She looked up from the book she was perusing. The only trace of her earlier tears was the redness in her eyes and the slight puffiness of her skin. Her face was otherwise composed, as it always was. "Gabe."

His remembered rage at Brendan rose up inside him. That story had been wild. How a man could be so needlessly stern and cruel to any child, let alone his own daughter, Gabe didn't know. "You should have told me you were back." He softened his tone immediately. "I mean, I wanted to make sure you were okay."

"I'm fine." She closed the book. "I apologize for worrying you with my outburst."

She wasn't fine. That formal tone, her stiff posture, the carefully precise way she was speaking. He got it now. It was part of her facade, like the closemouthed smile.

And it's none of your business. Who was he to think he could help? Even his closest relatives had made it clear he was nothing more than a shallow playboy.

Messy.

Yeah, it would be far too messy, and messy was intimate. So he plastered on his own mask and smiled. "I get it. We all have parental baggage."

She turned and put her book away. "Do you? Have baggage from your father?"

Her back was to him, so he let his grin slip for a

second. "My dad died when I was a kid." He had some fuzzy memories of Reggie Hunter, and lots of photos and stories from Sonya.

"Right. I'm sorry."

"Don't apologize." He frowned, and shook his head. Weird. He felt like he'd said exactly those words to her at some point recently. "Do you want to maybe eat dinner outside? There's a—" No, the fire pit would be too romantic. What was the least sexy place they could eat? "Stable."

She faced him, another book clasped to her chest. "You want to eat dinner in the stables?"

Fuck. "Uh. Sure."

Her lips curled up. "I think I'll spend the evening reading in my room, if you don't mind. I have a headache."

"Sure. I'll . . ." He held up his tablet. "I have some work to do." He'd lose himself in drawing all sorts of tiny, intricate designs. Ones that had nothing to do with her.

She came abreast of him, and he couldn't stop himself from grasping her arm. She stopped and looked up at him.

There was no interest or lust or sadness in her eyes. There was nothing. She was locked down, the perfect heiress. It was a mask, and he couldn't help but be intrigued by all the things swirling under it. "You're okay, Eve."

For a second, the mask slipped, and he saw confusion and yearning, but then it was gone. She nodded and slipped away, and he was left curling his hand into a fist.

Chapter 10

Eve stared out her window. She was glad she'd wound up with Gabe's room. It gave her a perfect view of the lake.

And Gabe, who had been slicing through the water for the past twenty minutes, the sun glistening on the water and his body.

She shoved the rest of the croissant in her mouth, barely savoring the taste of butter and blackberry jam.

Sneak.

Yes, she was a sneak. Growing up trying to fly under the radar meant that no one ever noticed her. Like when they were talking about business.

Or personal stuff.

I like Eve. She's a good person. Fun. Sweet.

She chugged her orange juice, unable to take her gaze off Gabe's flat stomach as he rose from the water like some kind of Poseidon.

She hadn't meant to eavesdrop yesterday. She'd only gone to the deck to tell Gabe she was fine and apologize for her tears. But then she'd heard her name through the flimsy doors.

He liked her. She knew she wasn't supposed to care what he thought of her, that she wasn't supposed to have her self-worth validated by someone else, but she'd been thrilled he liked her, even after her scene. She hadn't had time to relish that before he'd spoken again, though.

Getting involved with a Chandler would be messy.

Involved, like not platonically? She'd processed that sentence with the thrill it deserved. And then he'd utterly confused her.

Robert makes everything messy.

What did Robert have to do with Gabe?

She'd been so confused she'd instinctually run away instead of facing him. There was something niggling at the back of her mind, and she couldn't quite figure out what. It was like she was looking at a puzzle, and all the pieces were far too spread apart and disconnected, but the finished picture was right there. She'd turned over a couple of hypotheses in her head, but they were too absurd and far-fetched to be true.

She chewed her lip, watching him. Making a split-second decision, she threw on her swimsuit and cover-up, grabbed a towel and some sunscreen, and made her way downstairs.

Even if she couldn't solve this mystery, she could at least savor his company, knowing he still liked her. Also, she could stare at his butt. Clothed or not, it was a work of art.

By the time she reached him, he was working on his ever-present tablet in a deck chair on the bank of the lake. His hair was wet and down for once, trickles of water falling down his chest. He looked up with some surprise when she approached, then smiled.

"Eve. There you are."

"Hi." She dropped her towel and sunscreen on the chair next to him. Normally she'd be self-conscious about her brief swimsuit, but he'd already seen her in her bikini. Besides, he liked her.

Maybe that was why she couldn't figure out the puzzle, when she normally was so good at critical thinking. She was too distracted by the fact that he liked her.

She pulled off her cover-up and sat down, arranging herself on the lounger.

"How are you doing?"

She controlled her flush at his delicate question. Like she'd freak out if he asked after her state of mind. "I'm fine. You?"

"Good. The water's warm, if you want to go in."

She looked out at the lake. She always wanted to go in, but she'd rather take apart the mystery of Gabe. "Maybe in a little while."

"How was your book?"

"Huh?"

"The book you were reading last night?"

Oh the book. Or rather, the prop she'd grabbed when she'd heard his heavy footsteps coming down the hall to the room she'd hidden in. "It was great."

"What was it about?"

Organic chemistry. She hadn't so much as

cracked it open. She was smart, she wasn't a masochist. "Uh, a mystery."

"Maybe I'll borrow it when you're done."

"Cool." She made a mental note to find a mystery in the library later.

They lapsed into a comfortable silence, Gabe turning back to his tablet. She tried to surreptitiously crane her neck to see what he was doing.

"I'm drawing some flash designs," he said, which told her she wasn't as surreptitious as she'd hoped. "I do walk-in days occasionally."

"Ah."

He showed her the screen. He'd drawn two delicate birds on a flowering perch. She smiled. How such a large man could do such tiny, intricate work, she didn't know. "That's adorable."

"Thanks."

"I've thought about getting a tattoo," she admitted.

"Yeah?" He kept his gaze on the tablet.

"I don't know what I'd get, though."

"Do you know where you'd want it?"

She touched the side of her ribs, under the bikini. "Right here."

He spared her a quick glance. "Hmm. That's specific."

"I have a scar there." Why she was telling him this, she didn't know, except she supposed he made her feel comfortable in all situations.

He put down his pen and gave her his full attention. "From what?"

"When I was fifteen, I had pneumonia." Her father had ignored it. The housekeeper had checked in on her, proclaimed she had the flu, and Eve had been young enough and sick enough to not insist on professional care even though it hadn't felt like the flu.

Luckily, her brother had visited the house on a whim, had come up to her bedroom to see her. She had vague memories of Nicholas bundling her up and putting her in his car, the emergency room and people talking about antibiotics and surgery.

But she remembered the recovery very well, and her brother sleeping in her hospital room. Her father had stopped by twice a week, mostly so the hospital staff didn't gossip about how he wasn't visiting his daughter.

Nicholas was a good brother. There was a reason he was so overprotective and meddled so much in her life. In his eyes, she'd never stop being the fifteen-year-old kid who could have died without his intervention. "It was a long time ago, though. And it left no lasting effects."

Gabe fiddled with his pen. "Hmm."

She roused herself and grabbed the sunscreen. "Would you like some?"

"I don't really burn."

"Neither do I, but it's good to protect your skin anyway."

He made a face, but he accepted the lotion. She couldn't help but stare as he rubbed the lotion into his arms. His biceps flexed. The sun had already kissed his skin a shade darker.

Her eyes narrowed as she stared at that skin. The puzzle pieces all slowly clicked into place, leaving a hunch that was almost too ridiculous to believe.

Getting involved with a Chandler would be messy.

Anyone could say that, for any number of reasons. Granted, her parentage had traditionally been the reason men wanted to get involved with her, but she could see how, in Rockville, some people might be wary of her name.

But the rest of it . . .

Robert makes everything messy.

For Livvy and Nicholas, Robert Kane made things messy. If she'd ever gotten involved with Jackson, same. Robert Kane was a very specific wedge between the Kanes and the Chandlers.

But not between the Chandlers and anyone else.

So the one possibility was that she'd misunderstood, and he'd been talking about another Robert completely. Or that she hadn't misunderstood.

And getting involved with a Chandler was messy because he was a . . .

"How old were you when you were adopted?"

His eyebrows raised at her sudden question. He answered anyway. "Three."

"Were your parents looking to adopt?"

If she hadn't been staring at him, she would have missed how the skin around his eyes tightened. "That's how it always goes, doesn't it?"

"I suppose. Or sometimes there's other circumstances."

He placed his tablet on the chair, his pen on top of it. "Like what?"

Like paternity and secrets and cover-ups. "Do you know anything about your birth parents?"

He blinked once. "No."

He was lying. And there weren't many reasons for him to lie.

Had she thought him uncomplicated and simple?

She closed her eyes and opened them, and in the space of a few minutes, Gabe transformed from a beautiful, unattainable man to a breathing, three-dimensional human who had issues and problems and family drama of his own.

Her gaze drifted over his arms. The sleeves were made up of various elements—flowers, a steam-punk clock and gears, trees, a sword.

As beautiful as it was as a whole, her gaze didn't linger on any of that. No, it was the top of his right shoulder which caught her attention, a geometric design that had been worked so seam-lessly into the rest of the sleeve it was barely vis-ible on its own, except for the black ink arching over his shoulder.

She'd seen that design before. "Your sleeves. Did you design them yourself?"

"Yeah." He touched his right arm. "I got this one first, then the other."

"What do they mean?"

He smiled faintly. "Lots of things."

"I like that they're unique. Not the usual tribal—" She stopped, finally recalling where she'd seen that pattern on his shoulder.

Tribal.

It was a Hawaiian design. Jackson had it on his upper arm. And once, when she was a kid, she'd spotted it on Robert Kane's forearm. She'd assumed it held some specific meaning to the Kane family.

Genes were funny things. She was a carbon copy of her mother—there was no way to tell who her father might be simply from looking at her. Her brother was a mix of Brendan and Maria. Jackson and Livvy resembled each other a little, but people were often surprised to discover they were twins.

Eve thought about Robert as a young man. If she unfocused for a second and took some of Gabe's features and blurred them out, and swapped his darker skin for Gabe's lighter, slightly tanned complexion . . . if she changed his hair to a deep auburn instead of almost black . . . switched his eyes from black to green . . .

Oh shit.

She's like my sister.

Gabe's words about Livvy, when he'd been inebriated in the back seat of her car, came back to her. When she'd been young, Eve had had a tutor who deplored the word *like*, so much so he'd forced Eve to write an essay on good grammar whenever she used it.

She's, like, my sister.

Which was a different sentence than *She's like my sister.*

Oh my God.

She's, like, my sister.
She's my sister.

Eve closed her eyes, puzzle pieces sliding into place. That picture of Robert holding a baby on Gabe's shelf. If that baby was Gabe, it would explain why Gabe had that photo, in that place of honor, next to a photo of his adoptive family. It would explain why Gabe had been given privileges most wealthy families probably wouldn't have given the children of their help, like private schools and family vacations and new clothes and solo trips to get ice cream.

Gabe was a year older than Paul and Nicholas. Paul had been born almost exactly nine months after Tani and Robert had married. It was entirely possible Gabe could be the product of an affair that had occurred before Robert and Tani's marriage.

If he was Robert Kane's child . . .

Oh shit. What were the odds that she and her brother would both be obsessed with Kanes? Was this some kind of cosmic joke?

This wasn't just messy. This changed everything.

"Eve?"

She jumped. "I, um . . . I'm gonna go up to the house. I forgot . . . something . . ." She gathered her stuff up hastily, conscious of his gaze on her.

She didn't get far, barely clearing the first hundred yards into the trees before a hand wrapped around her upper arm. "Eve."

She stopped and breathed deeply, refusing to

face him. If he looked at her, he'd know all the wild thoughts racing through her head. Her facade was too cracked right now to prevent him from seeing everything.

He clearly didn't care about her facade. He exerted pressure on her arm and spun her around. His face was harder than she'd ever seen it, lips grim. She should have been terrified, but she was too shocked to feel anything but flabbergasted amazement. "What's going on in that head of yours, Eve?"

"Nothing."

"Liar."

She tried to wipe all emotion from her face, but she didn't think she succeeded. "I don't know what you're talking about."

He stepped closer, and she moved backward, each step making her feel like she was retreating from a suspicious mountain. "You're lying. Something is up."

She made a rough attempt to go on the offensive. "What do you think is up?"

He opened his mouth, then closed it again. His Adam's apple bobbed. "You know something."

"Nope. I don't know anything. I am knowledgeless. I—oh." The bark of a tree dug into her back. There was nowhere left to retreat to.

There was something dark and hot in his gaze, something that made her shrink back even more, even while a slow burn started in her belly. Who was this? This wasn't the Gabe she knew. This Gabe was almost . . . dangerous.

Dangerous and . . . really, really hot.

His big hands came up to brace himself on the tree on either side of her head. He leaned in close. She breathed in. She couldn't distinguish between the scent of him and the forest.

"Don't lie to me," he growled.

"I—I'm not. I don't—"

"Why did you ask me those questions? About my tattoo? About my birth parents?"

A spy she'd never be. "Don't know. Making conversation."

"Eve."

Damn it. She was literally between a rock and a hard place, except she wasn't sure which one of those descriptions applied to Gabe.

His shoulders blocked the sun. There was no room to do anything but stare at him helplessly, prey caught by the predator. "Your shoulder. Jackson has the same design tattooed on his arm."

His chest rose and fell. "So?"

"Robert did too."

His lashes lowered. "So?"

"I'm fairly sure the tattoo is somehow related to the Kane family, and you don't seem the type to appropriate."

He lowered his head so they were nose to nose. "What does that mean, then?"

"I—I don't know—" She gasped when his big hands wrapped around her arms, and gasped louder when he picked her up like she weighed nothing and brought her to eye level.

No one had picked her up since she was a child.

One boyfriend had even complained if she'd tried to straddle him.

Do not be distracted.

But he had *picked her up*. There was something very sexy about feeling small and dainty enough to be manhandled.

"Eve. Talk."

She licked her lips. "I overheard you on the phone last night." It was like someone had taken whatever filter had been in front of her eyes and ripped it off. She couldn't unsee the resemblance now. Gabe's broad forehead was a direct replica of Jackson's, his hair lit with Livvy's glossy sheen, despite the difference in color.

His nostrils flared. "What did you hear?"

"I heard you say it would be too messy to get involved with a Chandler."

"And?"

"Because of . . . because of Robert."

His hands tightened on her arms. "Shit. You guessed, didn't you?"

She trembled. "Gabe. Was Robert your father?"

She didn't need an answer. He paled. She immediately forgot her unease and grasped his biceps, seeking to comfort him. "It's okay. Don't freak out. I won't tell anyone."

He shook his head. She'd never thought a man so big and tough—a man who could pick her up, no less!—would ever look so helpless and distraught. "No one knows." His tone was bleak, the words tripping over each other.

"No one will," she whispered, though that

wasn't her place to promise. "I'll keep it a secret."

His laugh was a harsh bark. "What am I supposed to do? Just trust you?"

"Yes." She placed her hand on his cheek. It wasn't comfortable, being dangled like this, but it was exhilarating. The adrenaline in her blood spiked, and she leaned in closer, driven to comfort and consume him. "I'm very good at secrets."

He shook his head. "You don't—"

She had no idea what he was going to say, because she settled her lips over his. It was a ridiculous urge, born of panic and desperation and a deep-seated drive to calm him. Their lips fit together perfectly, and she moved them over his, tasting the faint hint of mint in his mouth.

Finally. Finally. Now she knew what kissing him felt like.

It was perfection.

He froze for a second, but then a growl came from deep in his chest. He tightened his hold on her, crushed her close, and kissed her back. Their noses mashed together until he moved his head, letting their lips and tongues work.

One hand grasped her hip and hoisted her higher. Small wasn't something she was accustomed to feeling and she wanted more of it. All of it. She wrapped her legs around his waist and he grunted, pressing her tighter against the tree. His fingers roamed under her cover-up, over her back, up to her bikini top strap, and she breathed deep, waiting for him to flick it open.

Instead, she got knocked back down to earth, quite literally. Her feet hit the ground as he untangled himself from her, ripping his mouth away. She pressed her hands to the tree for balance. He strode away from her, the green dragon on his back coiling as he ran.

Chapter 11

F<small>UCK</small>, F<small>UCK</small>, fuck.

How could he have been so fucking careless?

How had she been able to extrapolate the truth he'd spent his whole life hiding from two fucking overheard sentences?

She was smart.

Far too smart. She'd pieced together everything without him having to say a word.

And then he'd kissed her. Fucking hell.

He bounded up the steps to the back porch. Before he could open the door leading to the house, though, it flung open. "Uncle Gabe!"

He caught the six-year-old who flung himself at him automatically, picking him up and hugging him tight. He buried his face in the little boy's silky black hair, trying to compose himself.

Paul and Sadia had been childhood sweethearts, and they'd gotten married not long after the tragedy that had taken Robert's life. When Kareem was born, Gabe had been one of the first ones at the hospital. Paul had laid his son in Gabe's arms and laughed. *Meet your honorary nephew.*

It had been one of the few times Gabe had been tempted to reveal his secret. *He is my nephew.* His lips had formed the words, but fear had halted them. Instead, he'd tucked the baby close to him and vowed silently to look after the kid as well as any uncle could. Since Paul had died, he'd done his best to ensure Sadia and Kareem were happy and healthy.

Paul's son had all the best parts of him, with a heavy dose of Sadia's sweet charm. Every time Kareem called him uncle, his heart tightened a little.

Right this minute, it hit him particularly hard. He cleared his throat. "Hey there, kiddo. I didn't realize you were coming today."

Kareem pulled back. His cheeks were still round with baby fat, his black eyes dancing. He was a cheerful, bright boy. "The oven got fixed."

"Thank God." Sadia stepped out onto the deck. She was tall and curvy, with long black hair that rippled over her shoulders. Kareem looked a lot like her.

"Mom got mad at Uncle Jackson because she said he was more worried about his oven than he'd be over a human."

Sadia rolled her eyes. She and Jackson had been dating for months now, since he'd come back to town. No one who had ever seen the way Jackson looked at Sadia found it odd that he was in love with his brother's widow. "Kareem, stop telling everyone that."

"But it's funny, cause Uncle Jackson said to

Mom—" Kareem hunched his shoulders and growled "—'that's because there's only a few people I like more than this oven.'"

Gabe didn't feel much like smiling, but his lips stretched up. "Where's Jackson?"

"He made a beeline for the kitchen, as usual. The butler is showing him where it is." Sadia flipped her hair over her shoulder. Her skin was glowing. Love agreed with her. "Looks like you went for a swim."

"Mmm."

"Relaxing?"

"Sure." Until Eve had turned his world upside-down.

A little black puppy tumbled out of the house. The mutt was fluffy, one slightly smaller ear giving him a mischievously quizzical look. He chased his tail around twice, yelped, and came over to attack Gabe's feet. "Who's your new friend?"

Kareem beamed. "Aunt Livvy gave me a wedding present."

"Wait, wait." He lowered the boy and raised an eyebrow at Sadia. "You gave me grief for giving Kareem a drum set, but Livvy gets to get him a living creature?"

Sadia stepped in for a quick hug. "The puppy has been discussed before. The drum set was not."

"I haven't seen Uncle Gabe's drum set in a while," Kareem said.

"That's weird," Sadia said vaguely. "I'll look for it when we get home."

"What's the dog's name?"

Kareem squatted and petted him. "Smoke."

"You said you wanted to name him Cookie," Sadia observed.

"I like Smoke more now."

"Smoke's a good name." Gabe gingerly took a step away from the puppy. He was so small Gabe feared he would crush him. "Cute."

"Hello, Sadia, Kareem."

Gabe tensed at Eve's voice and tensed further when Kareem squealed, "Aunt Eve!" Kareem darted around Gabe to launch himself into her arms. "Hi."

"Hi there." She ruffled his hair and pressed a kiss on his forehead. For a second, when she looked up, their gazes met, and he forced himself to look away. He couldn't. His mask would crack.

Sadia embraced Eve. "You look like you got some sun. Sorry we had to sit out a couple of days."

"Yeah, I did." Eve tugged at the hem of her cover-up. Her legs were short and perfect.

He wanted them around his waist.

Gabe crouched down and scratched the puppy's ears, the silky fur not calming him. He had to control himself.

Eve shifted. "I'll go help Jackson in the kitchen."

Kareem brightened. "I'll come with you. Uncle Jackson says I'm a big help in the kitchen."

"I'm sure you are." Gabe didn't look up when she moved around him.

"Maybe we can all go for a nice walk around the lake after we settle in," Sadia said brightly.

Gabe didn't hear Eve's reply. He was too busy panicking.

He didn't want to hear Eve speak. He didn't want to see her move. He didn't want to go on a walk with her. He didn't want to be reminded that she knew.

Not with Jackson and Kareem around.

The circle of people who knew Robert Kane was his father had been limited to Robert, Tani, his parents, and Rhi. That was it. To the rest of the world, he'd been the housekeeper's kid, nothing more. For the first time in his thirty-five years, someone else was in the inner circle, and he didn't know how to compute.

He abandoned the puppy, who scampered after Kareem, and rose to his feet, facing Sadia. She smiled at him, the lines around her eyes crinkling. Even during some bad spots, Paul had always thought the world of Sadia and so did Gabe. "Sorry we were delayed," she said.

"No problem." He cleared his throat. "Actually, I got a call from work. There's an emergency," he lied. "I have to go check on the shop."

She raised an eyebrow. "That's an eight-hour round trip. They can't manage without you?"

"No."

"You know, Livvy's feeling better. Maybe she can go over and—"

"No, they need me." He cast around for something that only he, as an owner, could do. "A legal, financial . . . thing."

"A legal and financial thing?"

"Uh, yes."

"Oh. Livvy and Nicholas are arriving tomorrow. When will you be back?"

Tomorrow was Wednesday. If he came back tomorrow, he'd still have days to go before the wedding on Saturday. Days of being in Eve's company.

There was no help for it, though. He didn't want to upset Livvy. "I'll be back by then."

Sadia shrugged. "Okay. Don't stay gone for long. I could use another non-Kane-or-Chandler here."

His smile felt frozen. But at least it was there, hiding everything else.

EVE WALKED in on a minor crisis. Alistair stood inside the kitchen, wringing his hands, while a short, rotund man in an apron yelled at Jackson. "Who the hell do you think you are, coming in here and rearranging my kitchen?"

Jackson folded his massive arms—slightly bigger than Gabe's arms, but the same general musculature, Eve noticed—and stared at the smaller man. Smoke scurried over to Jackson and flopped himself over one of the man's large feet. Kareem pressed close to her leg. She cleared her throat delicately. "Is there a problem here?"

Jackson turned his gaze on her. He was so different from Gabe—his darker brown skin, the shape of his eyes, his distant attitude—but at the same time, he was so similar it made her head spin.

How had no one seen the resemblance before? And who on earth was Gabe's birth mother?

Okay, you have to shelve thinking about Gabe for like half a minute. Maybe even a full minute.

"The kitchen needs to be rearranged. It's a mess," Jackson said. The flat tone might have fooled people into thinking he was arrogant, but after months of getting to know him, Eve knew that wasn't the case. He was reserved, like she could be. He was also painfully introverted.

Alistair cleared his throat. "Our understanding was that Mr. Kane would be using the kitchen on Friday and Saturday evening, for the festivities. We have hired Chef Arnold for the remainder of the time."

Jackson shifted. Smoke growled and abandoned his perch, wandering off to sniff along the baseboard. "I changed my mind. I want the kitchen all week."

It took a second for Eve to understand what Jackson was saying. He *needed* the kitchen.

"Is this man even a chef?" Arnold spluttered.

Kareem gave a soft snort at her side and Eve almost echoed it, though silently. Jackson was a world-renowned chef. Well, anonymously. He traveled the world as the culinary genius behind Kāne, a pop-up restaurant dedicated to comfort food. Mac and cheese, poke, katsudon, curry—there was nothing the man couldn't do with fresh, humble ingredients.

Eve rested her hand on Kareem's head and launched straight into event planner mode, adopting a soothing tone. "Thank you, but we'll be okay handling our own meals, Alistair. Chef Arnold, why don't you take a vacation for the rest of the week? Paid," she tacked on hastily when the man's face turned red.

"That sounds fair." Alistair relaxed.

Arnold sniffed, his bulbous nose twitching. "Fine," he finally said, and stomped out, Alistair trailing behind him.

"Was that necessary?" she asked when they were alone.

Jackson shrugged and opened a drawer. "What else am I supposed to do around here for days?"

"There are lots of activities."

"Activities with other people."

"You know us, though."

Jackson paused. "No offense intended. I prefer having some alone time now and again."

"Uncle Jackson is shy," Kareem whispered in a tone that was louder than most people's shouts.

Jackson's face softened. "Sometimes."

Eve wondered now if Jackson's concern for the malfunctioning new stove had partly been a delaying tactic. "No offense taken. I understand needing alone time."

"Thanks for dealing with those guys. Ariel usually handles procuring kitchens for me. And, uh, generally talking to people."

Ariel was Jackson's business partner. Eve had heard a great deal about the older woman who managed the non-cooking side of Kāne. "That must be a full-time job."

"It is. Don't worry, she gets paid really well."

"She's coming to the wedding, right?"

"Yeah, for sure. Kareem, can you come here and rearrange the spoons like I like?"

"From biggest to smallest, yup." Kareem scampered to him.

"I'll go change, and I can help," Eve said.

"Not necessary. I'm sure you have things to do." He glanced up. "Or you can rest. I know Gabe can be a little exhausting."

"No, he's not. Gabe's wonderful."

He grunted. "He wants to be everyone's friend."

Which, to an introvert, was like a five-alarm warning sign. However, Eve's empathy with Jackson apparently ended at the suggestion Gabe was anything less than wonderful. "He's a good friend."

Jackson stopped, knives in hand, and stared at her. "I didn't say he wasn't. I like him."

"Why is there a chef yelling at our butler in the front foyer?" Sadia entered the kitchen and placed her hands on her hips. Then she took in her son, busily rearranging a drawer, and Jackson, examining the knives, and shook her head. "Jackson, we discussed this. You'd try to relax."

Jackson placed each knife back in its spot. "This is how I relax. Besides, I have to get used to the kitchen before the wedding."

Sadia made an annoyed noise. "Well, great, now Gabe's gone, and you're going to be in here all day."

Eve stiffened. "Where's Gabe?"

"He had some emergency at work. He said he'd be back tomorrow, when Nicholas and Livvy get here."

Eve's heart sank. She would bet money there was no emergency at work. Gabe had run away. From her.

The puppy came over to Eve. She bent down and picked up the creature, bringing him to eye level. He was a little funny looking, a proper mutt. She couldn't help but smile when the dog licked her nose, as if he sensed she needed comfort.

Eve didn't know much about puppies. She'd never been allowed to have a pet. Somewhat awkwardly, she cradled him like a baby and scratched his back. His furry head rested on her arm and his eyes drifted open and shut.

This is not about you. The rational whisper brought her relief. Gabe wasn't running because she was awful. He'd run because of his own issues. Because he was a three-dimensional human. Not a perfect flawless cutout she could impose a crush on.

"Looks like it's you and me and Kareem, Eve."

Eve wanted nothing more than to go to her room and get her head on straight, but she didn't want Sadia to suspect something was wrong with her, and trace it back to Gabe. She'd promised him she would keep his secret. He hadn't believed her, but that was fine. She'd protect him.

Besides, it might be good for her to get out. "Maybe we can go down to the village."

Sadia brightened. "Yes, I like that idea."

"I wanna stay here with Uncle Jackson," Kareem protested.

Eve's smile grew stronger. "There's an ice cream shop in the village. You can bring Smoke."

Kareem dropped the spoons in his hands. "I wanna come to the ice cream shop."

"Finish what you're doing first." Jackson's rebuke was mild, but Kareem immediately picked up the spoons.

"I'll go change." Eve looked down at the snoozing pup. The cloud of worry was diminishing with every stroke of her fingers over the baby's fur. "Smoke is very sweet."

"Yup." Kareem concentrated on carefully putting the cutlery away. "He makes everyone feel good. He's special."

"I don't want to disturb his nap." She clutched the small warm weight closer to her chest. "I can watch him while you all freshen up."

Sadia grinned. "That is an excellent idea. We'll meet you in the foyer in a little bit."

With each step away from her friends, Eve's worry over Gabe ratcheted up. But midway up the stairs, Smoke snuffled and licked her arm, and she calmed a little. There was nothing she could do about the man. Right now, she would do her best to distract and enjoy herself.

She hugged her unexpected bundle of comfort.

Because it wasn't about her. Gabe had his own demons, and she wasn't one of them.

Indeed, he liked her. Enough to kiss her. Her lips tugged up. In her emotional turmoil, she'd almost forgotten, and that wouldn't do. That kiss was worth remembering, even if she never got another one.

Chapter 12

W<small>HO'S</small> <small>MY</small> beautiful horsey? Is it you? It's you."

Eve brushed her horse, smiling at Livvy's nonsense cooing next to her in the large barn. Livvy and Nicholas had arrived this morning, and Livvy, fully recovered from her illness, had burst into Eve's room, where she'd been low-key moping, and dragged her to the stables.

The Kanes and Chandlers hadn't kept horses, but all of the children had grown up riding. She hadn't realized how much Livvy adored horses, though, until the other woman had squealed upon entering the barn. She'd claimed a dappled gray mare for herself named Polka.

"She is pretty," Eve agreed.

"Shh. You can't call another person's horse pretty." Livvy leaned over and checked her horse's hoof, her long braid swinging over her shoulder. "It'll give your horse a complex."

Eve looked into the wide-set eyes of her black horse. She'd chosen her because the creature looked calm. "You're the prettiest horse, Dot."

Livvy stroked Polka's side and whispered loudly, "She doesn't know what she's talking about."

Eve couldn't help her laugh. Livvy's silliness and Sadia's bracing practicality and Nicholas's constant check-ins that she was okay and even Jackson's silence. They'd all occupied her for the past twenty-four hours while she wrestled with what to do about Gabe.

He liked her as a friend, and then he liiiiiiiiiked her, and then it turned out he was the illegitimate son of her family's former enemy and no one knew?

She had whiplash.

She made sure none of her agitation was visible in the slow brushstrokes along her horse's hide. A lady didn't show the world her upset.

"There you two are."

Automatically, she pasted a smile on her face and glanced at her brother entering the barn. Nicholas looked relaxed and healthy. He'd gained a little weight since he'd started seeing Livvy, and it looked good on him.

"Should have known you'd be with the horses. Hey, Eve, you know how there's always one girl who draws horses all over everything she owns? That was Livvy."

Livvy stuck her tongue out at her fiancé, but didn't dispute that. "What do you want? I'm bonding with my darling."

Nicholas checked his watch. "Sadia sent me to fetch you. You have to go get your dress."

Livvy pouted. "But Polka and I have almost become one."

"You can take her for a spin later." Nicholas rolled his eyes. "Hell, we can buy you a horse later if you want."

She buried her face in the horse's mane. "Horses are expensive."

"We can afford it."

"We don't have stalls."

Nicholas shrugged. "We can buy a house with enough land to build stalls."

Livvy lifted her head and stared at Nicholas, but he was checking his phone. "Come on, Livvy."

"I'm a little scared the dress won't fit," Livvy admitted.

"There's no such thing as the curse," Eve said. "Besides, I think I already took one for the team with dress mishaps."

Livvy and Nicholas exchanged a glance, and Nicholas smiled. "She's right. It'll fit, and you'll come back happy. But if you don't go, you're going to have no dress to walk down the aisle with and then we're going to have to elope to Vegas like I wanted in the first place."

"Your poor grandfather would have never recovered. Fine," she muttered, and started putting her equipment away.

Eve tried to hide her disappointment. "Would you like to come for a ride with me, Nicholas?"

"Where are you going?"

"There's no set destination."

"So you're just . . . wandering?" Nicholas shook

his head. "No, thank you. I'll stay here and catch up on work. Why don't you check with Jackson? Or Gabe, when he gets back."

She maintained her smile, though the idea of talking to Gabe right now was a little unfathomable. *Hey, so. I know you're still pissed I overheard this explosive secret and horrified that I now know your parentage, and also we kissed, but would you like to go on a relaxing ride with me to the middle of nowhere?*

That would go over real well. "I'll see who I can find," she hedged.

Nicholas drifted closer, and pitched his voice low so Livvy wouldn't overhear him. "You haven't heard from Dad yet, right?"

She focused on her brush. "Of course not." After much debate, Nicholas had invited their father to the wedding.

She didn't know if Brendan would show up. As far as she knew, he'd avoided saying anything bad about the Kanes by completely ignoring the fact that his son and heir was with Livvy for the past eight months. Eve didn't know how tense work must be for her brother, but she imagined it wasn't easy.

"He's not coming, I'm guessing." Nicholas absentmindedly petted the horse.

"I'm sorry."

He shook his head. "I'm not. He knows the terms of his showing up. If he can't handle them, then he has no place at my wedding. Or in my life, outside of our professional ties."

Eve pressed her palm against her horse's mane. Nicholas's words were cold and pragmatic, but Eve caught the hint of longing in them.

Nicholas wanted their father to show up to his wedding. And why not? Brendan was their only parent, toxic or not. "Would you like me to call him?" She wasn't sure what she would say. She could count on one hand the number of times she'd called Brendan over the past few years, and she doubted she could prevail upon the man's better qualities. Of the two of his kids, Brendan gave Nicholas a smidge more respect.

Nicholas shoved his hands into his pockets. "Absolutely not. Don't worry about it. By the way, I got an email that Shel's going on maternity leave."

Willing to be distracted, Eve cocked her head. "Who?"

"Shel? She's grandma's sister's—oh, it doesn't matter. She's a relative."

Ah. The Chandlers did have an awfully large extended family, not that she or Nicholas knew many of them well. Their grandfather had always had a tendency to define *family* loosely, happy to claim anyone remotely related to him or his late wife. "That's great. Shall I send her a baby present?"

He shook his head. "My assistant already took care of it. The important part is that a job opened up."

"Head-hunting is work," Livvy said, coming out of the stall. "We said no work this week."

Nicholas casually draped his arm around his fiancée's shoulder and dragged her close for a kiss. "Not work. Just talking to my sister. Since I have a perfect candidate for Shel's job right here."

Eve's smile faded. "What's the job description, Nicholas?"

"Something in marketing."

Her heart pounded dully. "You don't even know what the job is. How do you know I'd be perfect for it?"

"Well, you won't know what you're perfect for until you try it." Her brother's smile was guileless, but he hadn't gotten to where he was by being sweet and innocent.

"Nico. We agreed you wouldn't bug Eve about this stuff." Livvy's face and tone conveyed her displeasure.

Eve knew her brother thought she was drifting, "finding herself" as he derisively called it, and maybe she had been when she'd first quit her cushy job, but that wasn't the case any longer.

Eve opened her mouth, ready to explain all of this to him, but he leaned forward. "Let me help you, Eve. I understand wanting to take a break, but you know . . . Chandlers, we work."

She drew back, her words stilled. She was well acquainted with the Chandler work ethic. "I'm aware."

His gaze was appealing. "I only want to make sure you're doing okay, kiddo."

Kiddo. Because she was a kid.

The business plans she'd made suddenly seemed childish and silly, like she'd drawn them in crayon instead of with spreadsheets. "Right. I'll look at the position," she managed.

Relief crossed his face. He gave her an approving smile, and despite her annoyance, she soaked it in like a sponge.

She wasn't stupid. She knew she had parental issues. Since she couldn't get her father's approval, Nicholas's had become the most crucial thing in the world. The last thing she ever wanted was for him to look at her with anything less than adoration. And she knew if she did propose her business idea to him, he wouldn't mock her. He'd pet her on the head and probably invest.

But she didn't want that. She wanted him to see her as smart and savvy and a success. She didn't want him to throw some money at her like she was a pampered trust fund girl with a shiny toy.

"Good," he said, and turned to walk away.

Livvy hung back for a second, and waited to speak until Nicholas was out of earshot. "I'm sorry. I've told him to leave you alone."

Eve looked down at her feet. They were clad in sensible boots. "It's not your fault he thinks I'm a kid." She glanced up. "I do have a plan for my life. I know it seems I've been aimless, but I have a purpose."

Livvy's gaze was sympathetic. "People thought I was aimless when I was traveling around the country, but I also had a purpose. Sometimes big brothers don't understand that not working is part of a larger plan. You're okay, Eve. Take your time."

It would be nice to confide in Livvy, but she

didn't want to put Livvy between herself and her brother. That wasn't the mature thing to do. "He thinks I'm a child."

Livvy grimaced. "Sometimes people need to be taught to see you as who you really are rather than who they think you are, you know? It's not easy."

She mulled that over, taking it apart, examining it from all sides. "I guess so."

After they'd left, Eve led her horse out of the barn, easily finding the trail through the woods. She started at a slow pace, but the worry inside her had her urging the horse to go faster and faster. The hooves pounded on the dirt trail, the wind stinging her face in the most pleasant way. It wasn't as good as swimming, but it was exertion. Her vision narrowed so it was only the five feet directly in front of her. She let the horse take her far away, her mind clearing with every step.

Eventually, she became conscious of an ache in her thighs. She reined in, finally taking stock of the unfamiliar surroundings. She'd gone way farther than she'd intended, leaving the private path behind. She glanced up at the darkening sky. Ugh. The forecast hadn't called for rain this week, but unexpected spring storms weren't unusual upstate.

She turned her horse around as the first drop of rain fell on her nose, and then another. And then another. She pulled her phone out, wiping the rain off the screen, but GPS was no good here—she was out of range of a signal.

She shoved her phone back into her pocket.

It was fine. She'd follow the trail back, and even if she couldn't make it to the house, she vaguely recalled spying a little cabin not far back. It had been one of those emergency outpost things the parks department maintained. If it wasn't open, she could take shelter from the rain on the porch there.

She kicked her horse into a trot when the rain started coming down in earnest, though after a few minutes, it didn't much matter—she couldn't get more soaked than she already was. Still, she leaned down and urged her mare into a gallop, her body moving as one with the horse.

But the most experienced horsewoman couldn't have predicted the bolt of lightning that struck down from the sky. She half-wondered if Dot would be all right, but then the creature reared. Eve tried to counter the animal's movements, but gravity proved too much for her. She slipped, the reins falling out of her hand.

There was a second of weightlessness, and she had the very clear, calm thought that this was it. The ground was rocky and hard. If she hit her head, she could very well not make it.

But it couldn't be it, because there was far too much she hadn't done yet. She was too young. She hadn't made her mark on the world, or proved herself to her brother. She hadn't spent enough time with Livvy. She hadn't learned every bit of wisdom she could from her grandfather. She hadn't properly kissed Gabe, or another man she desired as much as him.

Eve tried to twist, recalling what she'd learned about falling off horses, and when her body hit the ground, she knew she'd done her best to minimize broken bones and a concussion. Still, pain slammed through her when her back and head smacked hard dirt.

She didn't lose consciousness, though. She lay there, panting, shock running through her now that the immediate crisis was over. In the distance, her horse whinnied, its footsteps growing farther away as it raced hopefully back home to the barn.

Well, hell. Maybe she'd spoken too soon about that stupid curse.

Chapter 13

Gabe DIDN'T have to knock on the front door. It flung open when he raised his fist. Simultaneous fear and pleasure hit him as he took in tiny, beaming Livvy standing there.

"Gabe!" She embraced him, and he returned the hug, giving her a little extra squeeze. "If it isn't my favorite boss."

He closed his eyes and summoned every ounce of his acting ability, relief making him dizzy. On the ride up, he'd imagined all the worst case scenarios, and they revolved around Eve spilling the beans while he was gone. *He's your half-brother, Livvy and Jackson. No, I don't know any of the details. More tea?*

But that was unfair, and not really Eve's style, or at least not the Eve he thought he knew. When Livvy stepped away, he hoped his smile was as easy and relaxed as ever. He was Livvy's boss, and her friend, and nothing more. "Why are you out of breath?"

"I was trying to beat the butler."

He nodded like that was a normal explanation.

He was sure in Livvy's head it was normal. "Congratulations, kid. You look fantastic."

She smiled. She was pretty and adorable, her smart mouth one of the best things about her. She took after her Japanese American mother and was small in stature, though not in presence. Her hair had been freshly dyed for her upcoming wedding, natural black peeking through strands of opalescent blue and pink and lavender. The light danced on the iridescent colors when she turned her head.

She didn't look sick at all. She was practically glowing, her skin tawny and tanned. If he spent enough time in the sun, he turned exactly this shade of brown.

"Thank you, thank you. It's because I'm the bride, obvs. We get a little extra glow."

"You certainly do."

"Come on in!" She stepped aside and held out her hand. "Can I take your bag?"

He hefted his duffel over his shoulder and gave her a mock glare. The bag was almost empty. He'd only brought his electronics and a change of clothes to and from his home last night. "No. I'm a man. I can't let you, a mere lady, take my bag for me."

"Oh, that's good, because my fragile lady muscles would probably splinter into a million pieces," she said cheerfully. "You can leave it here, though. The help Nicholas hired will handle it."

She said the word *help* disdainfully, and after he parked his bag in the foyer, he tugged her hair.

"You used to have help, remember?" he asked lightly. His parents, for one.

"Yeah, yeah, but it's been a while."

"Better get used to it," he said. "You're marrying a Chandler. I can't imagine Chandlers don't have help."

"Nicholas seems to do fine on his own." She lifted a shoulder, and there was a hint of strain around her smile. "We still have some shit to work out, obviously."

He settled for a noncommittal sound. In his view, Livvy and Nicholas should have probably already discussed whether they would have a maid or housekeeper or butler after they combined households, but their relationship was outside the purview of what an employer or a friend could ask about.

"Sadia and I were about to head out. Dress fitting. Nicholas is in the library if you want to hang out with him. I think Eve went for a horseback ride."

He released the breath he hadn't realized he was holding. He would have to see Eve eventually, but she could wait until he figured out how to act normal around her. "Yeah, I'll go say hi to Nicholas. Thanks."

"No problem."

Nicholas sat in one corner of the library at a large desk, a stack of papers in front of him. He glanced up and smiled when Gabe entered. "Gabe. Good to see you." He rose and they hugged quickly, slapping each other on the back. One of the best things to come of Nicholas and Livvy getting back together had been being able to renew his friendship with Nicholas.

Over the past few months, Gabe had often felt a trace of guilt over their increasing chumminess, but he told himself Paul would have eventually reconciled with Nicholas. The man made Livvy so happy. She walked around with a perpetually sappy smile on her face. "Good to see you too."

"I have a quick phone call. Let me take it, and we can catch up."

It was no surprise to Gabe when Nicholas's one phone call turned into a few phone calls. Gabe checked his Ryde app, but Anne hadn't contacted him yet. He'd barely thought about his embarrassing escapade with his driver, until yesterday, when he'd felt Eve's body pressed up against him. The bracelet was tucked away in his bag, next to his electronics.

He put his phone down. He could go get his tablet but he hadn't been able to sketch anything since he'd kissed Eve. He'd realized that every little thing he'd drawn lately had been designs he could imagine on her. Delicate, flighty, whimsical things. Things she really wasn't. Or rather, that he hadn't really thought she could be, until he'd seen her in that cherry-dotted bathing suit.

That suit, that had cradled her lush, decadent body.

He shifted. *She is not for you.* He was not going

to think of the Baby Chandler, or that body or that little roll of flesh on her back. Especially not in the presence of her overprotective big brother.

Kareem burst into the room, his yapping dog at his heels. Kareem beamed at him and tried to tackle him. Gabe caught him with a pretend *oof*. "What have you been doing, kid?"

"Uncle Jackson and I went to the lake to go paddle boarding and then we came back and then we made cookies." Kareem smiled, revealing baby teeth stained with chocolate.

Jackson entered the room behind them, holding a tray of fragrant cookies. He silently placed the tray on the coffee table, and then wandered away to the bookshelf.

Gabe leaned over and swiped a cookie. He hated sweets generally, but he made an exception for these cookies. "I love these. I missed—" He cut himself off, because Nicholas had hung up the phone. Instead, he stuffed the cookie into his mouth, savoring the burst of bittersweet chocolate chips.

These had been called Sam's Cookies back when the C&O had been a joint enterprise, a recipe Sam Oka had brought to the store. After the split, Gabe hadn't gone to Chandler's to buy them. It would have been a betrayal, to shop at Chandler's.

These were even better than Sam's Cookies, though, because they were fresh, gooey, and hot from the oven. He polished off one, and reached for another. "What are you guys going to do now?"

Kareem leaned over and hoisted his puppy up. "I dunno. We're waiting for Mom to come back."

"Hmm." He petted the dog, who curled up next to him. "Gonna stare at the wall 'til then, huh?" The puppy tested his teeth on Gabe's thumb and Gabe smiled, letting the tiny guy gnaw on him.

Kareem frowned at his dog. "Paddles, no. We don't bite."

"Paddles?" Finally off his calls, Nicholas joined them and helped himself to a cookie. "You changed his name again?"

"He liked being in the boat."

Jackson returned, a deck of cards in his hands. "You want to play Go Fish while we wait, Kareem?"

"We should teach him poker. He can be a shark like his daddy was," Gabe said before he could think.

Kareem twisted around to look at him, one hand still on his dog's head. "What was Daddy?"

Gabe cleared his throat. Paul was a tough topic of conversation around these two men. Nicholas had been estranged from him the second the Chandlers had taken over the company. Jackson had left the country around that same time.

Paul had hissed about Nicholas and refused to speak much about Jackson. Gabe recognized that he'd been closer to Paul than either of them, and that wasn't quite right for any of them. He was sure it must hurt Nicholas and Jackson, how could it not? As far as they knew, or even as far as Paul had known, Gabe wasn't family.

His stupid unruly tongue. "Uh—"

"Remember when Paul and I were home from college, and we'd stay up all night playing?"

Nicholas's gaze was far away. He tucked his phone into his jeans, and sat down in the chair opposite them.

"You guys'd let me join sometimes," Jackson rumbled, and took a spot in the other chair. "So you could fleece me, mostly."

"Does that mean Daddy cheated?"

"Never," Jackson said swiftly before anyone could respond. "Your daddy was just really good at bluffing. Bluffing isn't lying," he said hastily when Kareem opened his mouth. "In poker, sometimes you pretend you have a better hand than you have, so you can get a little further in the game. It's okay in this one instance."

Gabe snorted. "Jackson. He was really good at bluffing you, because you were naive. The man had the worst tell."

Nicholas sniffed, and Gabe grinned, pointing his finger at him. "There you go. Before he played." Gabe gave a discreet sniff.

Jackson scowled. "No. I don't remember this."

"Naive," Nicholas agreed. "You were the easiest to—" His words faded. "Fool."

Gabe squeezed Kareem, leaning into the slightly awkward pause. "How about we teach you how to play, kiddo? We should start the next generation somewhere."

"Good idea." Jackson tapped the cards out, then casually shuffled them. Gabe raised an eyebrow when the cards flew back and forth between the younger man's hands. "I've learned a few things," Jackson said mildly.

More than a few things. By the time they finished a few hands, Jackson was up about three hundred dollars, symbolized by chocolate chips Jackson had fetched from the kitchen. Kareem, who had opted to join Jackson's team, whooped as they raked in their winnings.

Gabe pursed his lips as Nicholas sat back and folded his arms over his chest. "Clearly you're not as naive as we thought."

Jackson's face moved in an approximation of a smile. "Not anymore, no."

"Yoo-hoo." Livvy's voice preceded her appearance into the living room. She was almost hidden behind the large garment bag she carried. "We're back."

Nicholas jumped to his feet and pulled the bag out of her hands. "Took you a long time."

"Looks like you guys had fun," Sadia remarked. She raised an eyebrow at the crumbs on the tray of cookies. "You didn't leave any for us?" She perched on the arm of the chair Jackson sat in and tousled her son's hair, then draped her arm around her boyfriend's shoulders.

Gabe had to look away from the way Jackson gazed at Sadia. For such an emotionally reserved man, his face was nakedly soft when it came to her.

Kareem leaned into his mother. "We ate cookies and played poker, like men."

"Men aren't the only ones who can do either of those things," Sadia said archly. She picked up some of their winnings and popped them in her mouth.

Jackson ran his hand over his girlfriend's hair. "It's starting to rain, I see."

She draped her braid over her shoulder. "Yup. We used the umbrella to protect the dress on our run up to the house."

Livvy beamed at Nicholas. "Wanna see my dress?"

The "No!" that came from both Sadia and Nicholas made the rest of them jump.

"What are you doing?" Livvy's maid of honor demanded. "You can't let the groom see the gown before the wedding day."

"It's bad luck," Nicholas chided her.

"Uh . . ." Livvy looked back and forth between the two of them. "Could we have worse luck than what we've had?"

"Let's not jinx it," Sadia said.

"Agreed," Nicholas said. "I'll go put this in the bedroom." He picked up the dress, then glanced around the room. An odd look crossed his face. "Wait. Is Eve still out?" He pulled out his phone, dialed, and lifted it to his ear, his frown deepening. "It's going straight to voice mail." He tried again.

Livvy placed her hand on his arm. "I'm sure she's fine."

A crack of thunder went through the room. The lights flickered.

"If she's out in this, she's not fine," Nicholas snapped.

"Nico—"

"No." Nicholas pointed the phone at her. "I'm

not being overprotective. If she's still out riding in this storm—"

Jackson gently placed Kareem on his feet, then rose. "Let's check the house first, before we jump to conclusions. She might have already come back."

"Gabe, can you look in her room?" Sadia asked, and grasped her son's hand. "We'll go down to the pool."

His wariness drowned out by worry, Gabe nodded. He jogged upstairs and knocked on her door, but there was no answer. Feeling vaguely creepy, he opened the door a crack and peered inside. "Eve? Uh, are you in here?"

Nothing.

He opened the door wider and stepped inside. The room was a mirror image to his, complete with white bedding and furnishings. "Eve?"

Still nothing.

The place smelled . . . good. Like some light floral scent.

Nope, not weird at all for you to be sniffing her bedroom when you're looking for her.

Shamed, he gritted his teeth and made his way back downstairs, where Jackson and Nicholas had congregated in the foyer. "Any luck?"

Nicholas was pale under his tan complexion. "No. And I checked the GPS on her phone, and her last recorded location was about seven miles from here."

"You track the GPS on her phone?" Gabe asked. That was taking overprotective to an extreme.

"I'll go looking for her," Jackson offered, but Nicholas shook his head.

"Not in this rain. I'll go."

"Can either of you ride a horse in this weather?" Gabe asked skeptically. "Or were you planning on walking miles in a thunderstorm?"

Alistair cleared his throat. They all jumped, having not seen him hovering behind a column. Rhi was right, he was a little creepy. "Gentlemen, if I may intrude. There is an ATV in the garage."

Nicholas tightened his lips. "I've never ridden one before but—"

Gabe nodded. There was no question about avoiding Eve now. He had to go fetch her. "I've ridden plenty of ATVs. I'll go. Shoot me her last known coordinates."

"I'll go with you," Jackson interjected.

Before Gabe could respond, the butler spoke. "There's only one vehicle."

"Don't worry." Gabe clasped Nicholas on the shoulder and met his gaze, hiding his worry at the boom of thunder outside. "She's going to be fine."

Chapter 14

SHE WAS fine.

Eve tightened her arms around herself. She had to keep repeating that to herself. She was absolutely and totally fine. In the grand scheme of things, falling off her horse and getting a few bumps and bruises wasn't so big a deal. It could have been a lot worse.

It wasn't like she'd had a near-death experience or anything.

So why did she feel . . . different?

She leaned her hip against the porch rails of the small cabin. The overhang gave her just enough coverage to keep from getting more soaked by the torrential rain pour. Her phone screen had been smashed, but the phone itself was still functional. Once the rain slowed a little, she'd make her way down the trail. Eventually, she would get reception.

She winced, imagining what Nicholas would say when she called him and requested a pickup. He would fume and yell and stomp around. That was always how he expressed his worry for her. She appreciated his worry so much she didn't have the heart to tell him she hated how he yelled it.

She examined the dark sky, the heavy clouds that had blotted out the afternoon sun. It might be a while before the rain slowed. She might as well try to warm up. Eve flexed her frozen fingers and reached into her hair, wrestling a pin out. Then she turned and bent to the cabin's door.

A few months ago, Jackson had been teaching Kareem how to pick a lock. It would have been unseemly for her to ask him to teach her, but she'd paid close attention and then practiced that night. Silly, but it had looked cool.

Of course, that had been on her bedroom door, for kicks, and this lock was different and—

She heard the tumblers click and she smiled. The principle was the same, it appeared. There it went. The knob turned in her hand and she opened the door, peeking only her head in first. She'd worried there might be a wizened old man inside, clutching a shotgun, but the place was as deserted as it looked from outside. It was one room, the floor bare plank. The furnishings were limited to a hot pot in one corner, a lantern, a battered couch, armchair, coffee table, and bookcase. It wasn't the Ritz, but it was dry, and that was enough.

The slight whine of an engine had her pivoting back to the clearing. An ATV came roaring through the foliage, its rider draped in a black rain coat, a big helmet covering his face. Before she could scurry inside, he took the turnoff into the small dirt clearing. She tensed. Too late to hide, he'd probably already seen her.

The bike stopped a few feet away and Eve waited, braced for anything, a shot of fear running through her as she took in the biker's big body. She could run inside and lock the door, maybe push the couch in front of it.

The rider got off the bike and lifted his helmet. Her tension dissolved at the sight of his face.

Had Gabe ever looked so beautiful?

"There you are," Gabe shouted. He walked closer and ducked under the overhang, which suddenly felt much smaller and more crowded than it had before.

He was soaked, his hair plastered to his face. She inhaled. "You came looking for me," she said dumbly.

Like a knight. Or a prince.

She eyed the ATV. It wasn't exactly a trusty steed, but she had no doubt her fantasies would feature that muddy bike instead of a stallion now.

He ignored her statement to eye the ajar door of the cabin. "I see you got some shelter."

"Oh. Oh yes." She stepped aside to let him enter, then followed him in. She cupped her elbows, unease replacing some of her joy. He didn't look as thrilled to see her as she was to see him, but that made sense. He was still probably annoyed and wary of her, while she was just happy to have some company in her bruised, cold, wet state. Handsome company to boot.

"What is this place?"

"It belongs to the park. It's an outpost for rangers. They have them all over." She'd have to make sure they left it in the condition they found it in. Maybe she would make a donation to the parks department. "There was one near our old lake house. When I was young, I would go play—" She cut herself off. He didn't care about her lonely childhood and how she'd created fantasy worlds around a sad state-owned cabin.

Gabe fumbled beneath his raincoat and pulled out a radio wrapped in a waterproof zipped bag. "Your brother's probably going nuts. I had to ride a while past your last coordinates."

Her brother had the annoying habit of tracking her phone. She'd known about it forever, but she hadn't raised a big stink yet. She figured in an emergency it was good for him to know where she was. Right now, it seemed less annoying and more brilliant.

Gabe pressed the button on the side. "Yo."

"Did you find her? Where is she? Is she hurt...?"

"I found her. She looks perfectly fine, and ..." He glanced around the cabin. "We have some sort of shelter. We're inside a little cabin a few miles farther up the road. The ranger outpost. We'll wait it out here until the rain thins a little. Or at least until the lightning lets up."

Static came through the radio, and then her brother's tiny voice. "Give Eve the radio."

She was an adult. So she felt more than a little foolish when she hastily shook her head and mimed zipping her lips.

Gabe raised an eyebrow and spoke into the radio. "Uh, sure. She's right here."

She gave him a disgusted look, but accepted the radio. "Hey, Nic—"

"How could you—"

"I'm fine," she said quickly. "I'm fine, Gabe's fine, and we'll see you soon, okay?"

"The rain isn't going to let up for hours. Maybe overnight."

She bit her lip, not looking forward to trying to make her way through this mess when it was any darker than it already was.

But a night? With Gabe? All alone in the woods?

Ahhhh, this was great. Or terrible. She wasn't sure yet.

Gabe took the radio from her. "Nicholas, we can stay up here 'til the morning. There's a fireplace and some supplies. Don't worry."

"Thank God you're with her. Okay, keep me posted on when you head back."

The relief in Nicholas's voice was more than apparent. Someone had rescued his baby sister, and all was okay with the world.

This wasn't the romantic kind of rescue. This was a "someone take care of this kid" rescue. Her lips turned down. She'd managed to rescue herself fine, but all she would hear about from her big brother was how foolish she was to put herself in a position where she needed any kind of rescuing.

Gabe dropped the radio on the couch. "How'd you lose your horse?"

"The lightning spooked her. She threw me."

"Threw you?" Gabe took a step closer. "Are you okay?"

"Yes, I'm fine."

"Did you hit your head?"

"Only a little," she admitted.

He took another step, then another, until he was standing right in front of her. He captured her chin. And her breath.

His fingers were rough on her skin as he pressed his hand against her skull. She knew he was looking for a bump, that this was a clinical exam, but she couldn't suppress the thrill at his fingers running through her hair. "No bumps." His tone was a little different now. No longer as cranky.

"I mostly had the breath knocked out of me."

"Hmm. Look at me." He produced his phone out of another plastic bag and turned the flashlight on, peering into her eyes.

"Do you know what you're looking for?" she asked, curious.

"I played football in high school and college. You learn about concussions real fast." He let her go. "Your pupils look okay, but we'll keep an eye on you. Sometimes it creeps up on you later."

She licked her lips. "I'm sorry," she said.

"For what?"

Ah, that frost was back in his tone. It made her want to curl into a ball. *Go to bed, Eve.*

Gabe placed the radio on the couch and pulled his wet outerwear off. "Let's get a fire started."

Wait. Something she could contribute. "I can do that."

"You know how to start a fire?"

"I did. I was a Girl Scout." Her father hadn't wanted her to join the organization, but her mother had insisted, wanting her daughter to have a normal life. As normal of a life as she could when her last name was Chandler.

As an adult, she now wondered what negotiation her mother had had to do in order to get her way. What had Maria given up so Brendan would budge on his daughter mingling with the masses?

"I wasn't a Boy Scout."

Well, clearly.

He gave her a quick once-over, like he was trying to figure out whether her hands could ever strike a match. "I can do it."

"Um, it's not like rubbing two sticks together." She pointed at the box next to the fireplace. "They have matches."

The Gabe she'd known would have smiled and cracked a joke, but this grim-faced Gabe only nodded.

With every step away from him, her unease grew. He seemed mad, and she knew how angry men could react. She crouched in front of the fireplace. Her fingers were frozen and she was dripping water everywhere, but she could manage piling the logs and opening the box of matches.

"Sorry to put you in this position. I know this is your vacation."

"That's fine."

"You're all wet now."

He grunted. "Haven't had a chance to ride an ATV for a while. A dirt bike is best when things are dirty."

Her fingers fumbled open the box of matches. "You could have been hurt."

"Unlikely."

After months of driving him around and talking to him, speaking to him like this, without looking at him, felt so normal, she almost deepened her voice to hide her identity. She caught herself and struck a match. It didn't light. "You could be in a luxurious house right now in front of a fire instead of this ratty place."

"I've stayed in worse places."

His tone was short, but his words didn't sound like the words of an angry man. The disconnect only made her more anxious. She struck the match again, but it still didn't light.

She couldn't concentrate on this, not when she was waiting for him to fly into a rage. Why wasn't he yelling at her? Why wasn't he telling her she was dumb and foolish?

Her lips tightened, her temper oddly cranking high. She should be trying to make herself into a ball and disappear. She didn't know why she wasn't, but this anger felt good.

She tossed the matches to the ground, stood, and whirled to face him. "If you're going to get mad at me, can you do it now?" Her words were almost a shout, shocking her. The rain and the bumps and bruises had eroded her self-possession.

Gabe stared at her. "Get mad at you about what?"

"About being stupid and going riding by myself." She could script what her father would say. *You foolish girl. You could have died, and how would I explain that?*

When she arrived home, her brother would shout at her as well, though his lecture would be born of genuine agitation for her well-being. *Jesus Christ, Eve. How could you do this to me? I was worried sick.*

What she couldn't comprehend was why Gabe's grim expression was slowly transforming into puzzlement. "I don't know much about horseback riding. Are you never supposed to go alone?"

Again, there was a disconnect between his questioning words and the snappish tone. "No." She'd gone on plenty of solitary rides. "I would have been fine, except for the rain."

"Are you a riding novice?"

"No."

"You're a grown woman. Why would I yell at you?"

"Because I inconvenienced you."

His brow relaxed, his tone gentling. "This is like the dress, isn't it?"

She linked her cold fingers together. "I don't know what you mean."

"Are you scared of me?"

Yes. She hadn't been when she'd confronted him about his parentage, though he'd looked more ferocious and intimidating at that time than he did now. Adrenaline and excitement had taken her mind off of fear then. "A little."

"Do you think I'll hurt you?"

"Not physically, no."

"Has anyone ever hurt you?"

"Not physically," she whispered.

His lips pressed tight, and he looked pissed again. But she didn't think it was directed at her. "So, here's the thing. I'm really protective of my mom and sister. But they'd murder me if I so much as thought about chastising them for any decision they made. Besides, yelling's not really my style. Yeah, maybe next time you might check the weather forecast before setting out on a ride, but I've done way stupider stuff than getting caught in a thunderstorm."

"You can yell at me about eavesdropping on your conversation, if you like," she said. If she was braced for a reckoning now, she might as well get it over with.

His lips kicked up. "Anything else I can shout at you about?"

Yes, but he didn't know about Anne. "I am sorry I overheard you."

He sighed deeply and looked into the fire. "I'm sorry too."

"I swear I will never tell anyone about your secret," she said, her voice low and intense.

"Your loyalty is to Livvy. I understand that."

"Livvy has, evidently, lived her whole life without knowing about you. Running and telling her now wouldn't help much, would it?"

He stared at her for a long moment, then huffed out a disbelieving laugh. "How about we table that discussion for tonight, Eve?"

"I would rather get it all over with right now."

"I get that. But I'm seriously not going to yell at you. I promise, even if I stomp around and look mad, I don't blame you or anything. This isn't your fault. It's the situation, and you had nothing to do with that."

She inhaled, the relief making her light-headed. Each of her romantic relationships had ended with a single fight, because she'd feared a man's anger too much.

It had made her feel weak and foolish, but her self-esteem was like a fragile, tiny bird. She couldn't risk harsh words stripping it away.

He started to rummage through the chest in front of the couch while she turned back to the fire. The match finally caught a flame, and she lit the logs, blowing on the tiny spark until it grew.

He tossed the old blankets he'd found in the chest on the couch, his boots squishing water.

She imagined saying in her sultriest voice, *You're all wet. You should take your clothes off.*

"We're both soaked," he remarked. His tone was casual. He really had decided to table their issues for the night, it seemed. He was back to being mild, calm Gabe. "I didn't think to bring clothes, but looks like there's plenty of towels and blankets in this chest, if you want to dry off. I know I do."

She swallowed, then swallowed again. "Sounds good," she squawked, and gave him her back, focusing on the fireplace.

She liked him. She knew he liked her. Possibly liked her like *that*.

And now they were going to engage in platonic nudity? *Or maybe not platonic.*

Things were getting unzipped and uncovered behind her, and her imagination was zooming into overdrive. Wet fabric fell on the floor. She tensed as his heavy footsteps came closer to her. She didn't have to see him to know when he was standing by her side. Heat radiated off of him hotter than the heat from the fire.

She turned her head slowly, and looked up. He'd wrapped a blue quilt around his waist, and slung a gray towel around his neck.

"You okay?" He draped a shirt over the fireplace screen first, and then his wet jeans, and finally his socks.

No underwear. Was he still wearing it? Did he not wear any? So many questions.

He dried his hair briskly with the towel, and she tried not to stare, transfixed, at his bulging biceps. He was so big. There was a light smattering of hair on his chest, darker than the hair on his head, but his tanned skin was otherwise smooth.

Crouched as she was, she was on eye level with

his thighs. She could easily tug that blanket away, see what was under there.

She'd barely kissed him.

She shuddered. She wasn't a dramatic person, so calling her being thrown from the horse a near-death experience was a little too much for her, but that split second when she'd twisted in the air had clarified something for her. The fact that one of her regrets in a dangerous situation was not touching and being touched by this man—well, she ought to at least try to rectify that, right?

He stared down at her, and an odd look crossed his face. "Eve?" He shook his head. "Why don't you get out of those clothes? You're soaked."

Have you ever wanted something you couldn't have?

It was happening. Finally. Her moment. She couldn't predict what his reaction would be, but she could control her own behavior.

This isn't low-risk.

Worst case, he'd reject her. She wouldn't die.

Sometimes people need to be taught to see you as who you really are rather than who they think you are.

She swallowed and rose to her feet. She wasn't sure how, that was the problem. She'd had exactly two boyfriends in her life, and both had been men—boys—who had known her. Her main draw, for them, had been her wealth. She hadn't exactly had to seduce either of them. Her trust fund and connections had been seduction enough.

But getting naked was probably a good precursor for seduction.

She walked to the chest, trying to make her

walk as sexy as waterlogged clothes would allow
for. Not that he'd notice. He'd turned his back to
her, as interested in the fire as she'd been while he
was undressing.

His back was sexy too, a vast landscape of
muscle and ink and bone. A blue-green dragon
stretched from shoulder to shoulder, poised for
flight. She wanted to trace his shoulder blades
with her tongue, kiss her way up his neck.

She slowly whisked her shirt off, the fabric raw
and rough on her oversensitive flesh. Every noise
she made sounded louder than it needed to be, but
she was glad about that. She wasn't paying attention to her clothes at all, but to his muscles. Was
there a contraction when she undid her zipper?
Was there a relaxing when she shimmied the fabric down her legs?

She hesitated over her bra and panties. They
were wet too, but it seemed a little too wild to go
butt naked under a blanket. She compromised by
keeping her panties on and removing her bra.

She dried off with a towel quickly, rubbing the
thin terrycloth over her goose-pimpled skin, and
then wrapped a blanket around her, tucking it
under her arms and leaving her shoulders bare.
Since that felt scandalous as well, she draped another blanket over her shoulders.

"I'm decent," she said, and walked her wet
clothes over to the fire. He turned. If she hadn't
been so attuned to him, she would have missed
the quick once-over he gave her, but every bit of
exposed flesh burned.

She arranged her clothes next to his to dry, and daringly draped her bra so it was visible. Daring . . . ha. Her daring meter was definitely out of step with most people. She hadn't had anything daring happen to her in a while.

The light from the fire brought out the red in his hair. She angled her body toward him, supremely conscious that they were both wearing very little clothing.

"We're going to be here for a while," he murmured.

She cleared her throat. "It seems that way, yes."

"I don't have a cell signal. Otherwise I'd suggest we stream a movie or something."

"I don't have a signal either."

His lashes fluttered. They were long, those lashes, tipped in red, like his hair. "We're going to have to entertain ourselves the old-fashioned way, I guess."

Oh. Well.

Eve pressed her fingers to her neck, but there were no pearls to clutch. "Um." Yes, it was happening, and it had been so easy.

This is a bad idea. You can't have sex with him and walk away from him.

But do you want to ever feel regret like today again?

Her two sides—caution and need—were at war, and she wasn't sure which one to listen to. Caution was smart and how she lived her life, but need was hungry.

Need had felt that big body plastered on top of hers before, and it had had more than one dark car ride to talk to him and like him and, hell, smell him. Need wanted this.

He leaned closer and his well-formed lips formed words she was dying to hear. She swayed closer, eager and scared. "Monopoly?"

What. "Huh?"

"Do you want to play Monopoly or Clue?"

Eve drew back, the urge to laugh bubbling up in her. Jesus, she'd been picturing him naked and driving into her, and he'd been talking about board games. "Monopoly is fine," she managed. He gave a curt nod and made his way to the leaning bookcase, which held a couple of old games.

She was relieved, funny enough. But she was also disappointed.

The night is still young. Be brave. Take what you need.

She took a deep breath and let it out in a slow exhale. No regrets.

Chapter 15

Someone needed to give Gabe a fucking medal for not blatantly staring at the bra draped over the fireplace screen.

He'd only glanced at it once, but it was seared in his retinas. It was a large bra, capable of holding her heavy breasts, plain and no frills, but it was a hot pink he hadn't expected. What had he expected? He wasn't sure. Beige, maybe, or white. Not satin and pink, with a little charm at the gore. Though he probably should have readjusted his expectations after he saw those cherries.

"You owe nine hundred dollars."

He snapped back to attention. Eve had freed her hair from its complicated knot and the strands had dried in waves around her face. He wanted to stroke them away from her flushed cheeks.

He clenched his fists. That was a ridiculous urge, one he had to control. Along with all his other urges.

He could write off that kiss yesterday as an anomaly, born of frustration and buried desire, but he wouldn't be able to write off making out with her or sex with her. That was a level of complication their situation did not need. Even if he had tabled discussion of his parentage, it still loomed over them like a relentless thundercloud. "Uh, what?"

"Nine hundred dollars." She held out her hand, and the blanket she'd blessedly draped over her rounded shoulders parted to reveal her naked forearm.

She was dressed more conservatively than most women in a bar or a beach. He saw flesh all day long at work. He would not get all caught up in her lush bare arms again. Gabe averted his gaze and carefully counted out his money.

"Are you sure you aren't cheating?" he teased, trying to distract himself. The board game was set out on the chest that doubled as a coffee table. He'd grabbed the ratty armchair and dragged it over. They'd dined on the granola bars and water bottles Alistair had shoved into a waterproof bag and handed to him before he'd left. The remnants of their dinner were in a neat pile next to the game.

"I don't need to cheat at Monopoly." She carefully tucked the money he gave her into her fat stacks of fake bills. She'd had a few setbacks here and there, but she'd only increased her wealth. "I know the secret."

"There's a secret?"

She rolled and moved her piece, sitting pretty and safe as a jail visitor. They'd bought up all the land over an hour ago, and were now building property and trading cards. He controlled most of the board. She had two monopolies and a single utility she was stubbornly refusing to trade him.

"There are a few. I researched this a long time ago."

"You researched the secret to cracking Monopoly?" That distracted him from the bra. "What is it?"

"If I told you, it wouldn't be a secret."

"Let's trade. You can ask me something." He paused. "Unless it's about my parents or birth. Any of my parents," he tacked on hastily.

Her eyes were deep, dark pools of melted chocolate. They were really pretty. Big, innocent, framed by long lashes. "What was your major in college?"

His shoulders relaxed. Safe enough. "Art history."

"That makes sense."

"What about you?" That was cheating, asking her more questions in addition to the silly Monopoly one, but he couldn't squelch his curiosity.

"I majored in business."

"Did you plan to go into Chandler's?"

"No. My father made it clear there was no place for me at Chandler's."

There was no inflection in her voice, but he couldn't prevent his immediate desire to plant his fist in Brendan's face.

That asshole.

"I wouldn't want to work there anyway." She looked down at the board. "I actually want to start my own company."

He lifted his eyebrows. "Your own empire, huh?"

"If I'm lucky. Some day."

"What kind of business?"

She shrugged. "Still chewing on it."

"When are you going to open it?"

"I want to tell my brother first."

"That's the only thing stopping you?"

"Well, yes."

"You should tell him. Or not. You're a grown-ass woman. You don't need his permission."

Her lips parted. "What did you call me?"

Had she taken offense to the grown-ass part? He cleared his throat. "A woman. An adult."

"Oh."

Had it gotten warmer in here? Or was it just the way she was suddenly looking at him? He tapped the blue cards he held. "Back to the game. I know the secret, by the way."

Her lashes lowered. "No, you don't. Or you wouldn't be losing."

"The losing is a fluke." He held up a blue card. "I mean, I control Park Place and Boardwalk."

He was teasing, but she answered seriously. "The probability of landing on Boardwalk or Park Place is actually very low. They're high in value but the return on investment isn't there. Your turn, by the way."

He rolled and groaned when he realized he was only moving two spaces. Right onto the other property she controlled, complete with a hotel on it.

"Having an orange monopoly is the best monopoly to have," she continued conversationally, and held out her hand. "The probability of landing on orange is pretty high. Second to green." She tapped her green cards. "Which I also have. But green takes longer to earn out, because you have to shell out more for building on it. One monopoly is a long-term investment, the other quicker. Though if you have both monopolies, you can do very well no matter how long it takes." She fanned out her cards, the orange and green mocking him.

He riffled through his remaining cash. "Okay. Well. I don't have almost a thousand dollars to pay you in rent."

"Figure it out," she said heartlessly. "Mortgage your properties. Or . . ." She shrugged. "I'm happy to take your railroads and utility in trade and call it a day."

He snorted. "Happy to do that, are you? I'll be left with nothing."

"You'll have Park Place and Boardwalk. As well as all your other . . ." Her lip curled. "Assets."

He narrowed his eyes and leaned forward. "You only *look* cute and cuddly, don't you?"

He hadn't planned on the flirtatious tone in his voice. Her smooth skin darkened, the gold undertones turning reddish. "I . . ."

He didn't want her to retreat. He liked this aggressive, smart, somewhat predatory Eve. She was fun. "We're both businesspeople here." He spread his hands. "Let's work something out, hmm?" He gave her his most charming smile, the one that generally made grown women fall all over him.

"You can't leave me with no cash and no way to work it off."

"Of course I can."

His smile slipped. "Little shark there, aren't you?"

"Not a shark. Fair."

"Uh-huh." *Chandlers, man.* He could hear Paul tsking in his mind. *Can't trust them.*

Except Eve was right, she was winning fair and square.

She shifted and the firelight danced over her skin, like a sun meeting flames. His brain flashed to that roll of flesh under her bikini top that he'd glimpsed the other night. He'd thought about that roll way more than he should. His gaze cut to the hot pink bra, and then back to her. It was a split-second, nothing more, but she stilled.

Slowly, she placed her hand on top of the cards. "What are you proposing?"

It took him a moment to clear his throat. The game. He had to keep his head on the game. "An IOU. Personal loan. Let me pass Go, collect my money, and I'll pay you back with interest. Ten percent."

"Twenty percent interest."

He drew up, mildly offended. "That's highway robbery."

"It's not a bad counter."

"Terrible counter. Give me another one."

Her tongue flicked against her lips, wetting them, and he almost dropped his tough act and gave in.

But then he didn't have to, because she looked him dead in the eye, and shrugged off the blanket around her shoulders. She still had the one tucked around her torso. It covered her to her feet. But there were those far too tempting round shoulders and arms, laid out for him like a buffet.

He dropped his fake cash. She was warm, that was all. This wasn't a come on. "Eve . . . ?"

Another swipe of that tongue on her lips, and she loosened the knot on her breasts. The blue quilt dropped to pool around her wide hips.

He couldn't misconstrue this.

There were a million words he could and should say right now, and he was going to get to all of them, but in a moment. He needed at least that long to stare at her breasts.

They were more beautiful than he'd imagined, full and round, the nipples a perfect light brown. Her areolas were big and a little puffy. Perfect for kissing.

His mouth went dry, the saliva disappearing completely. He felt light-headed and drunk, though not off alcohol. No, his blood had all just gotten redirected to his dick.

He wanted to shove the board game and the chest aside and drop to his knees in front of her. He wanted to bury his face in between those breasts, and then his cock. He wanted to lick, bite, suck those impetuous nipples.

She rose, but kept that blanket wrapped around her waist with one fist. Her first step was a little hesitant, but then she grew in confidence, walking around the table to come stand in front of him. She was short enough that her breasts were on eye level for him.

"Eve," he said hoarsely, and her name was the splash of cold water he needed. Eve. Not a woman who wanted nothing more from him than a single night of fun.

She was Eve. A Chandler. And he had far too many problems to get tangled up in a Chandler.

He swallowed, then swallowed again. "Ah, Eve—"

He was going to let her down gently. He really was. He had the words on the tip of his tongue. They froze there, though, when she placed her hand on his naked shoulders. An electric shock ran through him. He wanted to drag her hand lower, over his chest. Down to the erection straining against the blanket.

The erection that was wrong, on so many levels. He tore his gaze away from her breasts and grasped her hand when it started moving over his pecs. "Eve. No."

He watched her shutter, power down. First it was her skin, paling slightly, then her eyes going blank. Oh Jesus. He hadn't meant to kill that tiny spark of heat in her. He opened his mouth, uncertain how to explain.

I can't have an affair with you, and an affair is all anyone wants me for.

She grabbed the blanket and hitched it up high. He was treated to a flash of pink panties and a slice of her belly, and then she was covered again, her breasts tucked away. She took huge steps backward, and it was like there was a canyon between them instead of a few feet. Damn it. "Eve."

She shook her head, hard, her wavy hair tumbling around her face. "No, I—I don't know what I was just doing. I misunderstood."

"It's okay."

"No, it's not!" To his horror, her eyes grew shiny. He rose, but then he remembered his own blanket. The knot had loosened and it fell before he could grasp it. Her gaze dropped down to his boxer briefs and the erection tenting the fabric, and then she whirled away.

"Listen, you don't have to be embarrassed—" he started.

"No," she said sharply. "I don't want to talk about this. Can you respect that, please? I—I want to go to bed."

He grimaced. On the one hand, he'd be happy to never talk about this. On the other hand, her breasts.

They're never going to be in either of your hands.

"Yeah," he said.

"Please turn around."

He did just that, so she could adjust her blanket. She was silent for a second. "Thank you."

He glanced down at the board game, allowing himself a grim smile. Her system was solid. While she hadn't bankrupted him, she'd most definitely won.

Chapter 16

THE WORLD was working against Eve. She wanted to put her clothes back on, but they were still soaked. She hadn't thought this gambit through, logistics wise.

She lay on the old couch on top of a bunch of blankets, to keep contact between herself and the old sofa to a minimum. She'd take these blankets to the house and wash them, return them with thanks.

She closed her eyes. She'd turned her back to Gabe, who was sitting against the wall near the fire. It had grown warm in the little cabin, but their clothes needed to dry and it was better than being cold.

Gabe moved, his blankets rustling. She wished she could block him out completely, but that wasn't possible.

She'd been able to read the rejection in his eyes, before he could tell her to cover up. He hadn't wanted her.

Did it kill you?

She frowned. Well, no, but it had hurt.

But it didn't kill you. She could have actually died earlier today. This had been bearable.

She chewed her lower lip, half-hating the context her analytical brain automatically put everything into. This wasn't the end of the world. She was a grown-ass woman. And she would deal with his rejection. She couldn't ignore Gabe forever.

She rolled over to look at the vexing man and cleared her throat. He glanced up from fiddling with his phone. Why he was bothering, she wasn't sure. They were completely cut off out here. She rose up on her elbow and said the first thing that came to her mind. "What's your favorite color?"

It was the type of question she might have asked as Anne, and for a second, she wondered if he knew. But his lips only quirked up. "Green. You?"

"Pink."

"Sounds right."

"Does it?"

"Yup." He dragged his leg up and rested his elbow on it. "You okay?"

She fought her blush. "Yes. Sorry for . . . being a pain. Again."

"At some point you should stop apologizing for having emotions and expressing them." He smiled, which took the sting out of what could have been interpreted as a rebuke. "You're a human. You can be human."

"I'm sorry I hit on you. I do feel foolish. I am quite aware now that you don't want me like that. It'll never happen again."

An odd look crossed his face. "I didn't say I don't want you like that. You overheard me on the phone, didn't you?"

"I did, but . . ." But she'd gotten used to doubting herself. Retreating. That turtle shell.

He looked away, into the fire. "You're hot. That cherry swimsuit of yours is a little absurd."

No one had ever called her hot before. Well, her girlfriends, yes. But not a man, at least not to her face.

All she could think to say was, "I have one with apples all over it too."

His groan was a half-laugh. "That's not helping."

"Sorry." She wanted to giggle, which was unusual. She wasn't given to giggling. This giddiness was foreign to her, though she imagined it was normal for most twenty-something women.

His smile faded. "I don't really do relationships, Eve. I'm also not into hurting women, though."

She tried to parse that. "You only have physical relationships."

"Yeah. And the dynamics between you and me and all of our overlapping connections—that would make any kind of physical relationship impossible." He gave a short laugh. "And that's not even factoring in the age difference."

"You're not that much older than me." She'd never felt young, not really. She'd had to grow up fast in a household that was, by turns, viciously cold and dramatically loud, punctuated with tragedy and upheaval.

"A dozen years." He made a face. "I was in middle school when you were born. Hell, I *remember* when you were born."

"Let's not think about that," she suggested. The last thing she wanted to do was for him to think of her as anything but a fully-grown, consenting woman.

"I haven't, lately. It barely occurs to me anymore. I feel like we're equals."

She rose up on her elbows. "That's good."

"No, it's not."

She bit her lip, trying to think. He'd admitted that he wanted her. Probably not even a tenth as much as she wanted him, but did it matter? "If the age thing isn't bothering you, and if we don't let the family stuff get between us, I don't see why we can't have a purely physical relationship," she said.

He raised an eyebrow. "I don't think that's really your style, is it?"

"I don't know if it is, to be honest. I've never tried it. But I'm an adult and you're an adult, and if we're both attracted to each other, there's no reason we shouldn't get together." It was hard to squash the little romantic yearning in her heart, the part of her that hoped they would have sex and he'd fall in love with her, but she'd had a lifetime of killing that yearning, so she did it somewhat ruthlessly now.

She'd be practical, and practicality said that nothing would come of this, but she could enjoy it while it lasted. She'd never had great sex, probably because she'd never been with anyone she desired as much as Gabe. She could change that.

Right now.

"Is this a weird rebellion thing? Against your brother?"

She drew back, mildly annoyed. "Ew, my brother has *nothing* to do with my sex life."

"Just checking," he replied. His eyes had grown warmer. They lingered over her shoulders.

She took a deep breath. "If I show you my breasts again, will you reject me?"

"Eve."

"Will you? I'd like some sort of guarantee." Silly, but she wanted to keep the risk low, even while she desperately wanted to prove to herself that she could take the initiative.

His leg straightened. "I won't reject you."

Okay. She pushed the blanket down, and she was gratified by his sharp inhale. Feeling, for the first time in her life, seductive and sexy, she cupped her breasts, touching her nipples. She rubbed them until they were tight points, hungry for his hands on her. "Gabe," she whispered.

He rose to his feet, his blanket held at his waist with one hand. He came over to the couch and stared down at her. His face was wiped clean of expression, but his eyes were hard emeralds.

She grasped his wrist. "I need . . ."

Her breath caught, because his fingers smoothed over her breast. He squeezed her flesh. Not rough, gently, like he was weighing the heft. "What do you need?"

"I need . . ." *You*, but that might scare him away. "Sex."

He swallowed and sat down on the edge of the sofa, still fondling her. He leaned in and pressed his mouth against hers.

The kiss was better this time around. Hotter, wetter, not rushed. He dipped his head and kissed along her throat and chest, until he got to her nipple. He traced the areola with his tongue. She shook. "I've been dreaming of this," he muttered.

He had? Dreaming of her?

Not like you've been dreaming of him. Cool it.

"These tits," he moaned, and rubbed his face over them. "They're so beautiful. God, I want to lick them. Suck them. Fuck them."

Her face turned red-hot. It seemed Gabe's talkativeness extended to the bedroom. "O-okay," she murmured.

He gave a choked laugh and captured her nipple in his mouth. She shivered. Her breasts had never been extraordinarily sensitive, but that felt nice. Especially since it was Gabe.

He moved to her other nipple, and she rested her hands on his shoulders. Her body softened and grew wet for him. Ah, yes. She wanted to revel in him forever, but this had an expiration date.

That was okay, though. A few orgasms to bank for her fantasies. She could settle for that.

He shouldn't do this, but here they were, locked away from the outside world. Away from his unknowing family, and hers.

Away from who they were outside this cabin.

He slid his hand down her arm over the softness of her flesh. He liked her upper arm, how he could squeeze it and the flesh gave under his fingers. He wanted to bite her there. He would bite her there.

He pulled away slightly, tracing his tongue over her lips. She followed him. She was so hungry. "You're a really good kisser."

Her lashes fluttered open. "I am?"

"Mmm-hmm. Hasn't anyone told you that before?"

"Oh. No."

He frowned. "Uh, you aren't a virgin or anything, are you?"

She shook her head. Her eyes were heavy-lidded, her cheeks flushed. "Virginity is a social construct."

"I don't know what that means."

"It means no, I am not a virgin, in that I have had a penis in my vagina before."

He contemplated her face, his abs clenching. "Can you say penis and vagina again?"

Her face flushed darker. "We can do it instead of talking about it, you know."

His smile faded. "Eve. This is . . ."

"A bad idea, I know. But . . ." She hesitated. "Have you ever had sex with someone who you don't see a future with? But someone you mutually respect and desire physically?"

How to explain that described his entire sex life? *Several-night stands.* He scratched the back of his neck, feeling vaguely jaded. "Yes. Of course."

"Can't we do that? I know it'll be complicated. But, um. I really want to . . ."

"Yes?"

She looked him dead in his eyes. "I would really like your penis in my vagina multiple times, please."

The clinical, blunt words should have made him laugh. But instead, his cock grew harder than it had ever been. He fit his fingers under her chin, lifting her mouth to his. "If anyone finds out . . . things would get complicated," he said, and the thrill of forbidden desire ran through him. Or maybe that was just desire, because he was so close to her and she was so soft and he could have her.

"I understand. This is for us alone." Her fingers climbed up his back, and she pressed closer. "Please."

How could he deny that plea? He lowered his head and captured her lips, kissing her harder than maybe he should, but she responded. Deep, drugging kisses, working his lips and tongue.

He had to stop kissing her when he stood. He tossed his blanket on the couch, leaving him only in his boxer briefs. She sat up and his knees went weak when she started kissing her way down his chest. She was eager instead of experienced, but that didn't matter when she slipped down to her knees, her nimble fingers edging under the waistband of his underwear.

Her face on level with his crotch was a sight he couldn't quite handle. "You look good right there," he said, his tone guttural. He cradled her head and brought her closer to the bulge in his shorts. "Tease me a little with your mouth."

She pressed her lips over his cloth-covered cock. He couldn't feel anything but the pressure, but that was enough. He gasped. "Yeah. Press harder. With your teeth. That's right, baby."

She drew back and he allowed it, especially since she was working on getting him free from the strangling cotton. When her cool hand grasped his cock he groaned in relief, then shouted in pleasure when her hot mouth slipped over the tip.

Again, eager more than expert, but that was fine. The thought of teaching her made every single spare blood cell redirect to his erection.

He pressed his hand to the back of her head and helped her find a rhythm as gently as possible. He'd never been one to linger on blowjobs—they were fine, but the main act was where his interest usually lay.

Right here, right now, though, he'd be happy if this went on forever. This was erotic on every factor: the tight wet suction, her fingernails pressing into his ass, the visual he had looking down at her small curvy body from his greater height. Her lashes were crescents on her cheekbones, and her cheeks hollowed every time she sucked him. He felt like a god. Especially when he cradled her face and tilted it up. Her eyes were big and wide, an innocence that was belied by the cock driving in and out of her mouth.

Innocence ruined wasn't his kink, but the excitement in her gaze was. She was enjoying feasting on his body. "You like this? You like me fucking your mouth?"

Her cheeks heated beneath his palms and he went a little deeper, the tip of his cock flirting with her throat. "Tell me. Nod."

A second, and she gave a single dip of her head. He growled. "Let me see. Touch yourself while I give you a mouthful."

She whimpered around his cock, the reverberation making him shudder. For a second, he wondered if she would comply or if it would be too much for her.

Silly to wonder. She wasted no time in shoving the blanket aside, her fingers slipping under the waistband of her panties, depressing the softness of her belly. He gripped her hair tighter and grew more aggressive, especially when he noted her fingers moving faster.

She liked it a little rough. Jesus save them.

He pulled out of her mouth, and her eyes blinked open, dazed and confused, when he hauled her up and pressed his cock against her belly. Her lashes were wet, and he realized it might have been from his roughness. He kissed her eyes. "I didn't hurt you, did I?"

"No," she said, her voice raspy. "I liked it. I wanted to take you deeper."

The confession was soft, and he shuddered, pushing her panties down her legs. "Next time.

You can deep throat me next time." He heard what he was saying and almost slapped himself.

His brain fritzed when he got excited during sex, to a point where he couldn't often remember what he said, but those were sex words. This was a promise that there would be more, and how could he go back on that?

Now, though, he was desperate to get inside of her, but a second of clarity stopped him. "No condom, damn it." For all of his enjoyment of sex, protection was one thing he was obsessive about. Which made sense, given his background.

She shook her head. "I have two in my wallet."

"You carry condoms with you?"

"I'm prepared for everything," she said primly. She moved away from him and to her jeans, grabbing a slim wallet from the back pocket. He eyed her big ass. Like this. He'd fuck her just like that, bent over.

She dumped the contents of her wallet on the couch and he raised an eyebrow, impressed despite his desperate desire. She was prepared for everything. She held up a foil packet triumphantly, and he forgot literally everything else.

He grabbed it and tore it open with his teeth. She watched with fascination as he rolled it down over his length. "Turn around and grab the back of the couch," he said gutturally. "I've been dreaming of seeing that ass jiggle when I fuck you."

She complied so quickly he wondered if he wasn't the only one who had been dreaming of that. She bent over, and he wished he had a mirror so he could properly see her breasts move as he rammed into her.

He dipped his knees and ran his cock over her wet folds. So perfectly open for him. He pressed inside, and she gave a muffled shout. He stopped halfway inside. "Are you okay?" he rumbled.

"Yes," she gasped. "Please, more?"

"So polite," he said, and gave her another inch. "More what?"

"More."

"Say the word," he demanded, and withdrew completely.

She mewled. "Cock."

"Good girl." He rammed inside her, loving how she shook. He grasped her hips and set a steady rhythm, fucking her long and deep.

She pressed her forehead against the couch, cries of pleasure falling from her lips. He bent over and slid a hand under her body, finding her clit under wet curls and plucking it with every thrust.

He slid his lips down her spine, finding the inch of skin that had so fascinated him when he'd seen her in her bikini. Her position somewhat flattened the cute roll out, but he could still rake his teeth over it. He nibbled, then licked the spot. Later, he'd give it every bit of attention it deserved.

"I'm so close," she whispered.

He lifted his head. "What do you need to get there?"

"I don't know."

He alternated fast strokes with slow, keeping

his thumb on her clit, paying careful attention to the noises she made and the way her body reacted to his every move.

He wrapped an arm around her and pulled her upright, making soothing noises when she startled. "Like this. Let me try fucking you like this. Tell me if you like it."

"I like everything you do."

He pressed his lips into her hair and smiled. "Tell me if you *like* like this." He withdrew and then thrust back in short, rapid strokes. She rose up on her toes, but it wasn't to get away. He anchored her tight against him and continued pounding. "Tell me," he muttered against her neck.

"I love it. Don't stop fucking me. Like that. Like—" He pinched her clit. She shivered and came around him, her contractions milking his cock, a shuddery "Fuuuck" falling from her lips.

He pressed her back down to the sofa and thrust deep once, twice, and finally let the pleasure spiral up his spine. He had the presence of mind to catch himself on his hands and keep his much larger body off her.

It took a few deep breaths before he felt steady enough to leave her. He took care of the condom, then scooped Eve up and collapsed on the couch with her on his lap, careful to keep their wettest bits away from each other.

She pressed her head against his chest and he breathed deep, taking in the scent of her and him and sex. Her hair tickled his nose, the mahogany strands more wild than he'd ever seen them.

Which was appropriate, since she'd been more wild than he'd ever seen her.

She lifted her head. Her drowsy eyes were soft and vague. "Wasn't that nice?"

He laughed, but a sense of unease ran through him. "Yeah." He pressed her head against his shoulder.

"We're cool, right?"

No one would find out. He ran his fingers through her hair, letting the various shades of brown reflect the firelight. "Yeah."

Her smile was wavery but hopeful. She placed a sweet kiss on his cheek, and then snuggled close, falling asleep within a few seconds.

He covered the spot she'd kissed with his hand. Nothing had changed. He had sex with women all the time. Casual. Uncommitted. Nothing shared other than their bodies. This was no different.

His stomach sank. So why did it feel like he wanted it to be different?

Chapter 17

Eve DIDN'T want to wake up. She was so nice and toasty warm here, snuggled up against Gabe.

She sighed and lifted an eyelid. She was sleeping on top of him on the narrow couch, her nose pressed against his chest. His lashes fluttered open when she raised her head. "Is it morning?" he asked hoarsely.

A bit of sunlight streamed through the dusty window, highlighting exactly how grim their little rescue cabin was. "Yes." The rain had vanished overnight.

A big hand stroked over her back, down to her bottom. He squeezed her gently, and she inhaled, but he gave her a sheepish smile. "We should go back."

"Right." The night of privacy was over, and they had to return to the rest of the wedding party.

And her brother. Nicholas was going to be a ginormous pain.

She got up reluctantly, and they both dressed in silence. Their clothes were stiff and still a bit damp. Eve grimaced and adjusted her bra. What she wouldn't give for having breasts that could occasionally go without support.

Gabe stopped her at the door. "Hey . . . you're okay, right?"

"Totally." She'd gotten exactly what she'd set out to get last night. Her body was relaxed and tingly. The sex had been amazing.

She'd worry about her crush on him later. For now, she was going to do her best to protect her heart and stay out of her shell. She captured his hand and squeezed. "I'm not going to freak out. I will still keep your secret."

He studied her face, and then squeezed her hand back. "Thanks."

She couldn't keep her post-coital buzz going for long. With every mile they got closer to the mansion, another nerve tightened. Not even the novelty of straddling the ATV, pressed tight against Gabe, could distract her from the impending doom of her confrontation with her brother.

Nicholas walked out of the house when they drove up to the garage, which meant he'd probably been pacing the foyer for hours waiting for them. She hopped off the bike before Gabe could help her. He halted her before she could move away. "Why don't you let me talk to him first?"

That was what her mother had often done, intervening on her behalf with her father. She was sure Gabe hadn't meant to hurt her, but her cheeks burned. She wasn't a child, and he wasn't her mother. "No. It's okay." She cast him a wan smile.

He stepped up close and placed a hand on her

waist. The familiarity of it thrilled her even as a part of her brain fretted over what her brother might think. "You're not a little girl. Don't let him chastise you like one."

She twisted her fingers together. "He means well."

"Sometimes it's harder to go against people who mean well." His gaze was far away, and she wondered who he was thinking of. "People you feel like you owe."

She took a deep breath. "I've got this." She moved away from Gabe, though it pained her when his hand fell away.

While they'd spoken, her brother had come stomping closer, so she didn't have to walk far up the driveway. She did her best to straighten her shoulders and not feel as tired and bedraggled as she probably looked.

"Jesus Christ, Eve. I trust you won't go riding off into a thunderstorm again?" A forbidding frown creased Nicholas's face. He was so big and he could be loud and intimidating. She was none of those things. She touched her wrist, stroked the bare skin there, and tried to not shrink away.

Livvy slipped out of the house, her half-made-up face telling Eve the other woman had rushed downstairs to intercept her fiancé. Everyone thought she needed protection. "Nico," Livvy said warningly. "We talked about this."

Nicholas grunted. "I can't not say anything."

Eve swallowed, conscious of everyone's gaze on them. It was one thing to have her brother upbraid her, but it was somehow more mortifying to have Livvy and Gabe witness this. "It's fine, Livvy. Let him speak his piece."

Livvy cast one fuming look at her fiancé and stepped back.

Nicholas gave her a narrow glance. "Eve, you can't ever do something like that again. You could have been hurt, or worse. It's lucky we had a bike here so Gabe could fetch you."

Fetch her. Like she was a forgotten hat or a troublesome child. The tiny part of her that was fragile and weak shriveled up, and she opened her mouth to apologize, but then she caught sight of Gabe's fingers.

They were wrapped tight around his helmet, so tight his knuckles were white. She glanced up to his eyes and found the kindness that had greeted her gone. He was frowning. But not at her, at her brother.

You're a grown-ass woman.

She straightened. She was, wasn't she? And she hadn't done something so terrible. She'd gone for a ride. Accidents happened, and she couldn't predict every bad thing that could or would ever befall her. "I didn't need fetching," she said, and she was surprised at both the words and her tone. It was hard. Assertive. Tough enough to make everyone still.

In her peripheral vision, she could see Gabe lean in. She waited for him to back her up, to tell Nicholas she had been fine without him, but he didn't.

*Be proud of your accomplishments. No one will be
proud of them for you.*

Actually, it was good Gabe was silent. She could
tell Nicholas everything herself. "I saved myself,
thank you. I stuck to the trail, I minimized my in-
juries when the horse spooked, and I had shelter
from the rain until Gabe got to me. Had he not
come, I would have waited for the rain to slow and
walked down the path until I had a cell signal—
which is basically what we did. I wasn't dumb or
stupid. I did everything right. I couldn't foresee
any of what happened happening, and I coped
when it did, and . . ." She trailed off, realizing she
was starting to repeat herself, and rocked back,
pressing her lips tight together.

Nicholas was staring at her like she had grown
a second head. "Eve—"

"Stop scolding me. I'm a grown—" She hesitated. "I'm a grown woman, not a child. Do me
the courtesy of treating me like one."

"She's right," Gabe said into the silence. "Not
that you need corroboration. Eve did everything
right. All I could bring to the table was a ride
back."

Eve flushed and looked at Gabe full-on. The
lines around his eyes were crinkled up.

She loved those lines. The worst part of driving him in her Ryde had been that she hadn't gotten to stare at those lines as he talked. She could
only look in the rearview mirror so much without
risking an accident. "I didn't mean to minimize
your—"

"No, no." Gabe lifted his hands. "You had shit handled. I provided some comfort." His smile slipped as he looked at Nicholas. "Cut your sister some slack, man."

Livvy smacked Nicholas on the arm, but she was beaming at Eve. "I told you the same damn thing, you overprotective lug. Good job telling him off, Eve."

"I didn't—" She hadn't meant to tell Nicholas off, not exactly. She quieted. Actually, whether or not she'd meant to tell him off, she was glad she had. She was grateful to Nicholas for how he'd raised her, but he needed to let her live now.

Nicholas opened his mouth and closed it again, nonplussed.

"I'm wet and gross," she said. "I need to get changed. I'll see you at breakfast."

Before he could answer, she swept past him, and into the house.

The bright sunshine on the all-white decor in her room made her grimace. She hated the color white, and not because it denoted virginity. It reminded her of her bedroom growing up. She'd loved that room as a child, but then around fifteen or so, she'd worked up the courage to ask her father for a different color scheme. She'd done her research, had brought paint samples and examples of different bedding she might like. She'd even priced it out.

He'd sat her down in his study and given her an hour lecture on not being frivolous and girly and wasteful. He'd told her how lucky she was to have the things she had. And then he'd sent her off, with that vaguely disappointed air, like he couldn't believe he'd spawned a child as foolish as her.

She'd had white furniture until she'd left for college. This past year, as part of her revamp of her life, she'd purged her bedroom of every white furnishing and textile. Purple sheets, a multicolored comforter, pink drapes—she'd gone all out. A statement of independence no one would see except her, but it had made her happy and she'd refused to feel guilt over that happiness.

She would not feel guilt now. She was done being scared and frightened. She'd stuck her neck out and gotten the best sex of her life. Today she was going to tell her brother about her business, and damn his reaction.

She showered quickly and then stood in front of her bathroom mirror, critically examining her makeup. She slicked on foundation and mascara. She never wore too much makeup, for fear of sticking out. But today, she used lipstick instead of lip gloss, the added pigment giving her courage.

She turned away from her reflection and scurried to get dressed in a pressed dress shirt and navy pants. It was boring and neutral, but that was okay. She had her secret escapade with Gabe in her heart and bright pink lips and that was good enough.

"Good morning," she said when she entered the breakfast room.

She got a chorus of good mornings in return.

Gabe broke off the low conversation he and Livvy and Sadia were having and gave her a big smile. "Hey, Eve."

She immediately flushed. This affair stuff wasn't as easy to hide as she'd hoped. Eve gave him a distant nod and moved to the breakfast buffet, served herself, and sat down next to Livvy. Her soon-to-be sister-in-law wore leggings and a raggedly cut crop top. At some point while Eve had been changing, Livvy had finished applying her makeup. Her eyeliner winged dramatically on each eye. "You look pretty."

"Thanks," Livvy responded, and forked a bite of scrambled eggs in her mouth. "Love that necklace."

Eve touched the turquoise necklace around her throat. "It's not—" She bit her tongue, having spent far too long demurring any compliment. Saying thank you felt vain and prideful, but Livvy had slowly taught her how to accept the compliments she handed out like candy. Eve felt foolish every time she soaked one up like a sponge, but it had been so long since anyone had told her she looked nice. Nicholas, sometimes, but he was too busy to constantly build up her self-confidence. "Thank you." She took a bite of the perfectly seasoned eggs, and dared to sneak a glance at her brother. Nicholas was frowning down at his plate, but it was more of a preoccupied frown than an angry one.

Jackson walked into the room, Kareem by his side, his adorable puppy trailing along behind him. Jackson dropped into the seat next to Sadia, drawing the boy onto his lap. "Hi, Eve. Glad to know you're safe."

She relaxed. This was a much better reaction than Nicholas's panic. "Thanks. Breakfast is delicious."

Jackson inclined his head, like that would be a foregone conclusion.

"What are we doing today?" Kareem asked.

Sadia took a bite of her toast. "We have nothing planned. I thought we could relax, since it's our last full day before the rehearsal dinner tomorrow."

Jackson shifted Kareem so he could snag a piece of bacon from his girlfriend's plate. "We can play some more poker."

"How much of my money do you want to win?" Nicholas asked dryly.

Jackson gave her brother a thin smile. Anyone who didn't know Jackson might think there was a cruel edge to the other man's expression, but Eve could make out the mischief dancing deep in his serious gaze. They might not have the best relationship in the world, but Jackson didn't hate Nicholas. He did, however, love poking Nicholas, and Eve was annoyed enough at her brother that she didn't mind. "All of it."

"Maybe a game outside would be better," Gabe interjected. He leaned down and picked up the puppy.

Oh, this was far too much. The man was as attractive as a god. He didn't need to be holding a criminally adorable rescue mutt too.

"What do you think, Paddles? You think we ought to smoke everyone at volleyball or basketball?"

Kareem rested his head against his uncle's shoulder. "I changed his name to Bandit now."

"Ah, okay. He does look like a Bandit." Gabe raised the puppy to eye level. "I think Bandit is down for a physical game of strength." The man's eyes shifted to her. "What about you, Eve?"

She halted mid-chew, conscious of a blush coloring her cheeks. "I'll sit out, but watch. I had plenty of exercise yesterday." Gah. Even that sounded inadvertently sexual.

Be cool, Chandler!

Livvy patted her lips delicately. "You can watch me kick these boys' asses, Eve."

Sadia gave an exasperated sigh. "Livvy, for crying out loud . . ."

"*Ass* is a bad word," Kareem said cheerfully.

Livvy winced. "Sorry, sorry."

Gabe adjusted the puppy. "Bring it, sister."

Hmm. Gabe was so much better at subterfuge. He said that "sister" so lightly and casually no one would suspect Livvy actually was his sister.

Eve studied Gabe surreptitiously as she quietly finished her breakfast and the others argued over what game they could play. He was the picture of attractiveness, the weak sunlight bringing out the red in his hair. He'd changed out of his own damp clothes and his big frame was dressed casually, shirt rolled up to reveal the bright tattoos on his arms. Not the Hawaiian design, though. No, that was tucked away under the plaid. The puppy had flopped across his arms, his eyes closing as Gabe casually rubbed the creature's ears.

They made eye contact, and Gabe's smile hit her low in the belly. She fumbled her fork, nearly dropping it. Instead, she neatly placed it on her plate.

Nicholas leaned back. "I need to make some phone calls before I can play."

"No work," Livvy said firmly.

"It's some tiny fires I have to put out. Promise, it'll only take an hour. You can figure out what we're going to play while I do that." Nicholas dropped a kiss on her head. His gaze drifted over Eve, and he frowned again, giving her a brusque nod.

"If you'll excuse me," Eve murmured after he left, and got to her feet. "I'll go change into something more appropriate, if we'll be outdoors."

"Wear a hat. You don't want to burn," Gabe remarked. "Your face'll be all pink in the photos."

She touched her face as she left. With Gabe at her side, and their secret fling in her brain, her face would be pink in those photos no matter what.

Chapter 18

Eve DUCKED her head into the living room, where Nicholas had created a mini workstation. Her brother had spread out reams of paper and was busy typing something furiously on his laptop. "Looks like you had more than a couple phone calls."

Nicholas jumped and glanced up guiltily from his computer, like she'd caught him doing something illicit. "I—uh—"

"I won't tell Livvy." She came inside and shut the door behind her. "Though you should probably inform her that you won't be taking off work even when you say you are."

"Nah. I'm not going to be like Dad."

Eve smiled sourly. Nicholas could never be like their father. "Of course not."

"I mean, when it comes to work. I'll take off when I say I will. Livvy says I need a healthy work-life balance." He shrugged, sheepish. "But when she's off doing something, and I'm bored, I might as well answer some emails."

Eve nodded. A low hum of tension invaded

her body. She'd come in here to have a chat with Nicholas, and that was what she was going to do. She simply didn't know where to begin. "You're coming out to the game?"

"In a few." He hesitated. "Eve, are we . . . okay?"

"Of course."

"I know I can get overprotective. Livvy has pointed it out. Many times." He paused. "Many, many times."

Say what you feel. "You can. Sometimes when you yell . . ." She linked her fingers together. "It's a bit intimidating, even if I know it comes from a good place."

His face darkened. "I had no idea. I'm sorry."

"Please don't be sorry." She started to explain it was her, not him, and she was sorry she was so timid, but Gabe's voice reverberated in her head. *Stop apologizing for having emotions.*

"Why don't you have a seat?" He gestured to the chairs opposite the desk. "Livvy takes a while to change and stuff. We can talk. Maybe about that marketing position."

His tone was so conciliatory. Her fingers tightened, and she almost said yes, but then she took a deep bracing breath. "Actually . . ." She walked to the chair and sat down, perching on the edge of the seat. For a second, she imagined she was sitting in front of her disapproving father, across from his massive desk in his dark study. She grasped her bare wrist and willed the image away.

No. There was nothing to be terrified of here. "I don't want the marketing position."

Nicholas ran his fingers through his hair, leaving the dark strands standing straight up. They'd both inherited their almost black hair from their Greek mother. "Eve—"

"I know, I know. Chandlers work. I've been working for months. I have an idea for a business."

"Oh yeah?" He steepled his hands under his nose. "What is it?"

Now. Tell him everything now. "A ride-sharing service."

"Like *Ryde*?"

"Better than Ryde."

"A lot of services market themselves as better than Ryde. What makes yours different?"

She was clenching her wrist so tight she might leave bruises. She forced herself to stop. "It would be fair."

"I don't understand."

"The current businesses are unfair. They're unfair to drivers and passengers. They don't give the drivers enough of a share. They allow tips, but most riders don't actually tip or tip well, especially in smaller markets like Rockville. After taxes and gas and vehicle upkeep, the drivers aren't taking home anywhere close to a living wage. They're not treated as employees. They don't get benefits, even if they work more than the equivalent of a full-time week in any other industry. It's not fair, when the business wouldn't exist without them."

"Hmm. But there's probably a reason they don't pay the drivers more."

"Greed." She lifted a shoulder. "The apps make

their money off of volume and keeping rates low. They know that means cutting the drivers out of a little extra bit of the pie." She leaned forward, warming to her subject. "There's also the safety and accessibility angle. Currently, drivers are given a cursory background check, but anyone can sign up to be a passenger. I'd change that, make things safer, especially for more vulnerable members of the population. I'd also create an app that's simpler and more user-friendly, even for people who aren't technologically adept, and give the drivers incentives for—" She stopped, seeing the skepticism on her brother's face. "You think it's dumb."

"I think you're entering an overcrowded market."

"Just like Grandpa and Sam did decades ago," she countered. "And I'll do it the same way. People. Quality. Fairness."

"You'll probably have to charge customers more," Nicholas pointed out.

"Yes. And they'll pay, like people pay a little more sometimes at Chandler's. Because deep down, people are good, and they like to support good things."

"Hmph."

"I've researched this thoroughly. I even have someone standing by to start app development."

But his frown was unrelenting and she leaned back in her chair, feeling the sting of disapproval. Still, she rallied. "Will you at least look at my business plan?"

"You have a business plan?"

"Yes." She wouldn't tell him about the market

research she'd conducted. No need for him to be distracted by the fact that she'd been driving around for one of those supposedly unsafe apps.

"I'll look at the plan," he allowed. "I—"

A knock came on the door and they both glanced over as Alistair opened the door slightly. "I beg your pardon for interrupting, Mr. Chandler, Ms. Chandler. Ms. Kane's mother and aunt have arrived ahead of schedule, and she wished for you to join her. Immediately."

Nicholas swore and got to his feet. "Sorry, Eve. We can continue this later. Livvy might kill Tani if she says a single word about this curse."

"Sure," she allowed. She should be anxious about her brother not immediately being excited for her business idea, but like Nicholas, her mind had immediately jumped to what Tani and Maile's entrance meant. Not to Livvy, but to Gabe.

Before the tragedy, she'd been too young to ever note how Tani and Gabe interacted. She didn't completely know the circumstances of his birth yet, but she assumed Robert had had an affair. Whether it had been before or after their marriage, it couldn't have been easy for Tani to have her husband's illegitimate child growing up under her nose.

And if it hadn't been easy for Tani, she imagined it must have been actively hard for Gabe.

GABE CAME down the stairs, having changed into basketball shorts and a T-shirt to play volleyball. He took one look at the woman in the foyer, and nearly deployed an about-face to go hide in his room. Dark eyes looked up and met his. "Gabe! How nice to see you."

Too late. He continued down the stairs, slower now, and gave the older woman as genuine a smile as he could imagine. "Ms. Maile. Nice to see you too."

Maile Kane was large boned and wide-shouldered, her long hair still inky black and braided into a single plait down her back. Her face was broad and creased from smiling. She looked like Robert, which meant she looked a little like him.

Genes were so weird.

He accepted the hug she gave him, being careful not to hang on too long. Maile had been a loving constant in the Kane home. While he hadn't gotten the same affection from her as she'd doled out to her brother's acknowledged children, he could well remember snuggling up next to her while she read them a story.

He'd avoided her since Paul's funeral. The talk eventually turned to reminiscing over her late nephew, which wasn't the problem. Talking about Paul brought grief, but he could do it, and it helped. No, Gabe had avoided Maile because he'd grown increasingly disturbed by how often he'd felt tempted to clutch the hands that looked so much like his and tell her everything. He'd almost spilled it all when he'd sat next to her at Paul's funeral and she'd wept into his shoulder over how she'd lost her eldest.

You didn't lose your oldest nephew. I'm right here.

"Stop calling me Ms.," Maile scolded. "You're a grown man now. Makes me feel old."

He called her Ms. because he couldn't call her simply Maile when she looked so much like his biological father, but there was no way he could explain that. "Yes, ma'am."

"None of that either," she said dryly.

He forced an answering smile. "I thought you weren't coming until tomorrow?"

"Tani's been anxious since she saw the weather report yesterday. I've told her this curse stuff is nonsense, but you know how she is. She wanted to drive up while the weather was beautiful." She linked her arm with his and led him to the living room. "Sorry if we're crashing you young people's party."

"Not at all," Sadia said from where she was serving tea off a tray. "It's good to see you."

Tani was already sitting on the couch, Jackson next to her. Livvy was perched on an armchair, rubbing her hands on her jeans. There were nerves and a touch of fear in her eyes when she looked at Tani.

Gabe got it. Part of him couldn't help but regress to being a child around Tani. He'd been cheerful and rambunctious, and every time he'd crossed paths with this woman, the blast of coldness he'd received had been confusing and hurtful.

As an adult, he could understand. Tani hadn't been required to permit his presence in her home, under her nose, but she had. She hadn't protested Robert enrolling him in her children's pri-

vate school or making sure he got to participate
in many of the same privileges they had—even
though it had been her family's money facilitat-
ing those privileges. Robert Kane had been firmly
middle-class when he'd fathered Gabe, the son of
local small business owners. He'd married into
the Oka fortune.

Gabe didn't hate or resent Tani, not at all. That
didn't mean they were friends. He inclined his
head to her. "Ms. Tani."

She accepted his greeting with a regal nod of
her own. "Gabe. It has been a while."

Since Paul's funeral actually. He'd avoided
Maile. He didn't have to avoid Tani, because she
rarely left her house. "Yes, ma'am." Tani wouldn't
tell him not to ma'am her.

Maile patted Gabe on the shoulder and moved
to the chair. "I'll wait to get the rest of our bags,
Tani."

"I can get them," Gabe offered.

Maile flashed him a bright smile. "No, sweetheart. Nothing essential in them."

Nicholas entered the room and made a beeline
for Livvy. They often did that, Nicholas and Livvy.
Sought each other out in the room, as if to ensure
the other was okay.

Sadia perched on the arm of the sofa, next to
Jackson. They did the same thing.

Gabe stuck his hands in his pockets and rocked
back on his heels. That sharp ache he was feeling
wasn't loneliness or hurt. Surely not.

"Did you have an okay trip?" Nicholas asked politely.

Tani took a sip of her tea before answering. "It was adequate."

Livvy leaned forward. "You'll love your room here, Mom. There's a big tub, and I made sure it faces the east, since I know you like the sun in the morning."

"I can't get into and out of tubs easily anymore. My hip. And I actually prefer to sleep in in the mornings now."

Livvy deflated. "Oh. Well. It has a nice closet."

Tani glanced around the room. "This place looks old and drafty."

Nicholas rested his hand on Livvy's shoulder and squeezed. "It's only a decade or two old actually."

"Young people always want newer houses. Things aren't built like they used to be."

"I think it's lovely," Maile interjected, and Gabe didn't miss the warning glance she gave her former sister-in-law. Maile clearly wasn't blind to how curmudgeonly Tani could be. "Was that a barn I glimpsed?"

"It is." Livvy brightened. "We have horses. I haven't had a chance to go riding, but Eve went yesterday."

"In the storm?" Tani asked.

"Uh, she got caught in it a bit, but she was fine." Livvy leaned against Nicholas. There was an air of desperation in her tone, and Gabe wondered if she was trying to head off any more talk of a curse from her mother. "Isn't that right, Nicholas?"

"Yup. Fine."

Tani sniffed. "Hmm."

As if summoned, Eve slipped into the room. She'd changed out of her pressed slacks and shirt into a tidy but more casual outfit of a T-shirt and jeans. Her gaze darted around, until it landed on him. She gave him a long look he couldn't quite interpret, then turned to the newly arrived guests. "Tani, Maile," she said smoothly. She gave them both light hugs. "How lovely to see you."

Tani perked up marginally, her gaze warming as it rested on Eve. She clearly liked the younger woman, which wasn't surprising. In a lot of ways, Eve's quiet reserve was probably more comfortable to her than her daughter's vivaciousness. "You look well, Eve. Very alert. The air here agrees with you."

Eve drifted slightly closer to where he stood holding up the wall, and avoided his gaze. But her cheeks pinkened a bit and he wondered if she was thinking about what they'd done last night and how it might contribute to her bright-eyed appearance today. God knew, he'd run every single minute of their time together in that cabin through his brain a million times already. "Thank you," she murmured.

"You all seem to be heading out for some fun activity," Maile said brightly.

Eve smiled. No teeth, lips up. "We were going to go play volleyball in the backyard."

"Kareem's already out there with the puppy," Sadia said with a smile. "He's excited to keep score."

"Well, don't let us stop you," Maile exclaimed. "Let me get my knitting, and we'll watch."

His gaze met Tani's for a second. It was strange, interacting with this woman after so long. He and Tani had bought into the lie that he was simply an orphan adopted by her housekeeper so well, sometimes he forgot it wasn't the truth.

Eve shifted closer, so they were standing barely a shoulder width apart. He glanced down at her shiny hair. This, he didn't have much experience with. Another person in on the secret that had governed his whole life? He felt raw and exposed, but weirdly . . . like it was right Eve knew and could give him comfort.

Her fingers brushed against him. The touch was so light and fleeting, he wondered if he'd imagined it, but then it came again. It brought with it a burst of warmth and comfort, like someone had wrapped his soul up in cotton and hugged it. Was this how Jackson and Livvy felt when their partners were near them?

Not that they were partners, of course.

The next time her hand brushed his, he looped his pinky around hers. She stilled and they both kept their heads forward. The others in the room continued to talk, working out the logistics of their next activity. They were forgotten here. He stroked his finger against her palm, up and then down.

Slowly, she interlaced their hands together, and gave him a squeeze. He squeezed back. Though it pained him, he released her, and not a moment too soon, because Maile looked directly at them. "Eve, can you show me to my room so I can freshen up?"

"Of course," she said.

As Eve moved away from him, Gabe balled his hand into a fist, as if he could capture the feeling she'd given him. He didn't want that warmth to disappear. It should scare him, how badly he wanted to keep it for himself.

The fact that it didn't scare him was even scarier.

Chapter 19

ONCE UPON a time, when Eve was a senior in high school, she'd wandered past a field where a bunch of men were playing football. Gabe had been amongst them.

It had been the first time she'd seen him since she was a kid. She'd recognized him instantly, the sun glistening on his sweaty skin and tattoos and muscles. She'd stood there for a long time, watching him. Perving on him.

When her friend had said she wanted to get a tattoo a few years later, Eve had jumped at the chance to go with her. Of course, Gabe hadn't seen her as a woman then. Or when she'd thrown herself at him at the bar, that one embarrassing night he didn't even remember. Now that she thought about it, though, those were good things, points in his favor. She'd been too young then to tangle up with an older man.

She lifted her glass of iced tea, tracing her finger over the condensation on the outside of the glass. Gabe and Jackson and Nicholas and Livvy were all playing volleyball, Sadia and Kareem sitting on the sidelines, cheering and keeping score. Gabe had his shirt off, so she was pretty much useless.

Not much had changed. Here she was, all these years later, still perving on him while he played a sport. Only this time, she was definitely a woman. And she'd felt that body against hers. In hers.

Eve took a big gulp of iced tea and tried to let it cool her overheated body.

"Did you finish the yellow, dear?"

Eve started and looked down at the ball of yarn in her lap. She placed her drink hastily on the table and put the wound ball in the bag next to Maile's chair. "Yes, ma'am. What color is next?"

"You don't have to sit here, helping me." Maile's knitting needles clicked and flew, spinning yarn between two needles. "You can go play with the other kids."

Eve automatically smiled at the thought of someone calling her and her contemporaries "kids." It wasn't hurtful at all, coming from Maile, who had held all of them as babies. "No, I'm fine, thank you. Swimming and horseback riding is about as active as I get. I don't love sweating."

Maile smirked. She was dressed in a soft lavender spring dress, a cropped cardigan around her shoulders. "Neither do I. That's why I learned how to knit."

"I'd love to learn how to knit someday."

"Well, you're family now, so I'll teach you my secrets," Maile said companionably.

Family.

She clutched the word close to her heart and gazed out at the others, playing merrily, none of them aware that Gabe was also part of their family. She wished . . .

No, no, no. You are not to get involved. You promised. She cleared her throat. "What are you making?"

"A blanket."

"Is it a gift?"

"No, not this one. It's for sale."

"Oh, I didn't realize you sold some of your creations."

"I sell most of them." Maile wrapped the fine mohair yarn around a needle. "Tani helped me create an online shopfront years ago. We make enough to support ourselves."

"Ah." Eve had simply assumed that the money Tani had made on the sale of the business and the Oka-Kane mansion had been enough to support her and her sister-in-law indefinitely, though now she felt foolish about that assumption, like she was a rich girl with no concept of money. "That's great. Where is Tani anyway?"

"Probably resting up. We do have the rehearsal dinner tomorrow."

Ah, yes, tomorrow was Friday and the rehearsal dinner, and then the wedding on Saturday, and then the weekend would be over.

And so would her affair or onetime fling or whatever with Gabe.

She ignored the pang of sadness. "Do you think—"

"There is almost no staff in that house." Tani settled into the chair on the other side of Eve. "It's far too big to get along with no help."

Eve rubbed her hands on her thighs. She hadn't felt particularly nervous around Tani over the past few months, since the families had largely reconciled. Knowing a secret about the other woman changed things. "We asked to have the minimum staff this week. More help will arrive tomorrow, ahead of the wedding, though."

Tani gave her a distant nod, and then looked out at the yard. Eve wondered what she thought of when she looked at Gabe. "Good." Tani leaned forward and poured herself a glass of iced tea.

"The wedding will be beautiful," Maile enthused. "This place is perfect. What a view." She glanced at the slice of glimmering lake, not far away.

Tani sniffed. "Hopefully the view will distract everyone from gossiping over why the two of them are rushing to the altar. In my day, that only meant one thing."

"You and Robert got married six months after you met." Maile's tone was sweet, but the reminder was pointed.

The lines around Tani's lips deepened. "And plenty of people counted backwards on their fingers when Paul was born."

Maile shrugged. "Livvy told you. She wanted to have the wedding on her birthday. The date has some sort of significance for them."

Eve had a hunch as to what that significance

was—her brother's annual disappearances around this date made a lot more sense, in retrospect— but she wasn't about to snitch to Livvy's mother. "People get married quickly all the time now," she said instead. "No one will be gossiping." Anyone who might be cruel had already been culled from the guest list.

"Hmm." Tani took a sip. "And your father? Have you heard from him?"

Another person might be fooled by the older woman's forced casualness, but Eve was not. John and Tani had easily reconciled, but John hadn't masterminded the takeover of her half of the company. She doubted there was any way Tani was looking forward to sitting across the aisle from Brendan. A man she'd grown up with, shared family with, and who had promptly screwed her over when she'd been grief-stricken. "No, ma'am. I have not. I don't think Nicholas has either. I'm pretty sure he won't be coming."

Tani bowed her head, her straight black hair hiding her face. "Very well."

"My grandfather will be arriving tomorrow," she offered, in an effort to cheer Tani.

Maile made a small sound of pleasure. "And Sonya and Rhiannon, yes?"

Eve licked her lips. She hadn't known if she could bring up Gabe's adoptive mother and sister to Tani. "Yes."

"It will be good to see those two again."

Eve cast around for something neutral she could say. "I vaguely remember them from when

I was young." *Don't poke. Don't prod. This is none of your business.* Besides, she liked Tani. The last thing she wanted to do was hurt her.

"Sometimes I forget you're younger than the others. You weren't even born when Gabe was adopted." Maile clicked her tongue. "My God, what a sad story that was. Eve, can you hand me the green?"

Eve leaned over and grabbed the green yarn from Maile's bag. "Oh?" Despite her best intentions, Eve turned toward Robert's sister, wondering if the older woman knew that her brother had fathered Gabe. "How so?"

"The way he was found, of course."

"That's enough," Tani said. "Gossiping isn't ladylike."

"You gossip worse than me," Maile returned smartly. "We went to high school with his birth mother actually. Linda. I never liked her, but I didn't know her well. She should have given Gabe up the second he was born instead of mistreating him like she did for three years."

Eve bit her lip, her heart aching with confirmation that Gabe's start in life may have been more difficult than she could fathom. She knew she should end this conversation, it wasn't fair, but she was so hungry for information about him. "Did Linda have an addiction or something?"

"No. Plenty of addicts aren't terrible people, and plenty of terrible people aren't addicts," Maile said sourly. "I don't know what her deal was. She seemed fine at first glance, had friends and a social life, but there was always something . . . off with her. At least it seemed that way to me. Don't you think so, Tani?"

Tani was silent for a beat, but then she spoke. "That woman was cruel and evil."

The suppressed emotion in Tani's voice had them both looking over at the small woman. She took a deep breath. "I never liked her either."

Eve wondered why it had taken years for Gabe to be removed from the care of his birth mother, if she was so awful, but she didn't know how to ask that without totally invading Gabe's privacy.

"Anyway, then Sonya came along, and the universe made up for his terrible mother with an amazing one, along with a fantastic father for as long as Reggie was alive, and a devoted sister." Maile nodded at Tani. "Plus, you and Robert were more than generous, sending him and Rhiannon to private school."

From her vantage point, Eve could see Tani's fisted hands on her knees. "It wasn't generosity. Sonya's father worked for mine. She was family, as were her children."

Had Eve not been aware of the secret, she wouldn't have picked up on how rehearsed and pat that answer was. She took another drink from her iced tea.

A groan arose from Gabe and Nicholas as the game halted. Jackson and Livvy gave each other a high-five. "Told you I'd kick your ass," Livvy crowed.

"I kicked their ass. You were along for the ride."

Jackson flicked his twin's bundled-up hair. She growled and swatted at him.

"Guys," Sadia snapped, and glanced meaningfully at her son.

Jackson and Livvy both looked shame-faced. "Kareem, don't use the word 'ass,'" Livvy said, as they moved toward the patio.

"Never?" Kareem hugged his puppy.

Jackson swiped his hand over his brow. "I suppose, if you're discussing donkeys—"

"Never," Sadia emphasized, and gave her boyfriend a quelling look.

"Never," he parroted, and dropped into a chair at the table.

"I'm thirsty," Kareem said, and leaned against his grandmother. His puppy sniffed Tani.

Tani exploded into movement, grabbing the pitcher of iced tea. "I'll get us some more drinks."

Nicholas shook his head. "Don't do that. I'll have someone refresh it."

"You have a bell pull out here for help?" Livvy asked with a hint of bite in her tone.

Her fiancé glanced at her quizzically. "There's an intercom system."

Livvy rolled her eyes. "Jeez, the kitchen is right there, Nicholas. No need to drag Jeeves into it."

"I'll go," Tani interjected. She disappeared into the house before they could argue any further, Kareem and Sadia following her.

"What's your problem?" Eve heard Nicholas ask Livvy as the couple walked inside.

Jackson twisted around to look at Gabe. "You wanna get a beer and play some more poker?"

Gabe perked up, and Eve wondered if he knew how obvious it was, his hunger to spend time with Jackson. "Yes. Yeah."

"You're only allowed to talk for a total of ten minutes, though."

Eve widened her eyes. "What a brilliant idea."

She meant in general, to force people to adhere to a time limit of talking, but Gabe made a mock outraged sound. She knew it was mock, because his eyes were twinkling.

How she adored his easy-to-read face. She didn't have to worry if he was mad or pissed at her. She could just tell.

"I can't believe you all have such a problem with my mouth," Gabe retorted.

She met his gaze, and she knew the instant he realized what he'd said and the double meaning that could be applied to those words. "I don't have a problem," she said softly, and thrilled when his eyes darkened.

Tonight. Tonight she'd chuck her shell off again and knock on his door. If she could only have a few nights next to him, she'd pack in every second of pleasure she could.

Jackson came to his feet. The two men walked away, but not before Gabe cast one last look over his shoulder at her. Her stomach clenched. His eyes were definitely not twinkling anymore. Or if they were, it was a wholly different kind of twinkle. He swiveled his head to face forward, which was also okay, because she got to stare at that fine ass strutting its stuff.

"Hmm," Maile said, breaking Eve's contemplation of Gabe's butt.

Eve jumped, having forgotten the other woman was still there. She flushed at getting caught mid-ogle. "What?"

"Nothing." Maile carefully changed colors of yarn. "I said *hmm*."

"Nothing's going on," she said, and when the woman's lips curved up, Eve kicked herself for making it clear something was indeed going on.

Damn it.

"Gabe's a lovely boy," Maile mused. "Very sweet, friendly. Always had a smile on his face when he was young. Rose above his beginnings."

She tried to think of how anyone could call the huge, tattooed man sweet, but she knew it was the only thing you could call him. He was sweet. Principled. Generous. Ethical.

Some people might say the truth should come out, but she wasn't one of those people. She respected the secrets people held. Sometimes secrets were necessary and healthier than the truth. Whether that was true for Gabe's situation was something only he could determine.

She looked at the bag on the ground. "Do you want any more help winding yarn?"

"No, I'm fine, dear."

Eve glanced at the shimmering lake. She hadn't gotten to properly swim since she'd gotten here, and she suddenly, desperately craved sinking into water and letting exertion fatigue her muscles. "I was thinking of going to the lake for a little bit."

"If anyone is looking for you, shall I send them your way?" Maile asked slyly.

She grew overheated at the thought of Gabe coming to find her. He had said he liked her swimsuit. And more importantly, she wanted him looking for her. "Yes, please."

Chapter 20

Eve plopped down on her bed, wrapping her towel tighter around her. She'd opened her window a crack, and the laughter and conversation from downstairs trickled into her room. Everyone else was outside, enjoying dinner on the deck.

Gabe hadn't come looking for her at the lake, but she hadn't noticed him or Jackson at the big farmhouse-style table when she'd snuck in either, so she assumed the two of them had gotten caught up in their poker game.

She opened her messages and texted Madison. She'd been so wrapped up in all the new developments in her life, she hadn't updated her roommate. **Told my brother about my business.**

She didn't add anything about Gabe. It was too private and new. She needed time to process it.

Madison's response came immediately. **So proud of you.**

Eve smiled and set the phone down. She was proud of herself too. Was it possible to feel like a different person in the space of a week?

She got to her feet as a knock came on the door.

She cinched her towel tighter under her arms, frowning over the lurch in her heart.

It wasn't Gabe. It wasn't Gabe. She repeated the words to herself, echoing them with every step she took.

She was so certain it wouldn't be Gabe she was genuinely startled to find him outside her door. "Oh." She looked up at him, unable to think of anything else to say.

His gaze zipped over her. He'd showered at some point this afternoon, and changed into a pristine white T-shirt and jeans. His hair was pulled back and still wet, the red strands muted. "Maile said you came straight upstairs without eating. I brought you food." He held out a plate, wrapped in foil.

She searched his face, but she was unable to determine if this was basic human decency, the kind of caretaking her brother might engage in, or something more. "Thank you." She tightened the towel under her armpits and accepted the plate.

He didn't let go, though. "Can I come in?"

"Yes." The word maybe came out a little too fast, but she couldn't help it. A flame lit inside her belly. Their single night together had only stoked her desire for him. She closed the door, locking it as an afterthought.

She wasn't going to assume they would sleep together, but she didn't want to not assume that either. Better to be prepared.

He paused near the window and twitched the

curtain aside, looking down at the party outside. "One big happy family."

Not really hungry but unsure of what to do with her hands, Eve placed the plate on the desk, and moved the foil aside. She picked up a roll and tore it apart, chewing on a tiny piece. He didn't sound caustic, just tired. She swallowed. "Indeed."

He dropped the curtain. "What did you do today?"

"Went to the lake."

"Did you have fun?"

"I did."

"Nicholas laying off you?"

"Yeah. He actually, uh, apologized." She thought about their brief meeting in the office. "I told him about my business idea too."

"What's your idea?"

He'd asked before, and she'd brushed him off. If she told him, how long would it take for him to make the leap from a ride-sharing service to Ryde to Anne? Not long. And then she'd have to explain why she'd driven him around for months secretly like a weirdo. "It's not important."

He didn't pursue the topic, for which she was grateful. "How did he react?"

"Not well. I mean, he had a lot of objections."

"He'll come around. Don't back down."

She wouldn't back down, but that didn't mean she was looking forward to having to stand her ground. "What did you do all day?" Weird, how this felt like something a couple would do. She'd never really been in a relationship where she could tell her partner about her day. Both of the men she'd dated seriously before hadn't been interested in her days. They'd been interested in her name or her fortune.

Don't get used to this. They weren't a couple, she reminded herself.

"I hung out with Jackson." His shoulders relaxed. "I didn't realize you guys were such good friends."

"We get along well."

"He said he never would have thought he would like you as much as he does. That you were, and I quote, *better than most humans.*"

That was the highest of praise from Jackson. "Wow."

Gabe's lips quirked up. "Please tell me. What's the secret to cracking his code?"

"He told you. Don't make small talk. He's uncomfortable in most social situations. Too much friendliness, and he gets nervous and clams up."

Gabe smiled and turned back to watching the crew outside. "I must drive him crazy. I talk when I'm nervous."

She bit her lip, uncertain of how much she could overstep. He'd made it clear he didn't want to talk about his parentage, but his siblings . . . well, that was a bit of a gray area. "Is it weird? Knowing about them when they don't know about you?"

His nod was infinitesimal. Livvy's shriek of laughter filtered through the room.

She pressed. "You and Paul were so close. Did he know about Robert?"

"No. He died not knowing."

There was a wealth of pain in those words, the heavy grief of a beloved brother. "I'm sorry. I didn't know him well, but I'm sorry."

He cleared his throat. "Thank you. It didn't matter in the big picture, I guess. He treated me like a brother. Always had Kareem address me as *uncle*."

She hesitated. The words were practiced, like Gabe said them to himself a great deal. "Do you regret not telling him, though?"

"Every day."

The words were soft, but the emotion behind them was raw. "Have you thought about talking to Jackson and Livvy?"

His hand clenched on the curtain. "I don't know how to tell them. I grew up knowing I was a secret, that every privilege I had, that Rhi had, was by virtue of me keeping that secret. I can't let that go so easily." He lifted his shoulder. "And sometimes I think, why bother? What would I gain from telling Jackson and Livvy that their father had an illegitimate child he kept under their noses for their whole lifetimes? Nothing."

Except more siblings. More family.

She'd made a family with friends, and she'd never say they were more or less family than those of her blood, but she understood the feeling of wanting to belong.

"Besides, Tani wouldn't be happy." Gabe grimaced. "She's never been exactly warm to me."

Eve thought of Tani's fist tightening under the

table. "You know she was the one who suggested you be a part of this wedding party, right?"

He frowned. "What?"

"Yes. Our numbers were uneven, and she suggested you."

His scowl deepened. "Huh. That surprises me."

She thought of what Maile had said, about his birth mother. "Did Robert . . . did he cheat on Tani?"

"Not with my birth mother. She and Robert had a one-night stand before he met Tani. Robert and Tani were already married by the time I was born."

"But you lived with your biological mother for years. Until Sonya adopted you," she ventured.

"Yeah. I don't know what would have happened if she hadn't adopted me."

Eve wanted to say surely Robert and Tani would have made alternative arrangements for him, but who knew if they would have. "How—"

Gabe dropped the curtain. "That's enough. I didn't come here to talk about me."

"What did you come here for?"

He stalked away from the window, coming to stand in front of her. "You promised me apples," he growled, and she dropped the remnants of her roll in the plate he'd prepared for her.

His fingertip smoothed over the knot in her towel and hooked inside. He tugged, and the fabric loosened, then dropped to the ground, leaving her clad in only her bikini. She was grateful she had brought multiple swimsuits now.

"Oh yeah," he said, staring at her chest. "These are some nice apples."

Her face flushed red, but she didn't stop him when he grasped her by the waist and walked her backward. Her knees hit the back of the bed and she sat down on the firm mattress.

He grasped his shirt with both hands and pulled it off over his head, tossing it on the floor, revealing a tanned expanse of flesh and muscle. He was so big, not just his muscles, but his frame too. She slid her hands up his chest, and he froze for a second, then broke away to get his pants off. He wrestled them off and tossed them on the floor, then pushed her down so she lay on her back. He took a step back and surveyed her.

Music came from outside, and she flushed. "Shut the window."

"You don't think you can be quiet?" he teased her.

"I can absolutely be quiet. You can't, though."

He ran his palm over the bulge in his boxer briefs. His cock was erect and straining at the red cotton material, pulling the waistband away from his skin. "I'm not a moaner."

"You're a dirty talker. Like sex closed-captioning."

He snorted but he did go to the window and close it. "I've never heard it called that before."

"It's what you are."

"Maybe you inspire me." He prowled back toward her.

"Or you're filthy and I have nothing to do with it."

He crawled over her, his thick hairy legs on either side of hers, the motion shoving her farther up the bed. She looped her arms around his neck as he stared down at her, his gaze heavy-lidded. His weight was perfect. "You have everything to do with it. You look good under me, by the way."

She thrilled. "Do I?"

"Mmm." He dipped his head and kissed her neck, then moved lower, over her breasts. "I want to eat all these apples," he growled. She jumped at the first touch of his teeth through the fabric. He carefully bit each tiny apple. She whimpered when he lifted his head, though he made soothing noises.

Gabe moved down her stomach, and farther, until he was between her legs. He used two fingers to move the fabric of her bikini bottoms aside, and then his tongue was sliding over her, wet, hot. She clutched his hair in her hands, hoping she wasn't hurting him. He paused to pull the tie out of his hair and let it loose, so she assumed not.

His tongue stroked her clit and she inhaled. She'd never had anyone do this to her before. One boyfriend had been firmly opposed to oral sex while she'd denied the other one.

Why had she denied the other one? She wasn't sure now, because this might be her new favorite thing. His lips surrounded her clit and sucked and her legs trembled. As if he knew she needed the support, his big hands cradled her ass and held her tighter against his mouth.

She looked down her body. Her top was wet from his mouth, the white almost see-through, her nipples visible, the red apples garish now. She ran her fingers through the dark mass of his hair, tightening when she felt his thumb sliding along the crease of her ass. He moaned, the reverberation sliding right up her spine. "I like this," she gasped. "I *like* like it. FYI."

His laugh made her clutch him even closer. He settled into an easy rhythm of sucking her clit, his finger fucking her. The coil inside her tightened more and more, and she tossed, though he controlled her easily.

Just when she was ready to cry, desperate for release, he scraped the stubble on his chin over her clitoris. The rough contact was all she needed to detonate. Before she was even done coming, he lurched over her. She slitted her eyes open when she heard foil rustle. She was glad he was being so responsible, because she could barely move.

Though she did gasp when he rammed inside, his hips forcing her thighs wider.

His big hand covered her mouth, cutting off the sound. "Shhh," he whispered. "You don't want anyone to hear you, do you? Hear how I'm fucking you?"

Her moan this time was muffled, and helpless. The window was closed. No one would hear them. But the dark fantasy his words spun made heat curdle inside her again.

His hips picked up speed. "They'd hear how hungry you are for cock," he continued, still in that low voice meant for her ears only. "You're hungry, aren't you?"

She nodded frantically, fearful he would stop if she didn't answer.

"Whose cock are you hungry for?"

He released her so she could answer. "Yours."

"My what." His breath tickled her ear.

"Your cock."

He thrust harder. He rose up on his elbows and watched her breasts jiggle with every movement of his body. "You're amazing."

"Thank you," she breathed, and wrapped her hands around his forearms.

He gave a half-laugh and bent down. She thought he was going to kiss her, but instead he went for her breasts, shoving the cups aside and licking her nipples. She clenched on his cock harder. His touch turned gentle, sucking on her. "Can you come again? With me fucking you?"

"I don't know."

"Well, let's find out." His fingers slipped down her body and plucked her clit. Her breath came faster, her body heating not just from his penis, but from his hot gaze on every inch of her. There was no part of her that didn't seem to turn him on, and that turned her on.

"Come for me. Again." He adjusted his grip on her leg, pushing it up so he was hitting some new magical spot every time he bottomed out. Her cries rose in volume and frequency and he didn't attempt to stifle them this time.

His body hammered into hers, and she knew he didn't have long. Her toes curled and she came with a long moan. He froze, the heat rising off of him in waves, and then he shuddered in her arms.

She hoped he'd rest on top of her for a while, but he rolled right off as soon as he was finished, his chest moving up and down with the force of his breaths. Her swimsuit was bunched uncomfortably. She pulled the crotch back into place, and tidied the cups of her top.

She looked at him, and gently scooched closer. He made no move to embrace her, and she bit her lip, looking him over.

You don't need him to cuddle you.

No, she didn't, but she wanted him to cuddle her. Difference.

Her gaze rested on his shoulder and the black tattoo there. "This part of your tattoo . . . it is a nod to Robert, isn't it?"

He glanced at his shoulder. "Yeah. He showed me his tattoo when I was young, told me about how the design was intensely personal to the Kanes." His lips quirked. A sheen of sweat covered his tan skin. "Actually, looking back, that was probably the first time I wanted to go into the tattoo industry. I liked the idea of giving people something they love forever."

He was poetic in the oddest ways. "Did you get the tattoo before he died?"

The skin around his eyes tightened. "After. I went to Hawaii. Got it done the old-fashioned way, hand-tapping."

She didn't know what that was, but it sounded painful. "Did it hurt a lot?"

"Like a bitch." But he grinned, like the memory was good. "The guy I found didn't want to do it, initially. I guess he was tired of white guys coming down and getting Hawaiian ink. I had to explain." His smile faded, and her chest ached.

She knew what it was like, to feel like you didn't belong. She moved closer to him and kissed his shoulder. "I like it."

"Thanks." He pulled her closer, until she was almost on top of him. It was contact that probably meant nothing to him, but she luxuriated in the cuddle.

He frowned at her and she instantly grew worried. "Is something wrong?"

"No. I—hmm. I felt a bit of déjà vu for a second."

"How so?"

His hand drew up her arm and he tested the flesh there. "Never mind. Not important."

If he said it wasn't important, she wouldn't stress about it. She lay on his chest and listened to his heart beat. His arms were so big and secure around her. She snuggled deeper and drew her leg up between his, delighting in the way the crinkly hair on his legs abraded her smoother ones. "I could stay here forever," she murmured.

The muscles of his stomach tightened, something shifting in the air. Oh shit. Her stupid romantic soul.

She tried to cover it up by rolling away, though it hurt to leave the circle of his arms. It hurt more when he sat up immediately and swung off the bed, grabbing his underwear and jeans. She tugged the blanket up over herself, feeling a little too exposed.

Damn it. "I'm sorry."

He drew his jeans on. "It's fine. You didn't do anything wrong."

He was lying. She swallowed the lump in her throat. She didn't want him to leave like this. "I didn't mean—"

"Don't worry about anything, okay?"

She had to restrain herself from apologizing a million times, because that would only call more attention to her faux pas. He finished getting dressed and stepped close to the bed and dropped a kiss on her forehead. "Thanks," he whispered. "This was great."

Words he'd probably said to a million women. And now she had to grin and act breezy, even though she didn't feel like it, because that was how the game was played. So she smiled up at him. Corners up, no teeth bared. "Yup."

The relief in his gaze was a prick to her pride, but she buried it deep. This was fine. This was all she could have. And it would be enough.

Chapter 21

Livvy ran a brush through her hair and watched the black, purple, pink, and blue shuffle together in the mirror. She'd had her color done before she'd gotten sick, but the lighter colors were already fading. Too much sun and heat. She might have to touch it up before the wedding the day after tomorrow.

The day after tomorrow.

Her stomach lurched, and it wasn't from a virus.

It had felt right to have their wedding on her birthday. For ten years, they'd met secretly in various parts of the country on that date. She'd come to dread and anticipate the day in equal measure.

She didn't dread the day after tomorrow this year, because it wouldn't be a secret. She was excited. Thrilled. Scared.

Nicholas readjusted his body on the bed behind her. His knee joints creaked, reminding her that he wasn't nineteen anymore. She wasn't sixteen. They were adults, there was no curse, and the wedding would go off without a hitch.

Her gaze softened as she watched him in the

mirror. His brow furrowed, and she knew him well enough to surmise something on his tablet was upsetting him. "I said no work," she reminded him.

He glanced up. He was dressed in a white T-shirt and boxers, and he looked so blessedly normal and boring and familiar.

She'd imposed the no-work rule mostly because she didn't want the reminder, during this tumultuous week, about the company he ran—the company her family had once also owned. Sometimes she could simply revel in being with Nico, the boy she'd always loved. Then something—their families, work, the world—intruded. It was nice to have a break.

"It's not work. Eve sent me her business plan."

"Eve has a business plan?" Delighted, she spun around. She adored her younger soon-to-be sister-in-law. Eve seemed timid, but from the moment she'd marched up to Livvy and tried to defend her brother's honor, Livvy had known there was pure steel in that backbone. "What is it?"

"A ride-sharing service." He quickly ran through the proposal.

It sounded impressive to Livvy, but she didn't know much about business. "Is it not a good plan?"

"I didn't think it would be. There are a number of barriers to entry in any industry, especially a service industry like this. But . . ." He waved his hand at the screen. "This is actually good. She's really thought things through."

"Then . . . what's the problem?"

"I guess I assumed she would want to come work with me."

"Aw." She got up from the dressing table and went to sit cross-legged next to him on the bed. "Did you hope the two of you would run Chandler's together?"

"Maybe. But mostly I wanted her where I could keep an eye on her." He made a sour face when she gave him a narrow look. "I know, I know. You don't have to lecture me about patriarchal and patronizing attitudes."

"You ought to know better by now, Nico. I shouldn't have to lecture you."

His chin lifted. "I have the right to—"

"Nope," she cut him off. "You're her brother, not her keeper. Grown women don't get keepers, babe."

He subsided, his full lips dangerously close to a pout. She might have found it cute, if it wasn't so important for her future husband to get this lesson through his thick skull. What if they had daughters? She wasn't about to subject her future hypothetical girls to a father who smothered them. "You have no rights toward her except to respect and love her. You can do those things without wrapping her in cotton."

His jaw clenched and he tossed the tablet on the bedspread. "I'm scared for her."

She softened, because she knew how much that admission cost him. Nico wasn't accustomed to revealing fear. Or any emotions actually. "I know.

But she's not fifteen anymore. She's an adult, and you need to let her stand on her own two feet."

He pinched the bridge of his nose. "She said sometimes my overprotectiveness reminds her of our father."

Livvy chose her words carefully, because she could tell Nico was hurting. "I can see how that may be true."

"I am nothing like my father."

"Of course not." She interlaced her fingers with his. "But you know, sometimes, when you're in a stressful situation, your body reacts almost independently of your brain. It may not be so easy for her instincts to differentiate between you scolding her and your dad scolding her."

He paled, and she snuggled next to him. "You're not abusing her," she said firmly. "Just, like, listen to her, maybe. When you get the urge to chastise her, maybe ask if it's something you would do with a fellow adult, or if it's something you would do with a child. And then act accordingly. Don't treat her like a child. She hasn't been one in a long time."

He pressed his lips tight together. "Okay."

Warmth ran through her when she stuck her cold feet on his, because he grunted, but didn't move away. This was love, in its purest form. Letting her warm her feet on his. "Part of treating her like an adult is supporting her in this endeavor, if it's as smart as you say it is."

"It's smarter than that," he admitted grudgingly. "She'd make it work with her name alone, but she wouldn't need it for this. She's already hammered out so many of the kinks I'd worry about."

"Then help her. Don't block her. Let her grow. She's come so far. Look at the way she stood up to you today. She wouldn't have dared to do that a year ago, would she? It's good for her."

He tipped her chin up. "You've helped her, too, I think."

She scoffed. "The girl who stalked me to protect her precious brother has always been there. She's gonna be okay."

He pressed his hand on her belly. "Are you going to be okay?"

"Of course." She pressed her hand over his. "I'm healthy as the horse you're worried about me riding."

He ignored the second part of her sentence. "That's all I want to hear."

She grimaced, hating to ask, but unable to let it fester. "Have you heard from your father yet?"

Nicholas's eyes darkened. "No."

Unease slithered through her. Brendan didn't want his son and heir marrying her, and she didn't trust the man to not follow through on making his displeasure widely known. "Great."

"It'll be okay. We'll handle him if we need to." He stroked her cheek. "You got annoyed with me earlier today. Was that stress or about Eve, or do we have anything else we need to talk about?"

She cuddled closer. It wasn't easy for Nicholas to talk anything that might smack of emotions, but he did it anyway, for her. Because she badly needed it. "I don't want help after we get married."

He raised an eyebrow. "What?"

"I don't want to hire other people to do the things we can do for ourselves."

"Livvy . . ." he said slowly. "You grew up with maids and a chef and a housekeeper, like I did."

"Yeah. I haven't hired anyone for a long time."

He considered her thoughtfully. "This isn't about the help. It's about relying on anyone, isn't it?"

"What happens if the money dries up tomorrow, Nico?" She realized she was clenching her teeth, and she made a conscious effort to relax the muscles of her face. "I know how hard it is to go from having everything to having nothing, and I don't want us to have to go through that."

"*You* don't want to go through that, you mean."

"Can you blame me?" She picked at the comforter. "For the last six months we've been out in the real world, but we haven't, not really. We stick to your condo. We don't go to events. We don't go out to eat, really. We've managed to avoid reminders of who you are, who we are. Driving up here was like a nasty slap of reality. This house, the lake, the help, the horses . . . You're richer than we were when I was young, and it scares me."

He mulled all this over, his hand not stopping its stroking motion. "You know what a therapist would call this, right? Self-sabotage. You're looking for reasons to find things wrong with our life and the future."

She reared back in annoyance, but he tightened his arm around her. "You were the one who wanted to have this week up here, Livvy. Renting this place was an easy way to do it. As far as the help goes, did you think we could cook and clean for a dozen people? And have the place ready for a wedding at the end of the week?"

She winced. "No. But—"

"I hear you," he said mildly. "I never really thought about how losing your family fortune affected you because you always seem so blasé about it."

"I am blasé about it." Until she thought about those early lean years before she'd hit her stride as a tattoo artist. It had been hard to go from never thinking about money to budgeting every little penny. She'd managed to keep her head above water, but it hadn't been easy.

He was right, though. She'd survived losing a fortune once, she could do it again. This worry might be a little bit of self-sabotage. Because a lot of things were changing, and she was scared.

"How's this for a proposal. In the future, we confer on any help that's hired. We only do it if it's somebody who will ease our life, or do a job we cannot." He grimaced. "Because I'm not my grandfather, Livvy. I do not want to spend my days weeding a garden."

Her lips curved up. A lot of things were changing, but this man was her constant. He always would be. Just knowing he was willing to listen to her and calm her and compromise with her put her at ease. "Okay."

He pressed his forehead against hers. "See? It's not so hard to make decisions when you can talk it out." He kissed her lips. His fingers stroked her back, finding the compass tattoo there. A few weeks ago, after he'd proposed, she'd modified her ink. The day after their wedding, in lieu of an immediate honeymoon, they'd start work on the back piece he wanted.

He drew a square around her compass, boxing it in. "We're good?"

"Oh yes," she whispered as he slid over her. "We're very good."

Chapter 22

JACKSON CAME up behind Eve and glanced over her shoulder. "Very good. Make the carrots slightly smaller." With the ease of someone who had spent a long time training subordinates in the kitchen, Jackson readjusted her cutting hand.

Eve concentrated harder, focusing on the vegetables. She had no doubt Jackson didn't need her assistance in making the wedding eve dinner, but he hadn't turned down her help.

She'd accompanied him to town this morning. They'd had an almost silent car ride there and back, with only minimal conversation in town while they were picking up food. It had been glorious.

When they'd returned to the house, he'd strapped an apron around his waist. She'd watched, fascinated, as he methodically set about inspecting the entire kitchen, as if someone might have fiddled with his setup overnight. When he was satisfied everything was in its place, he started to cook.

She continued with the repetitive task of carrot chopping, glad she'd chosen to spend the day with Jackson in this sort of silent reflection. No one would have ever called them friends before, but they'd slipped into an easy—if quiet—camaraderie over the past six months or so.

The door opened and Gabe walked in. Eve promptly sliced right into her thumb. "Shit!"

"What happened?" Jackson barked.

"Are you okay?" Gabe asked at the same time.

Before she could blink, she had two large men backing her into the corner, both their heads bent as they examined her bleeding thumb. She looked from almost-black hair to reddish brown. The color of the strands wasn't the same, but the texture was.

She grimaced. "I'm fine, really."

Gabe grabbed a towel and took her hand from Jackson's. His touch was gentle as he wrapped the towel tight. "Doesn't look like you need stitches at least."

Jackson straightened. "No, it's not too deep. Stay here. I'll go get a first-aid kit. I think I saw one in the bathroom. Gabe, can you keep an eye on the pot on the stove while I'm gone? Turn the heat off if it starts to boil over."

"Sure," Gabe said, and blessedly moved away from her. "Keep pressure on that."

She tightened the towel around her thumb. "Yup." The sight of the red staining the white towel made her vaguely nauseous and she leaned against the counter, closing her eyes.

They flew open when he cupped her elbow. His face was close to hers. "Hey. You okay?"

"Yes." She cleared her throat and straightened, trying to not succumb to the light-headedness. "Yes, I'm fine. I—I don't like the sight of blood."

He cocked his head. "But you came to the shop with your friend because she didn't like the sight of blood."

"What?"

"Years ago, remember? You said you accompanied Madison to the shop when she was getting her tattoo for moral support."

No, it was to stare at you.

Wait, though. She hadn't told him that Madison didn't like the sight of blood. Madison had told him that. All those years ago.

He remembered a random meeting that well?

Her heartbeat accelerated, though she tried to calm it. This only meant he had a really good memory for his clients. "It's my own blood. I'm okay with other people's."

His forehead cleared. "Why don't you sit down?"

"I'm okay. I won't look at it."

"Hey."

She fixed her gaze over his shoulder and waited, but he didn't continue. After a moment, he grasped her chin and gently tipped her head so she had no choice but to look him in the eyes. A little annoyed her trick hadn't worked on him, she jerked her face out of his grasp, and he didn't press her.

"I'm sorry I ran out like I did yesterday."

She scoffed, though her heartbeat picked up. "You don't have to be sorry."

"I do. You . . ." He hesitated. "This is different, Eve."

Don't overreact. Don't read anything into this. "Different how?"

"I'm not sure." He lifted his shoulders. "The thing is, I don't know how to be anything but casual with anyone. That's what everyone says, at least, and I suppose it's true."

There it was. The shot of hope and the brush-off. She didn't want to deal with the sting of rejection right now. She tightened the napkin around her finger, until the pressure hurt. "Don't worry about it. I understand."

His eyes darkened. "Do you?"

"Yes. Of course. What we have is like a one-night fling."

"More than a night now."

"A few nights."

He nodded slowly. "A several-night stand."

She supposed the cold description fit. Ouch. "Sure," she managed. "I don't want anything more. Don't worry."

He drew away from her, each inch feeling like a canyon opening between them. "Right. Good. I'm not worried."

Jackson entered, a bandage and a tube of anti-biotic ointment in his hands. "Found it. Sorry that took me a minute."

"That's fine." Her voice was higher than she would have liked.

Gabe gave Jackson a tight smile. "My sister and mom should be arriving soon. I'll leave you two to dinner. Smells great, Jackson."

"Thanks."

Eve kept her head down while Gabe left the room. Jackson crossed over to her and competently dressed and bandaged her wound. "Eve?"

She glanced up at him.

His black eyes held a hint of worry. "Are you and Gabe okay?"

Oh jeez. The last thing she wanted was tension between Jackson and his half-brother—and over her? No way. "Fine. Blood makes me woozy." It wasn't a complete lie at least.

He seemed satisfied by that explanation. "Alistair caught me in the hall. Your grandfather is here, with your brother in the study."

"Already?" She'd wanted to be on hand to greet her grandfather and his care attendant when they arrived. She made it to the door, then glanced over her shoulder. "Aren't you coming?" Livvy and Jackson and her grandfather had a deep bond. The man had been their surrogate grandfather their whole lives, until the split.

Jackson shook his head. "No. I'll see him when he's alone."

That was a very Jackson thing to say. "Gotcha."

Eve scurried down the hall, her stress over Gabe somewhat buried under her anticipation. Her grandpa John was her favorite person in the whole world, maybe even above Nicholas. She pushed open the door of the library, smiling when she caught sight of the elderly man sitting in his power chair next to the luxurious couch.

"Grandpa, it's so good to see you."

He beamed up at her, his bushy white hair neatly combed. John tended to favor casual clothes, but he'd dressed up today in trousers and a navy sports coat. "There's my Evie."

John was a legend in Rockville, regarded with awe and reverence. There wasn't a single family who didn't either know him or know of him, one of the two men who had created the region's largest employer.

He had always been a larger-than-life figure for her, a gentle, affectionate, yet occasionally gruff father figure. She hugged him gently, a little alarmed at how weak his return squeeze was. Arthritis had made the power chair a necessity a few years ago. "I didn't know you were already here."

"Only drove up a little while ago. Chad's making sure my room's set up for me and the chair. Nicholas was catching me up on your adventures."

Eve's smile slipped slightly, and she glanced at her brother. She hoped he hadn't told their grandfather about her adventure in the rain.

John shook his head. "Volleyball and kayaking and horseback riding. I'm glad I didn't come up any earlier. I would have been tired watching you people."

Oh good. Nothing about her getting stranded, then. "You would have been welcome all week."

He patted her hand. "No. More important the next generation spends time together. I won't be around forever, you know. You need to form bonds again."

She hated hearing stuff like that. She wanted him to be around forever. "You'll outlive us."

"Why would I want to do that? Especially when my blood is carrying on the Chandler name so proudly." He beamed at Eve. "All this time you've been secretly plotting to put the rest of this family to shame in the business world."

Nicholas shifted. "Eve, Grandpa and I were talking about your company." His tone was carefully neutral.

"Is that right?" she asked warily, and braced herself for more criticism.

But it didn't come. Her grandpa looked delighted. "Nicholas had to explain some of the basics to me. I'd heard of these kinds of services, but of course I've never had to take one. Might be hard with my chair anyway."

"I want my company to be more accessible."

"I saw that in your plan." Nicholas grinned. "It was a good plan, Eve. You've done your research."

"I have. I've even driven for Ryde for a few months," she blurted out.

Nicholas pursed his lips. "You've been driving for the company you said isn't completely safe?"

John slapped his knee. "That's how you do it, girl. Get out there, get your hands dirty."

"That is how you do it," she said firmly, looking at Nicholas.

To his credit, Nicholas only looked a little green at the thought of her driving around the city with strangers. "Yeah. Right. Get your hands dirty."

"Chandlers don't quit and they don't sleep on opportunities. I'm so proud of you, Eve."

She soaked up the approval like a dry sponge. "Thanks, Grandpa."

"We need to sit down after dinner and go through the whole plan."

"Maybe after the wedding," Nicholas interjected. "We have a big day tomorrow."

John continued as if he'd barely heard his grandson. "We'll have to see what you need too. Investment-wise. Of course Nicholas and I will both contribute seed money."

"Of course," Nicholas echoed.

That should have made her happy. She shouldn't turn down capital. She opened her mouth to accept but instead what came out of her mouth was, "No. I want this company to stay mine."

Nicholas frowned. "It would still be yours—"

"No, it wouldn't, Nicholas. If you put money in, you'd have equity. And your big nose would be all up in it."

He harrumphed. "It would not."

"She knows us, son," her grandpa said, his blue eyes twinkling. "I respect you wanting to do this on your own, Eve."

"Grandpa—"

John held up his hand, and his grandson immediately clammed up. "It's Eve's company. Eve calls the shots. Promise, though, if you need any consultation, you'll come to me or Nicholas. We do want you to be successful."

"That's fine." She shot Nicholas a warning look. "But only if I ask for the advice. If I don't, you keep your—"

"I know." Her brother touched his nose. "It's not that big."

"It's the Chandler nose," John said. "It's large enough."

Nicholas smiled and dipped his head. "Very well, Eve. You have my support. My distant support."

Approval. It shouldn't feel so good. She almost squealed, "Really?!" but she didn't want to diminish her victory with an immature outburst. So she nodded demurely and kissed her grandfather on the cheek. "Do you want to rest for the afternoon, before dinner?"

"I'm not a toddler." But the annoyance was almost absentminded. A shadow moved over John's face. "Actually, that's why I wanted to see the two of you alone first. Your father is coming tonight. To dinner."

Her excitement deflated, but when she glanced at Nicholas, she knew she couldn't be churlish. Longing and anger warred there, and she understood them both. Sometimes, even when a parent was toxic to the extreme, it was hard to get rid of the hope that they would be kind or gentle or perfect *this* time. "Well, he was invited."

"I told him it might be best for him to just show

up for the ceremony tomorrow, if he really wished to attend the wedding to satisfy appearances, but he refused." John looked between the two of them, helpless. "I'm sorry."

"Don't be sorry. As Eve noted, I did invite him." Nicholas rolled a pen between his fingers. "I'll tell Livvy."

John placed his hand on the chair's control. "If you point me in Tani's direction, I'll break the news. I'll run interference through the night for her. I don't want Brendan to make her upset." Tani had always been like John's surrogate daughter. Over the past month, the two of them had made great inroads on repairing their relationship.

Mentally, Eve cursed her father. She understood why Nicholas had invited him—that stupid hope—but that hadn't meant Brendan had to come.

Eve allowed herself a few deep breaths. She wouldn't become overwrought by this. Nicholas and John didn't know the extent to which Brendan had bullied her when she was young—only Madison and, more recently, Gabe knew the more sordid stories—and she'd like to keep it that way. She'd manage her father the way she always managed him, with distance and shields.

She poked those shields. They didn't feel as strong as usual, which was worrisome. It was okay, though. Worse came to worst, she would stay silent and fly under Brendan's radar. She was good at that. "Tani's in the garden in the back. The deck is accessible, and there's a ramp for you."

"Oh good. I was hoping to see the garden."

"I can accompany you."

Nicholas rested his hand on the table. "Let me phone in for one meeting and I'll join you."

"Keep the meeting short. You don't want to miss out on life because you're working, Nicholas."

"Yes, sir."

The second they opened the door, a shout echoed through the hallway. "Grandpa John!"

John looked one way, then the other, a smile splitting his face. "Where is that boy?"

Kareem careened around the corner, his puppy yapping behind him. Kareem scampered into John's lap without a hint of hesitation. Kareem had a sprawling family on Sadia's side, including two grandparents who doted on him. He had quickly adopted John as Paul and Jackson's kin, and the affection was mutual.

John squeezed Kareem close. "There's my boy. And who's this?" He peered down at the puppy, who was sniffing the wheels. Eve bent, picked him up, and deposited him in her grandfather's lap as well.

"That's . . ." Kareem frowned. "I forgot what I named him last."

John scratched the pup's ears. "He looks like your grandpa Sam's puppy."

Kareem readjusted himself. He was always hungry for any stories about his late father and his family. "What was his name?"

"Rascal. I helped name him. Sam got him for a thirteenth-birthday present. I was so jealous."

"Because he was the best dog?"

"Yes." John's smile faded. "I took care of him for your grandfather when he was in the camp. He was indeed the best dog."

Kareem grew solemn as well. Sadia wanted her son to know as much of his multicultural heritage as possible—Pakistani American, Japanese American, and Hawaiian. Sadia and Jackson had matter-of-factly explained to Kareem how his grandmother Tani's parents had once been sentenced to an internment camp for Japanese Americans. Somehow, they'd struck a balance between not scaring the boy but still impressing the gravity of his history upon him. Eve was forever awed with Kareem's ability to process information. "Was he so happy to see Rascal when he got out of the camp?" Kareem asked.

John's eyes darkened, and Eve knew the situation probably hadn't been so simple. But he nodded, and Kareem didn't seem to notice anything amiss.

Kareem ruffled his dog's ears. "I can name my dog Rascal Two. But we can call him R2. Like R2-D2."

John cleared his throat. "Well, now. I think your great-grandpa would have liked that."

Eve smiled, thinking about how much Gabe would enjoy the pup's name as well.

Ah, stop thinking about him.

Impossible, especially when they came across him hugging two tall black women in the foyer. It took Eve a second to place Sonya and Rhiannon, and she immediately blushed.

She'd been daydreaming about making out with Sonya's son. She was allowed to blush.

The trio separated. "My gosh," the older woman exclaimed and put her hands on her hips. "Is this handsome little man Paul's son? Last time I saw you, you were tiny."

Kareem smiled beatifically from John's lap, accustomed to attention. "Hi."

"Sonya?" John boomed. "What is this? All of us are aging except you."

Sonya laughed, a throaty, deep noise. She was dressed in a pretty yellow dress, her hair braided tight. No jewelry, except for a worn wedding ring on her left hand and a pair of diamond studs in her ears. "You always were a charmer, John."

The two embraced, and John peered at Rhiannon. "I've seen your face on magazines. Are you too rich and famous for us yet?"

"Hardly," the younger woman drawled, and accepted the hug John gave her. Though she wore casual, almost grunge clothes, Rhiannon carried herself with an air of casual confidence Eve feared she would never have.

You are okay.

While Gabe greeted John, she shoved herself out of her shell, stepped forward and extended her hand to the women. "Hello. I'm Eve. It's been a while."

Sonya ignored her hand and pulled her in for a hug. "I could never forget you. You look like your mother. Maria was a dear friend, and I miss her every day."

Eve flushed again, with pleasure this time. "Thank you."

"Now that everyone's put the unpleasantness behind them, I'll dig out my old yearbooks when I get home. Maria's in them. I'll mail you copies." Sonya squeezed Eve's hands.

"Oh! That would be lovely." She didn't have anything of her mother's from that long ago, except for a few baby photos. If her father had kept old yearbooks, she'd certainly never seen them. She released Sonya and greeted Rhiannon. "Hello."

Rhiannon opted to shake her hand, her gaze assessing. "The Baby Chandler," she murmured.

No shells. Not today. "Indeed," she said. "And you're the woman who's reshaping love, one app at a time."

Rhi's lips curled at Eve parroting her last Forbes profile at her. "I'm trying, sweetheart."

Gabe rested his hand on his sister's back. "I was about to show the ladies to their rooms."

"Feels good to have the whole family here like this, doesn't it?" John asked Sonya. His tone was both wistful and self-satisfied. All John had ever wanted to do was unite the Chandlers and the Oka-Kanes.

"Very much so." Sonya's eyes were kind. "Everyone will be at dinner, yes?"

John's smile tightened, and Eve knew he was thinking about his son. Her stomach somersaulted. "Yes. One big happy family."

Chapter 23

GABE RESISTED turning around to stare at Eve as she left. Instead, he grabbed his mother up in another hug. She laughed and scolded him as he swung her around. She wasn't a tiny woman, but he'd shot past her in height when he was in middle school. "I missed you, Ma."

She laughed. "My precious little boy."

He doubted she'd ever stop calling him her little boy. That was okay with him. He bent down and accepted her kisses on both his cheeks, her expensive perfume twining around him. She'd always had style, and she had no compunction about using the trust fund Rhi had established to indulge it to the best of her ability.

He glanced at Rhiannon and grinned. Her black hair was long, the tight curls forming a halo around her heart-shaped face. Her nod to the occasion was switching out her blue jeans for black. Otherwise her black hoodie was in place, half unzipped to showcase a rock band's concert T-shirt, black combat boots on her feet. "Don't tell Rhi I'm your favorite right in front of her."

Rhi rolled her eyes. "I'm not sure why I missed you."

A throat cleared behind him. "Would you like some more time, or shall I show you to your rooms?"

Before he could answer Alistair, his sister peered around him. "You may show us to our rooms." She pointed at their bags. "We only have these."

Alistair sized her up quickly, and Gabe could tell the butler was doing the mental gymnastics to reconcile his sister's decidedly casual appearance with the ease with which she took control. Most people didn't know what to make of Rhi. She was complicated, and she preferred it that way.

Gabe grabbed the bags. "I can show them, thanks, Alistair. Come on, ladies."

"Chuck didn't come?" he asked his mom over his shoulder as they went down the hall to his mother's room first.

"No, he had a work emergency come up."

"Ah, too bad. I was looking forward to seeing him." Kind of. Being reminded that his precious mother had a boyfriend was more than a little weird for him.

"Next time."

He opened the door to the bedroom and set the suitcase down in the closet while his mother went to the window and opened the curtains. The place was decorated in light yellows and white. "What a beautiful home," his mother remarked.

"It's not bad." Rhi leaned against the wall. "We're both in here?"

"No, you're next door."

"Sweet."

"Can you close the door for a minute, Gabe?" Sonya sat on the small settee.

That wasn't good. Gabe wasn't sure what his mother wanted to discuss, but he closed the door.

"Good. Now, first, Gabe, please tell your sister to wear the dress I bought her tonight."

Oh. This. Gabe blew out a rough breath.

Rhi examined her nails. "Gabe, please tell our mother I will wear whatever I damn well please."

Sonya's nostrils flared. "Gabe, please tell your sister not to swear at her mother because she is not too old for me to send to her room."

He eased closer to his sister and squeezed her hand, easily falling into his role as mediator. "Ma, you know Rhi has an image she has to keep up. The hoodie's part of her brand."

"Her brand could easily be adorable dresses and sweaters."

"Kill me," Rhi muttered.

"But it's not," he told his mother, as firmly as he could, suppressing his urge to laugh. After more than three decades, he knew for a fact laughing around either of these women when they were annoyed would have them joining forces to turn their ire on him.

This was so blessedly familiar. With all of the upheaval and uncertainty in his life, slipping back into this dynamic was like putting on a pair of old jeans. Or a hoodie, for that matter. "She's comfortable like this. Let her wear what she wants."

"Hmmph." Sonya folded her arms over her chest. "I am so tired of this battle."

"Wouldn't be a battle if you didn't keep firing shots," Rhi remarked.

"People will think I didn't raise you properly." Sonya waved her hand. "You are richer than most everyone here. Dress like it."

Rhi rocked back on her heels. "I don't want to dress like it. I want to dress like me."

Gabe intervened. "Okay, how about we declare a truce on this topic for today and tomorrow? Mom, let Rhi wear whatever she likes. Rhi, maybe, could you possibly at least . . . lose the hoodie at the wedding?"

Rhi pursed her lips but rolled her eyes when he cast her a pleading look. "I know how to go to formal events with a bunch of rich people, Ma. I'll wear my nicest clothes, promise. No dress, but you won't be ashamed."

"And tonight? At the dinner with all the Chandlers and Kanes?"

His sister made a face. "I won't wear a sweatshirt."

Sonya sighed. "I suppose I can't ask for more."

Gabe smiled. "Come on, Rhi. I'll show you to your room."

"One second, please."

They both paused. Sonya stood and walked over to him and grasped his face. "Have you been okay, my love?"

"Sure."

She looked deeply into his eyes. "Has Tani been good to you?"

"She's been the same as usual."

"Cold, then," Rhi remarked. There was an edge to her voice.

"Can we blame her for that?" And that was the crux of the problem. He couldn't blame Tani for being awkward around him, because his existence was awkward. "And actually, to be fair to her . . . I heard she was the one who suggested I be in the wedding party."

His mother's smooth forehead creased. Sonya's comment to Eve about the yearbooks and Maria had prompted Gabe to wonder, for the first time, what Sonya and Tani's relationship had been like before he'd come along. They were of an age, and Sonya's father had worked for Tani's father. Had they been friends? Or had this wary formality always existed?

"That's interesting." Sonya nodded and took a step back. "Okay, love. Get Rhi settled in, and then you can give us the grand tour of this place."

Rhi immediately flopped onto the bed in her room like she was a teen instead of a millionaire in her mid-thirties. "What's the deal with you and the Baby Chandler?"

He shut the door hastily. "Shhh."

"Is it a secret?"

"Is what a secret?"

"That you two are banging it out."

He dragged his hand over his face. "Jesus, Rhi. Language."

"Oh, I'm sorry. Was that too coarse? Should I say you two are engaging in a union of souls?"

"I hate you. How did you know? Tell me you haven't created an app to figure out when people are intimate."

"Are you kidding me? I'd be a trillionaire."

"We're skipping over billionaire? Or did you already hit that?" he teased.

"Kid, you have no idea. P.S. don't think you can distract me."

"Yes, fine." He shoved his hands into his back pockets. "We're kinda talking to each other."

"It's a secret?"

"Not a secret. Just . . . no one knows." He replayed the words in his head. "So, yes. A secret."

"Uh-huh."

"A secret who . . . knows some of my secrets."

At that, Rhi sat up. "Oh really? She knows about Robert?"

Rhi would badger him until she got every little detail about him and Eve, so it was actually efficient for them to get this over with now. "Yes."

"Have you ever told any woman that?"

"No. I've never told anyone. She figured it out and I couldn't lie fast enough."

Rhi rolled over onto her belly and cupped her face in her hands. "What else have you told her?"

"That's all."

"Nothing else?"

"Oh, you know. I told her about Paul, and how he didn't know. And how I kind of wish I could tell Jackson and Livvy." He paused. "Actually, I guess I told her a lot."

"Interesting."

"No, it's not. It doesn't mean anything."

She held up her hand. "I didn't say it did. I said it was interesting. Cool your jets."

He leaned against the door. The subject of this talk wasn't comfortable, but the setting, their dynamic, that was familiar. He and Rhi could have been back in one of their bedrooms in the Kane mansion. "I like her. She's a good person. It's . . . I don't know what we're doing together. It can't go anywhere." The words tasted like ash in his mouth.

Last night, when she'd cuddled up against him and said those words—*I could stay here forever*—his gut reaction hadn't been to run away. On the contrary, he'd wanted to pull her tight, and say even more foolish words back to her. Words like, *Stay forever.*

The urge had been so strong, he'd gotten spooked. He'd run, yes, but only because he'd been terrified of how little he wanted to run.

You're supposed to be the uncomplicated one.

None of it mattered, though. As she'd made clear in the kitchen today, she didn't want anything more than his body. And if Gabe could be counted on for anything, it was always giving a lady what she wanted.

Rhi rolled off the bed. "Huh."

"What?"

"That's the first time you've ever talked about a girl with even the expectation that it could go somewhere."

He reared back. "No, it's not."

"Isn't it?"

He frowned so hard Rhi sauntered over to him. "Relax. It doesn't have to mean something."

"It is messy."

"Yeah, well." She shrugged. "Sometimes good things are."

Chapter 24

Lɪᴠᴠʏ ʜᴀᴅ nixed an actual rehearsal before the rehearsal dinner, citing her love of spontaneity, though Eve suspected it had been an attempt to cut out any further stressors and potential curse-rearing opportunities.

Eve wished she'd gotten a chance to speak with Gabe before dinner, but between the new guest arrivals, dinner prep, and making sure her grandfather and his attendant were comfortable in their accommodations, there had been no time.

She had stood in front of her and Gabe's adjoining door for a precious ten minutes after her shower, but ultimately, she'd quietly gotten dressed alone. Had she knocked, she wasn't sure what she would have said. They weren't at a place where she could confide her anxiety over her father and expect him to comfort her, were they?

They stood at opposite ends of the living room as they sipped drinks before dinner, Gabe, she noticed, sticking to water. Every time their eyes met, he would smile, and so would she, and she wasn't sure if her strain was being projected on him, or if he was also tense for some reason, but neither smile felt authentic.

The whole room was some level of agitated, Tani hovering around John as if he might shield her from anything terrible, Jackson his usual level of grim, Livvy and Nicholas leaning against each other. Sadia had chosen to dine with Kareem in their room, citing a headache and wanting rest before the wedding tomorrow, but Eve wasn't fooled. Sadia was protective of her son and no kid needed to be exposed to Brendan.

He's not an evil wizard, coming to curse them all.

Or was he?

By the time they took their drinks into the dining room, Eve was a bundle of nerves. When would Brendan get here? Would he come at all?

She smoothed her skirt under her and sat at the table. Rhiannon sat next to her, Jackson and Gabe across from them. She gave Rhi a tentative smile as they picked up their salad forks. She'd try to drown her anxiety in small talk. "How do you like living in California?"

"It's not bad. Weather's better." Rhi dug into her salad. "Nicholas said you're thinking of starting a ride-sharing company."

Guess Rhiannon wasn't one for small talk. Eve shot a glance across the table, but Gabe was engrossed in a conversation with Jackson. Or rather, Gabe was talking and Jackson was staring at his plate. The man had clearly forgotten her advice on how to win Jackson over. "I'm not thinking about it. I'm doing it."

"Cool. Shoot me your business plan."

Confused, Eve paused in picking through her salad. "Why?"

"Because I have oodles of money," Rhi explained, as if she was a simpleton. "And I like to invest it. Especially in other women."

"Oh."

Rhi speared a tomato. "Specifically, Nicholas mentioned your concept will be more responsive to women and other vulnerable populations. That's my area of interest. Too many of these companies are helmed by a bunch of dudes who don't know how anything works for anyone but them."

She turned toward Rhi, forgetting her earlier intimidation of this woman. "Yes, that's exactly the problem. Sometimes things that seem great in theory don't work out in the real world for everyone."

Rhi stabbed her fork at her. "Patriarchy."

Eve grinned. "Smash it."

"Nah." Rhi's teeth flashed. "Murder it dead."

Eve turned her head, exhilarated, and found Alistair walking into the room. That wasn't what made her stomach sink, though. No, it was the familiar dark-haired man behind him. Blood rushed through Eve's head, making it pound.

Like someone had hit a switch, the party quieted, but Brendan didn't seem to notice. He looked up and down the table. His gaze lingered on Tani's bowed head. Maile edged closer to her friend, her dark eyes narrowed on the newcomer's face.

Brendan was, as always, impeccably dressed in a tailored dark suit, his salt-and-pepper hair expensively cut. A perfect purple pocket square was his only pop of color.

In a few years, Nicholas would probably look like him. But he'd never be him. It was impossible for Nicholas to ever be this cold and remote.

"Hello, all," Brendan said, almost cheerfully. "Apologies for being late."

Eve's fingers tightened on her fork. Even in his best mood, Brendan wasn't cheerful. He was only mildly thawed. And he never, ever apologized.

Something was up.

John had sat at one end of the table, with Tani and Nicholas on either side of him. Alistair gestured to the only empty seat at the table, directly opposite John. No one had touched that seat. It was Brendan's seat, because above all, her father had a severe complex about his stature in comparison to his father.

Before the tragedy, Brendan had occupied Nicholas's role as president of the company. Sam and John had been co-CEOs, and then Robert had taken over Sam's spot when he'd married into the Oka family.

Eve figured that had always spurred part of Brendan's resentment of Robert Kane as well as his hatred of the Oka-Kane family, above and beyond the circumstances surrounding his wife's death. Robert, a relative outsider, born to a middle-class family that owned a café, of all things, had leap-frogged above him to essentially become his boss.

Until Brendan had "bought" Tani's shares and become co-CEO with John. That was when he'd started insisting on sitting opposite his father in a seat of equal importance. It didn't matter if they were in the board room or the dining room.

Nicholas finally cleared his throat. "Father."

Brendan's gaze slipped over Nicholas, and Livvy at his side. Ever expressive, Livvy's forehead was puckered. "Nicholas."

He didn't say anything to Eve, for which she was grateful. It meant she was already under his radar. She ran her fingers over her naked wrist. She should have worn some other bracelet tonight. It would have given her something to fidget with quietly, under the table, out of sight.

Brendan accepted the glass of wine Alistair handed him with a murmured "Thank you," looking for all the world like nothing more than a pleasant guest.

Gabe caught her eye across the table. *Are you okay?* he mouthed.

A burst of warmth spread through her belly. She gave an infinitesimal nod and let go of her wrist.

John cleared his throat and raised his glass. "Now that we're all here, I'd like to make a toast. To you, Nicholas and Livvy. My Barbara—" He swallowed, and Tani took his hand. "She used to say we had soul mates and maybe we do. But I know people who are meant to be can only truly be meant to be if the individuals choose to be. I am so happy you have chosen to be together. Though the path has been bumpy, you have weathered it with grace and kindness. May you have as happy a marriage as Barbara and I did. May it be filled with love and laughter."

Maile straightened and lifted her glass. "May you treat each other with respect, always."

Sonya beamed. "May you never go to bed angry with one another."

The room was silent. Tani hesitated, finally picking up her glass. Her gaze met her daughter's. "May your love be a light in the darkest of times."

Livvy's eyes filled with moisture, and she dabbed at them.

Eve had to blink back her own tears. They all lifted their glasses.

Except her father, she noted. Singularly unmoved, he sat back in his chair, and folded his arms over his chest.

She wasn't the only one to notice his lack of reaction. John leaned forward and glowered at his son, jerking his head at the man's wineglass.

Brendan raised an eyebrow.

"Stop acting like a petulant teenager, Brendan. And toast your son and his bride," John said between gritted teeth.

Nicholas shifted, lifting his hand, ready to mediate between the two men, like he'd had to do for years. "Grandpa, it's okay."

"No, it's not. Pick up your glass, son."

Brendan's chest expanded, and so did Eve's sense of dread. "I'd rather not toast this farce."

Maile inhaled sharply. "Why, you—"

Brendan barely glanced at her, but he did look at Alistair, standing by the door. "Everyone who isn't family can leave."

The staff immediately departed, but no one at the table stood.

"You don't order anyone around here," John said, his face growing florid.

"Yes, yes. Because there's one patriarch in this family, and it's you. Well, it can stay you. I'm done." Brendan paused. "Unless this ridiculous wedding is called off."

Livvy leaned forward. Sentimental tears gone, there was death in the other woman's eyes, and Eve didn't blame her. "Listen, ass—"

Nicholas rested his hand on his fiancée's arm. "Dad, we've discussed this," he said, and his pleasant tone sent a chill down Eve's spine. "You know what happens if you step over the line."

"You quit, I know. And that would be very difficult for me. If I was still half-owner of this company. But I won't be for long. I'm selling my shares. I'm ready for retirement."

Eve's stomach clenched. She had not seen this twist coming. Her father had done everything for those shares, had destroyed their families to swindle them out of a grieving Tani so he could be equal to his own father in equity and power.

"Now, I don't particularly want to sell to an outsider. So Nicholas has a choice he can make here. I'm happy to sell to him, at a fair yet discounted value, so long as he calls off this wedding."

Nicholas froze. "You can only sell to a Chandler or an Oka. Those are the restrictions."

"I have to first offer them to a Chandler or an Oka. If no one can meet the fair market price for them . . ." He shrugged. "I can go to an outside party. Dad, you really should have closed up that loophole, but I guess you and Sam could only be forward thinking on some matters."

The wineglass slipped from John's hand. No one made a move to tidy the spilled wine. "You would—" He wheezed. "You would threaten everything I built? Just so your son doesn't marry the woman he's always loved?"

"Don't be dramatic, Father. This is business."

"There's no choice to be made here. I'll buy the shares," Nicholas said. "And you can leave now."

Brendan examined his nails. "You don't have enough in liquid assets to afford it if I don't discount market value. And I won't discount unless you end your fraternization with the Kanes."

Eve's brain was racing, palms sweating, but finally she saw a place for her to speak. "I'll pool my trust fund with whatever he has," Eve said, but her heart plummeted when John grew tense.

Brendan finally looked at her, and there was nothing in his gaze. She understood John's dismay when her father addressed her. "Even if you withdrew every dime, penny, and quarter that you, your brother, and your grandfather owned, you could not begin to pay me the market value for my shares."

"I'll take a loan," she said flatly, too stunned to

even think about stepping lightly or hiding. "We all will. This maneuver won't stand in court."

Brendan's eyes slitted. "Don't be stupid, Eve."

"Don't talk to her like that."

They all looked at Gabe, who had been so quiet next to Jackson. His eyes were flinty hard, and he looked almost as impotently enraged as Livvy.

Brendan stared at the younger man. "Who are you again?"

"Gabe Hunter. More importantly, I'm the man who's going to murder you if you ever speak to your daughter in such a dismissive way again."

Eve should not feel her heart go pitter-pat, but . . . Gabe's body was coiled, his face set in hard lines. He looked scary and intimidating, not the funny gentle giant he usually came off as.

And he was outraged on her account. Hers.

Like a prince, rushing to her rescue.

"Gabe. Hunter." Genuine amusement appeared in Brendan's gaze and he turned his attention to Tani. It took a second for Eve to recognize the emotion in the smaller woman's eyes.

Fear.

"The housekeeper's kid?" A malicious smile curved Brendan's lips, and Eve leaned forward, terrified of what she feared her father would say next.

He couldn't know. If he did know, he'd keep his mouth—

"Robert's bastard?"

Chapter 25

THE ENTIRE table stilled. Gabe's ears buzzed, like someone had slammed their fist into his face.

Livvy was the first to speak. "You hate my father so much," Livvy whispered, "you would make up a lie like that?"

"You mean you don't know? It's not a lie." Brendan gestured at Gabe. "That boy's your half-brother. Raised right beside you, in your own house, under your mother's nose."

"Mom," Jackson murmured. His fingers shifted next to Gabe's on the table. "Mom, is this true?"

Gabe couldn't bear to hear Tani confirm the accident of his birth. "It's . . ."

"No." Sonya tossed her napkin in her plate. "Baby, you don't have to dignify these lies. Come on."

Gabe softened. His mother's face was taut with anxiety and fear. For him. She might have wanted him to come clean to Livvy and Jackson, but not like this.

It was okay, though. Brendan had already taken the choice of confessing his ancestry out of

his hands. The least he should get to do was confirm it. "It's true." The words hurt. "I'm Robert's
biological son." He dared to glance at Jackson. For
once, the younger man's emotionless mask had
slipped. He was staring at Gabe with horror and
disillusionment.

Another punch, this time to the gut. He'd
known, though, hadn't he? He'd known Jackson
and Livvy probably weren't going to welcome
him into the family with open arms.

"How dare you."

The word fell with the weight of a thousand
pounds of rage. Tani came to her feet, her small
body vibrating. "You monster."

Brendan's nostrils flared.

"You're wrong, Olivia. He doesn't hate Robert.
He never did, did you, Brendan?" Her eyes grew
wet. "It's me you hate. I'm the reason you can't
stand Olivia marrying your precious son."

Brendan came to his feet as well and braced his
hands on the table. "Don't flatter yourself. I can
hate your whole family."

"I've had enough of all these dramatics," John
said weakly.

"I'm sorry. I think we need one more minute of
drama," Tani said. "Don't we, Brendan."

The man's eyes narrowed. "What the fuck are
you talking about?"

"I've been quiet. Out of respect for your children and mine and . . ." Tani's gaze slipped over
Gabe. "And mine. But no more. If you want to
sell your shares, so be it. The rest of us together

will buy every single one. Do not think for an instant that you can ever attempt to come between my daughter and her husband again. Because we both know what I know."

"You don't know anything."

"I know you never really minded those rumors that Robert and Maria were having an affair. Because the truth would have hurt your precious image more."

Brendan stilled. "Shut up."

Tani's lips stretched up in the facsimile of a smile. "The truth is, Robert would never have been with Maria that night if I hadn't sent him out to help her. Because she was trying to leave you."

Eve drew in a breath. "Mom was leaving? Without me?"

Tani jerked out of the tense staring contest between her and Brendan. She turned to Eve, hand outstretched. "Eve, she wasn't abandoning you. Your mother asked me to bring you to her, to the lake house. She had bags packed. She even had fake passports for both of you, because she'd tried to leave before and Brendan had stopped her. Once she was somewhere safe, she was going to tell you, Nicholas." Tani's tears overflowed. "I didn't like to drive in the ice. So I called Robert, and I told him what was happening. He was going to help her, bring her to Eve, and get them to the airport. That was why he was speeding. That was why he was there. He was just trying to help our friend." Her face crumpled, and she wilted into her chair.

Nicholas's voice was raspy. "There was no baggage or fake passports found in the car."

"'Cause she's lying," Brendan said. His eyes were flat, as usual, but his hands trembled.

"Your father paid people off to make sure nothing would be found," Tani said to Nicholas, exhausted, but the rage she turned on Brendan wasn't weak at all. "You hated that I knew your wife couldn't stand you. You hated that I tried to help her. You took the company away and hurt my children when I was too depressed to fight back. But I will not let you hurt my children now."

"You're hysterical."

"No. I'm honest. Do you know what, Brendan?" She leaned forward. "I don't regret helping Maria. What happened that night was a terrible tragedy, but I would have done anything in my power to help your wife leave you. She deserved happiness. My conscience is clear. Is yours?"

Brendan had turned utterly white. His gaze finally dropped away from Tani. "I—" He focused on Nicholas. "My demand still stands."

Nicholas stood. "Your demand will be met," he said, cold as ice.

"Good luck."

"He doesn't need luck," said Rhi, who had watched the whole spectacle silently. Her deep, throaty voice signaled danger. She picked up her wineglass and swirled its contents, but her eyes glowed with anger. "I'll give Nicholas every spare dime he needs."

Brendan scoffed. "You can't have equity. You're not family."

"I don't want equity. It would be a loan. I have more than enough to buy you out a few times over." She smiled thinly. "Consider it my gift in return for you fucking with my brother tonight."

"Rhiannon . . ." Nicholas started, but Rhi shook her head.

"Later, Nicholas. We'll handle the terms later."

"No one wants you in this company anyway, son," John said. His voice was thready. "Sell us the shares already, discounted or not. There's enough of us to meet any demand you make."

Brendan's jaw clenched. He walked out without another word to his daughter or son. Eve slowly came to her feet, like she was in a daze, and she followed him out. A second later, Nicholas cursed and threw his napkin on his plate and strode after her, with John following not too far behind.

Gabe wanted to stop her, ask her what she was doing, but he was locked in his own nightmare.

Everyone knew. His secret was out.

He looked around the table at his adoptive family and his birth family. Livvy's tears had made her mascara run down her cheeks in black tracks. "Mom," she said, her voice scratchy. "I know a lot of things have come out but . . . Gabe?"

He cleared his throat. "It's true," he said again.

Maile had been silent until now, but she was also crying. "You kept my nephew from me?" she whispered to Tani. "All these years?"

Jackson exhaled. "How . . . ?"

"Robert and I got married six months after our first date," Tani explained quietly. "He had a relationship with Gabe's mother before we met. Gabe was the result."

"That doesn't resolve the question of why Dad never acknowledged him." Jackson's voice rose. "Mom, did you not let him?"

Before Tani could reply, Maile rose from the table and gazed at her former sister-in-law as if she were a stranger. "We have been roommates and best friends and business partners for a long time now. How could you not tell me?"

Tani stared her friend down. "I didn't want anything to tarnish Robert's memory."

"I don't give a fuck about my brother's memory," Maile said harshly.

"But he would have," Tani returned simply.

"Robert's memory did not trump my right to know about my nephew." Every word was slow and precise. Maile swept out of the room, her feet heavy.

Livvy rubbed her face. "God."

Tani stared down at the tablecloth. "I'm so sorry all of this happened on the eve of your wedding, Olivia."

Livvy's laugh was humorless. "It wasn't the best timing, for sure. This is the first time I've believed in the curse."

Oof. A curse. His existence was that bad?

Rhi leaned forward, probably to take issue with Livvy's framing, and he gave her a sharp shake of his head. There didn't need to be any more conflict. Not tonight. Without another word, he got up and left the room.

EVE WASN'T sure what she was planning on saying when she ran after her father. She should have a speech or a blueprint for what she hoped was a final showdown, but her brain was blank. Except for rage and fury and an odd satisfaction.

All these years, Eve had wondered why Maria and Robert had been on that road together. She'd had to grow up listening to gossip and wild speculation, smiling in the face of the cruelest comments.

Her mother had been leaving Brendan. She'd wanted to take Eve with her.

Silly for a grown woman to have abandonment issues over her mother dying. But those had eased, the mystery solved. Her mother had never meant to leave her.

And Brendan . . . She'd been so certain the man had hated her because she looked like her mother, because he'd loved the woman. But no. It made more sense that he hated her because he'd hated Maria. But either way, it had nothing to do with Eve. She wasn't the terrible one.

She might not need someone else's love to tell her she was lovable, but it helped to have it. And plenty of wonderful people loved her. This house was full of them.

She darted past Alistair and a maid, uncaring of what they thought about her tearing through the mansion. She cleared the front door and spied

Brendan almost at his car. "Hey," she shouted. It didn't sound like her, because polished, rich women didn't shout. They whispered or smiled sweetly or cut silently.

But shouting was effective as well as cathartic. Brendan halted and turned around, his face incredulous.

She came to a stop a few feet away and stared at him. The shell was there, waiting for her, and part of her wanted to crawl into it. She didn't fault herself for that part of her, though, because she finally understood the shell wasn't necessarily a horrible thing. It was a protective mechanism, that was all. It had kept her alive and functioning when the world wanted to poke and hurt her. It was a part of her, and maybe not a part of herself that she needed to find disgusting or bad.

"You're not my father." The words were flat, and she meant every single one. "I mean, I know you are, biologically, but you're not my father in any other way that matters."

"Don't be so—"

"I will be dramatic. You are cruel and unkind. You've hurt me in ways that no parent should hurt a child."

A muscle ticked in Brendan's cheek. "You're acting like I abused you."

He never raised a hand to me. Her usual excuse for this man. She wrapped her fingers around her bare wrist, her pulse giving her strength. "You did," she said softly. "When I was twelve, and you made me cut up that dress for no reason. When I was fifteen, and you told me to stop making a big deal out of being sick, that everyone got the flu. When I was seventeen, and the housekeeper told you I was sad that a boy was mean to me, and you told me I should consider losing some weight if I wanted to be even moderately appealing to men. God. I could go on and on."

His face tightened. "You foolish—"

"I'm not foolish. I'm smart. You underestimated me."

"Did I?" He rolled his eyes. "Evangeline, I am sorry I never heaped praise on you and gave you medals for breathing. I wanted you to be tough."

Her first instinct was to flinch away and hide at his caustic sarcasm, but she straightened. "I don't want medals or praise. I am tough and smart, and it's no thanks to you."

He snorted, and turned away. Maybe it was how mad she was on Gabe's behalf, or maybe it was anger for herself, but she saw red at the clear dismissal. "I'm smarter than you." She nodded when he glanced at her. "That mysterious leak to the news about Chandler's using prison labor for some of their goods? Who do you think did that?"

A footstep scraped behind her. She glanced over her shoulder to find Nicholas and John standing there, staring at her nonplussed. "Eve, you undermined our company?" Nicholas said in disbelief.

Uh-oh. A bit of rational thought pierced her rage. She hadn't particularly intended to confess this, but since it had stopped her father in his tracks, she couldn't take it back. "No, Nicholas. I made it possible for you to get what you needed." She shook her head. "Managing this asshole—" she hooked her thumb, loving the sputtering that came from their father as well as the swear word on her lips "—was taking all your time and resources. So yeah, occasionally I leaked a little news to put pressure on him. So you could do what you needed to do."

"You—"

She glared at Brendan. "You made me feel scared and small and timid. You made me question every emotion I ever had." She blinked, not caring that tears were streaming down her face. Those tears were cleansing. Powerful. "You made me feel like something was wrong with me. But nothing is wrong with me. I'm fine. And I feel nothing for you. No desire for a relationship. No hunger for affection. I did, once. But not anymore." It was like something inside her uncoiled as she spoke, freeing her. Her voice dropped to a whisper. "Goodbye."

A big hand settled on her waist, and Nicholas stepped up next to her. His gaze was as distant as she felt.

A soft, wrinkled hand grasped her right hand, and her grandfather came to her other side. "You heard the girl," he said gruffly. "Go on now. We'll discuss anything that needs to be discussed through our attorneys."

Brendan cast them all a searching look, perhaps expecting more lectures or rebukes, but none of them had anything left to say. His jaw tightened, and he stalked away.

She felt . . . nothing. And it was amazing.

Nicholas cleared his throat when the roar of their father's car had faded. "Eve, I appreciate your assistance, but please do not resort to corporate espionage ever again."

Her laugh was more of a sob. She turned in her brother's arms and pressed her face against his chest. John patted her back as she cried.

Here was love. Deep, unconditional love. And she deserved it.

Chapter 26

Eve opened the door to her room, pausing when she caught sight of the man sitting on her bed. She didn't say anything, merely closed her door and walked over to him.

Gabe had let his hair down, and it was mussed, like he'd dragged his hands through it. He grasped her hips and drew her close, looking up at her. There was pain and sadness in his gaze, but also heat and need. "Are you okay?" he rasped.

She checked herself. She was okay, oddly enough. "Yes. Are you?"

"As okay as I can be."

"Good." She waited a beat. "Can you take off your clothes?"

The air between them grew taut. He came to his feet and she took a step back to give him room.

First came his shirt, then his pants, then his underwear, every article of clothing that he took off revealing another inch of tanned, delicious, perfect skin.

She walked around him, coasting her hand

over his broad shoulders, the dip at the small of his back, his round buttocks. Bubble-y indeed.

She came full circle, and smoothed her hand over his belly, down to his thick cock, and grasped it tight. He exhaled, the muscles of his stomach contracting.

Her dress was demure, navy blue and white, and buttoned from hem to neck with fabric-covered buttons. She stroked him leisurely as he undid the row of buttons.

He opened it to her waist and then leaned in and kissed the curve of each breast. "Can I have you?" he murmured.

She smoothed his hair back. "Yes."

The word was barely out of her mouth before he started yanking and tugging at her dress. As soon as she was naked, he hoisted her high in his arms, spun them around, and pressed her against the bed. Her body was already wet for him, but he tested her with a single finger, then two. He spread his fingers carefully, widening her. She was full, but not full enough. "Fuck me," she gasped.

He captured both her wrists in one hand and shoved them over her head. She gasped when he thrust inside her. He held still for a second, letting her adjust. "You're so tight," he murmured.

She swallowed. "You're so big."

His erection dragged over her most sensitive tissues. "Too big?"

"No. I mean, only for the first moment or so, when you push in." She thought for a second. "I wonder if there are exercises I can do. To make taking you easier."

His shoulders shook. "Masturbation. That's the exercise."

She stretched up and bit his earlobe. His laughter stopped. "I could buy a larger vibrator."

His breath came faster. "Yeah? Tell me what you'd do with it."

A flush infused her whole body, but she didn't feel self-conscious. This was another kind of freedom. She whispered right into his ear. "I'd rub it all over my clit. Then I'd fuck myself with it, deep and hard."

He released her wrists and pushed inside her. "Like that?"

"Yes."

"I can be your vibrator," he muttered. He pulled out, then sank in again, the thick head of his cock bumping right against a particularly sensitive knot of nerves.

She gripped his shoulders tight, hungry and selfish, the motion of his hips making her toes curl. "I like that."

"Good. I want to give you everything you like." He leaned up on one elbow and ran his thumb over her clitoris and she bit her lip. A couple strokes was all it took for her to come, her breath breaking as he fucked her through one orgasm and then a second, smaller one, before he shuddered in her arms.

He collapsed on top of her. They lay in silence

for a long time, his breathing tickling her ear. She nestled close, pulling him in tighter despite the fact that he was crushing her. This was exactly how he'd fallen on her that night he was drunk and she drove him home. Except this time, they were both naked, and he was still inside her.

It was heaven.

"Are you really okay?" she asked.

He didn't answer, just buried his face between her breasts. She stroked his hair, unsure of what to say. "If anyone said something cruel to you . . ." She paused. "It's because it's a shock. Give them time."

He shook his head. "No. Everything's fine." He withdrew from her and rolled away, taking care of the condom and dropping it into the wastebasket at the side of the bed.

She was cold, but she warmed instantly when he pulled her back into his arms and adjusted the covers. She rested her head over his heartbeat while he tucked the comforter around her shoulders.

"Why did you chase after your father?"

She closed her eyes. "I had to tell him something."

He stroked her back. "What?"

The whole evening was taking on a hazy quality, like it was already a distant memory. "That he abused me and he means nothing to me."

His thumb stroked over her shoulder. "Do you feel better?"

She inhaled. "Yes."

"Nothing quite like confronting an abusive parent."

She craned her neck. Gabe sounded like he knew what he was talking about. "Was Robert—"

"No. He was as good of a father as he could have been, in secret."

"Your birth mother, then."

He gave a tiny nod.

"I heard she gave you up."

"She just . . . left one day. They found me wandering around an alley, barely clothed, trying to find food in a dumpster. She didn't report me missing for hours."

Eve flinched, trying to imagine the sweet apple-cheeked toddler in that photo on Gabe's shelf, digging through scraps. "My God, was she arrested?"

"My understanding is Robert and Tani made sure she wouldn't face legal charges in exchange for her giving up her parental rights."

"Have you ever spoken to her?"

"Yes. I wanted to see where I came from." He grimaced. "I felt guilty for even looking. But I grew up not quite looking like anyone around me. For once, I wanted to see a resemblance. Feel like I belonged."

"What was she like?"

"My biological mother?"

"Yeah."

"Uh, she tried to blackmail me, so not great." Eve reared back in shock and he raised his hand. "It's fine, I'm not still upset. She seemed nice at first, and a part of me actually thought she might have just been young and dumb and made a mistake when she abandoned me. Then she demanded money. So I cut all ties."

It was unlikely his birth mother's abandonment and betrayal hadn't left its mark on Gabe, but it wasn't Eve's place to second guess Gabe's feelings. "That's awful. I'm sorry."

"It's fine. Blood doesn't make parents."

"It certainly doesn't." Brendan was living proof of that.

They were silent for a little while. He shifted, his leg slipping between hers. She rubbed her thigh against his crinkly hardness. "Eve," he murmured.

"Yes?"

"We talked about how . . . this was sort of casual."

Uh-oh. Had he seen something in how she looked at him? In the things she'd said? Had he realized how much she liked him? Her stupid crush?

It had been bad enough when he'd rejected her briefly in the cabin. To be rejected now, because he suspected her troublesome emotions? That was unthinkable. She wouldn't be able to bear it, not on top of all the other tumult in the day.

The shell. Yes, fine. She was going in the shell. Because sometimes you needed the protection of a shell. "Yeah. Of course. It was such a great idea," she said in a rush. "This was fun, right?"

He inhaled. "Yeah, fun."

"I mean, it's not like we could have anything more, ever," she said, and her heart cracked. "But this was great sex."

He pressed his face against her hair and gave her a kiss. "That's what I'm good for."

"I . . . I enjoyed myself a lot."

He was smiling when he pulled away. "I'm glad." He squeezed her. "I should go to bed. We all have a big day tomorrow."

It was on the tip of her tongue to ask him to stay here, and sleep with her, but she stuffed that desire down. "Right. Sure."

Slowly, his arm left her, and he rolled out of bed. He drew on his boxers, and gathered his clothes. She pulled the blankets up over herself, the bed frigid without him.

When he looked at her, his eyes were calm and clear. He bent over and kissed her forehead. It was the kind of kiss you might give someone when you never expected to run into them again. "Good night."

"I'll see you tomorrow."

He stroked her cheek. "Yeah," he said, and then he walked away, shutting his door behind him. He didn't see her sniffle, or shed a single tear. It was over, she told herself. And that was fine.

She closed her eyes, and let her tears seep into the pillow. It was fine.

Chapter 27

Eve walked down the hallway and scrubbed at her eyes. She was sure she had huge bags. It would require a mountain of makeup to get rid of them.

She met Sadia outside Livvy's door. The other woman looked slightly more rested than Eve, but not by much. She probably hadn't gotten much sleep either, though she'd missed being present for Brendan's dramatic revelations.

"Hey," Sadia said, subdued. "How are you doing?"

"Okay, I guess."

Sadia squeezed her arm, which surprised Eve. "I know last night must have been especially hard on you. We can talk about it later, if you like. It might help to decompress with someone who has a little more perspective on both your families."

Eve fiddled with her shirt. "I . . . Thanks. That means a lot." She bit her lip. "You know, thanks for not holding how stupid I was with Livvy when she came back here against me. It's really cool of you."

Sadia raised her eyebrows. "I would never have done such a thing. It was an emotional time for all of us, I get it."

Eve wasn't accustomed to talking about emotions like they were an acceptable reason to behave erratically, but she was learning. "Thank you."

Sadia pulled her close for a hug. "We're sisters now, Eve. God knows, I don't have enough of them."

She gave a watery smile. "Oh. Okay."

"Shall we see how Livvy's doing?"

Eve nodded. They knocked and received an immediate summons. They walked in and paused. Livvy had looked shell-shocked last night, but today she sat at the vanity in a silk robe. The sun streamed through the room, highlighting the pale silk of her wedding gown, hung carefully on the wardrobe.

She glanced over at them and continued smoothing lotion over her arms. "There you two are. Did you sleep at all?"

"Yup," Sadia said cheerfully.

"Like a baby," Eve agreed.

"Liars." Livvy smiled and came to her feet. "We are going to be the most terribly fatigued wedding party in the history of the world."

"You're okay, Livvy?" Eve asked, and perched on the bed. "I mean, you're not—"

"Depressed? No. Oh, I had a bit of a rough patch last night. I started thinking maybe this was all too complicated and hard and we would never get through it all, and wouldn't Nico be better off without me?" Livvy walked to her wedding gown. "But then I woke up next to Nico, and he still had his arms tight around me. Life's gonna be complicated and hard no matter what, but if he's by my side I think we can make this work." Her face hardened. "Besides, I'll be damned if I let some asshole—sorry, Eve—take today away from me."

"Don't be sorry," she murmured. "He is an asshole." The word felt freeing, so she repeated it. "A giant asshole. And I'll be so happy if he really does sell the company to us." It might deplete most of the capital she'd planned on using to start her own business, but that was okay. She'd figure something out. She was resourceful.

Livvy sniffed. "You're growing up, Eve."

"It's been a long time coming."

"Well, if we're all ready to start getting dressed, let me see what Jia and Ayesha's ETA is. If they aren't too close, they can stop and get us some coffees." Sadia pulled out her phone. Sadia's younger sisters were arriving to ride herd on Kareem while they all got ready. Plus, Jia was a makeup and style icon and would be doing their hair and makeup.

Livvy examined her face in the mirror. "That would be nice. Did you guys eat? Sadia, can you grab us all some fruit before we get terribly busy?"

"On it."

Sadia had barely closed the door when Livvy spoke. "I know you and Gabe are a thing. Are you okay, after last night?"

Eve stared at Livvy's reflection. "Uh, what?"

Livvy rolled her eyes and turned to look at Eve. "Do you think I'm new? I know last night's news might complicate your relationship. I don't think you should let it."

Eve swallowed, uneasy. "We don't have a relationship. We were—you know. Messing around."

Livvy lifted her hand. "If you both made an adult, consensual decision to have an affair, it's not my place to judge."

"Yup. That's exactly what happened." It was, damn it. It couldn't be helped that she wanted more.

"Okay," Livvy said, and drummed her fingers on the table. "I'm a little surprised, is all."

"Because I don't seem the type to engage in a fling?" She couldn't help the little bite that accompanied her words.

"Nah. It's not about you." She shrugged. "I was surprised because he doesn't seem the type to mess around with anyone he considers more vulnerable than him."

"You're making me sound weak."

"I don't mean to. Can I give you some sisterly advice? From someone who has been in this situation before?"

Eve readjusted her position. "Sure."

"Be honest with him. Whatever your expectations or needs are. Sex, love, whatever. It always works better that way."

"I've been honest with him." Sort of. Kind of.

"And be honest with yourself too." Livvy's smile was rueful. "That's the first step, really. Don't just think about what he wants or what you think he wants. Think about what you want too." She looked up and smiled as Sadia slipped into the room with a tray of food. "Ah, good."

Think about what you want too.

For so long she'd been fixated on what other people wanted from her, a hypervigilance that she wasn't properly filling whatever role they needed from her. Living like that was exhausting, and she wasn't planning on continuing it any longer.

But living for herself was scary in its own way.

A knock sounded on the door, and Tani came in, followed by a quiet and subdued Maile. They were both in their robes. "I know you told us we should get dressed here with you, but I can do it in my room, if that's better," Tani said politely.

"Why would you do that?" Livvy asked, confused.

Tani glanced around the room, barely making eye contact with any of them. "Because I assumed you were all still mad at me."

"We can be mad at you for keeping secrets and still love you and want to be around you," Maile snapped. She took a deep breath and pasted a smile on her face. "Apologies. I am working through my anger."

Livvy drifted over to her mother and grasped her hands. "What Aunt Maile said. I'm getting married, and I don't want to hear any negative talk about past feuds and curses or anything. I want us all to be happy."

Sadia came to stand next to her mother-in-law.

She put her arm around her. "I understand trying to take care of ghosts as well as the living," she said quietly. "It can be exhausting."

Tani squeezed her hand. "Yes."

"It's okay, Mom," Livvy said gently. "It's good the secret came out. That's how we can all move forward in a healthy manner."

Tani tsked. "Therapist talk."

Livvy's eyes narrowed for a second. "You feel really bad, right?"

"Of course."

"Then this is a good time to tell you I *am* pregnant."

Eve and Maile gasped. Sadia didn't look all that surprised, but she was closer to Livvy than anyone.

Eve clasped her hands together. "I'm going to be an aunt?"

Livvy beamed and accepted Maile's hug. "Yes. I found out last week when I went to the doctor."

"Did the flu—"

"Nope." Livvy patted her still-flat belly. "Me and the muffin are fine."

Tani drew herself up. "I *knew* you were rushing this wedding because—"

"No, no, no!" Livvy raised her hand. "You are not to say *anything* right now that can be construed as crowing or chiding."

"You're taking advantage of my guilt."

"I am," Livvy agreed.

Tani sniffed. Tentatively, she stroked Livvy's arm. "Well. I suppose that's okay this one time."

"Good." Livvy rested her hand on her belly.

"I'm only telling you this now because I want the future to be tangible. Sadia, Eve, you can go ahead and start getting ready. Can you and Aunt Maile come with me, please?"

GABE AND Nicholas got dressed in about ten minutes, tops, and then Nicholas turned on the news.

"Why were eight hours set aside for putting our suits on?" Gabe asked.

Nicholas shrugged and flipped through the channels. "I think it takes the women a little longer. I don't know."

Gabe drummed his fingers on his knee. He felt restless and out of sorts, and only partly because half his attention was on wondering what Eve was doing and if she'd slept at all.

The rest of his attention was focused solely on the other people in this house. He couldn't joke or laugh his way out of last night's reveal. He had no idea what the Kanes were thinking about him.

Panic rose up in his chest, that same panic that always came with the thought of revealing his parentage, and he tried to distract himself. "Hey, man." Gabe sat on the ottoman near the couch. "I'm sorry about the drama yesterday."

Nicholas cast him an incredulous look, putting the remote down. "Uh, I'm the one who should be sorry. That was my father who outed your secret."

"Yeah, well." He grimaced. "Still my secret."

Nicholas swiveled. "You're a Kane. And even before the biological thing came out, you were a

Kane. Despite my father's best efforts, Kane business is Chandler business. Especially after today."

He swallowed. Nicholas looked tired, but Gabe had never seen someone so grimly determined to get through a day. No one was going to screw up Nicholas and Livvy's wedding. "Thanks. We're cool, right?"

Nicholas's smile was broad and unusual on the reserved man's face. "Yeah."

"Good."

Jackson stuck his head inside the door. He was dressed in casual clothes still, but since he was overseeing the food for the reception, that was to be expected. He ignored Nicholas and focused on Gabe. "Hey, can you come with me?"

He had been expecting a summons like this, but from Livvy, not Jackson. Still he got to his feet and followed the other man into the hallway. "I know you have lots of questions."

"I do, but can you not talk for a second and follow me?"

"What's going on?"

"That's talking."

He shut his mouth, mystified, and nodded. Jackson gave him a searching look. With a satisfied grunt, he started walking.

Gabe grew more confused as they made their way to his mother's room. Jackson knocked, and then opened the door.

The room was large, but it was filled. Sonya and Rhiannon sat on his mom's bed. Tani and Maile perched on the couch, and Livvy leaned against a wall, dressed in her robe still. They looked somber, but Livvy grinned when he walked in. "What's this?" he asked.

Livvy took charge. "I'm sorry to corner you like this, but I thought at least a quick talk before we all get up in front of strangers might be good."

He stuck his hands into his pockets. Normally he loved talking, but he dreaded this. "Sure. I owe you that, I suppose."

"You don't owe us anything," Jackson muttered.

"We only wanted to welcome you to the family," Maile said softly.

His chest tightened. "Ah."

"About damn time," Sonya muttered, and his sister elbowed her.

"It is about time," Livvy agreed. "I'll never understand why Dad didn't acknowledge you—"

Sonya snorted loudly, and Livvy looked at her. "Do you know, Sonya?"

"Not for sure, no. But I think it's pretty clear that the husband of one of the town's princesses couldn't have possibly sullied the Oka name by bringing an illegitimate child into the home." Sonya jutted her chin out at Tani. "Tani didn't want me to even adopt Gabe."

"I didn't," Tani agreed when everyone looked at her.

Maile gave a disgusted noise. "I swear to God, Tani. The way you half-answer things, it's like you want people to think you're the villain. Tell them what you told me last night." Maile turned to the rest of them. "Tani didn't want Sonya to adopt Gabe—"

"Because *I* wanted to adopt him." Tani finally looked at him, and he was shocked at the tears in her eyes. "The second he walked into my house, I wanted him. I loved Robert so much I could never have turned his child out."

He rubbed his chest. "You didn't like me being out in the sun, because my skin darkened. I looked more like Robert."

Tani frowned. "Gabe, my mother died of skin cancer. I didn't like any of you children out in the sun without protection."

Jackson ran his hand over his jaw. "That's true. She was always on all of us."

"Please never think I didn't want you. I was so mad at Robert for not telling me about you the second you were born, for keeping you a secret for years. If I'd known, I wouldn't have let you stay with that ditz of a birth mother for one second longer than necessary."

"So why didn't you adopt him?" Sonya's indignation had been replaced with wary confusion.

Jackson answered for his mother. "Dad stopped you."

"Yes. He was . . . He cared about appearances far more than I did. I finally agreed to let Sonya and Reggie adopt him, so he could stay in the house at least. Besides, I could tell Sonya had fallen in love with him the second she held him." Tani's lips trembled. "But please don't think harshly of Robert, Gabe. He loved you dearly, and he came to regret his decision. He just didn't know how to fix it. And he thought he had time."

"You're still protecting him," Livvy observed. "You don't need to, Mom."

"I do." There was a finality in her voice. "His memory is all I have. I'll keep it for as long as I can."

Maile rose and came to Gabe, capturing his face between his hands. She searched his face, as if she were looking for something. "Gabe. We can't change the past, but we can make the future. We can tell everyone, or we can keep it in the family, whatever you'd like. But we would like you—and Sonya and Rhiannon, of course—to be a part of our family. Formally. Publicly."

His secret was out.

And they wanted him.

It hurt to breathe. "Excuse me. I need some air." He moved around all of the people in the room and stepped out onto the balcony. He rested his hands on the porch railing, breathing in the lilac-scented air. This side of the mansion didn't have a lake view. There were no calming blues to look at. He focused on the trees, the mix of hunter and forest greens.

A second later, the door behind him opened and shut.

Livvy came to stand on one side of him, Jackson on the other.

"What I just can't understand," Livvy started, "is if you knew you were my half-brother, why were you always flirting with me?"

He reared back to stare at her, horrified, shocked

out of his panic. "What the hell are you talking about? I never, ever flirted with you."

"Sure you did. You even winked at me."

"You have been with the wrong men if you think winking constitutes flirting. I probably had something in my eye."

"I don't think you've ever flirted with me," Jackson mused.

"I have never, ever flirted with either of you," he said emphatically. He finally caught the twinkle in Jackson's eye, and his lips inched up, finding the humor in the twins' banter. "Trust me."

Livvy inched closer and brushed her arm against his. "Did Paul know?"

He swallowed. "No."

Jackson cleared his throat. "But you guys were so close."

"He loved me. He had his issues, yeah, but . . . man, when he loved someone . . ." Gabe smiled, remembering Paul's grin, the way he'd slap his back, his groan of despair when his team lost the playoffs.

The way he'd handed Kareem over to him, that day at the hospital, with the utmost care and adoration, like he was entrusting Gabe with his most prized possession. "He loved me like a brother, though he didn't know," he said huskily. "He loved me like he loved you two."

"Did he love us?"

"Of course." Gabe frowned at Livvy. "Was that ever in doubt?"

"We didn't know him like you knew him.

Maybe you can tell us about him," Jackson said. "Like you tell Kareem."

Gabe straightened. Here was something he could do for his biological half-siblings. Something that would ease him as well. "I'd like that."

They were silent for a little while, all of them contemplating the trees. Finally, Gabe looked down at Livvy. "You're practically on top of me, Livvy. Are you trying to tell me something?"

Jackson peered around him. "She wants a hug," he translated.

"Are you sure you won't think I'm flirting?" he asked dryly.

She elbowed him, and something tight unraveled inside him. He grinned, lifting his arm to wrap it around her. Her voice was muffled against his side when she spoke. "I'm sorry Dad never acknowledged you."

He shook his head. "I'm sorry too." That anger and resentment and love that made up this complex ball of emotions toward his father would probably always remain.

But the resentment he'd always felt toward Tani had eased significantly. She had wanted him. With no blood ties to him at all, she'd wanted him. He didn't know if this would change his relationship with her, but it definitely made him view her in a different light.

"Can we acknowledge you?" she asked. "Privately or publicly."

It took him a moment to speak. "Do you want to?"

Jackson placed his hand awkwardly on Gabe's shoulder. "We lost one older brother. Might be nice to get to know another one properly."

He nodded, hating the sting of tears in his eyes. "Yes. That would be nice." He cleared his throat. "Now, Livvy, don't you need to go get married?"

"Yup. Let's go do that."

Chapter 28

Eve FIXED her dress and glanced up at Gabe. They stood just inside the house, Tani and Livvy adjusting Livvy's dress behind them. John was already at the altar, an arch of flowers and vines. Sadia stood in front of them, fussing over Kareem, who would carry out the rings, his puppy on a leash at his side. "A rehearsal would have been handy, Livvy," Sadia fretted.

"Nope." Livvy cracked her neck. "I'm a single take kinda gal."

Sensing Eve's attention, Gabe looked down at her and smiled. There was a new, relaxed light in his eyes that hadn't been there before. "You look beautiful," he whispered.

She smiled, her chest swelling. Mr. Perez's dress fit her perfectly. She'd said a little quiet "fuck you" to her father when she'd put it on. It had felt better than eating a delicious piece of cake.

He stilled, his expression unreadable. "What?" she asked.

He brushed his thumb over her lower lip, and

she forgot to worry about who was watching them. "Nothing."

The beginning chords of music came through the slightly ajar doors, and Gabe's touch fell away, leaving a trace of heat.

"Okay, go time everyone," Sadia whispered, and shoved her son out onto the deck.

Gabe escorted her down the aisle, and then she went to stand next to Nicholas while he took his place next to Sadia. He waggled his eyebrows at her, and she flushed. Someone would see, and get the wrong idea.

What's the right idea?

That they were friends. Really friendly friends.

Livvy came down the aisle and Eve refocused on her brother and a wedding ten years in the making. Everyone held themselves together admirably well, until it came time for the two to recite their vows.

Nicholas pressed Livvy's hands to his chest. "Livvy, I have loved you since before I knew what love was. I carried that love with me every second we were apart, and I will carry it with me for all my days. You have made my life brighter and sweeter. I promise to cherish you for all my days and nights."

A tear trickled out of Livvy's eye. "Nico, last night, my mother said we should be each other's light in the dark. That's what you are and always have been for me. My love for you makes me stronger, which is how love should be. I won't thank you for loving me, because you *should*—" always a comedienne, she paused for the burst of tearful laughter from the audience before finishing "—but I will always be grateful you are in my life."

Without looking behind him, her grandfather passed Eve his handkerchief. Eve discreetly patted her eyes, hoping her makeup hadn't run.

What do you want?

Her gaze met Gabe's. His eyes were as damp as hers.

Have you ever wanted something you couldn't have?

This. She wanted exactly this. She was worthy of this.

Why couldn't she have it?

Chapter 29

Eve MOVED through the guests at the reception, smiling and nodding at the people she knew, fielding compliments on her flouncy dress with grace and gratitude. As Mr. Perez had promised, she had more than enough room to eat and dance.

She stopped next to Jackson, who was standing in a corner, scanning the crowd as if he were mentally calculating how quickly he could get out of there and back to his room. Which probably wasn't far from the truth.

He gave her a nod. "How are you holding up?" she asked.

"I'm surviving. I hate people. You?"

"I'm surviving. People are tolerable."

They grinned at each other. The reception wasn't as crowded as a Chandler and Kane event could have been. Nicholas and Livvy had tried to keep the wedding to around one hundred guests, which was the lowest they could get away with once they accounted for the extended Chandler clan and business partners Nicholas couldn't snub.

Not that either bride or groom was interested in talking to anyone. They'd accepted everyone's well-wishes, but they'd been on the dance floor more often than not, lost in each other's eyes and arms.

"Everyone's complimenting the food," Eve said.

Jackson inclined his head arrogantly, like compliments on his food were to be expected. And maybe they were. "I could have made a better cake."

"I'm sure you could have. But I'm glad you didn't have to worry about one more task. You should get to enjoy yourself a little."

"I'll dance with Sadia once she's done micromanaging everything. That's all I want to do." He nodded at Nicholas and Livvy. "Their vows were nice. Your brother's okay."

Eve hid her smile, lest Jackson think she was laughing at him. This was high praise. "Thank you, Jackson. I promise, he grows on you."

"Like a fungus."

"Yes, but a kind, gentle, loving fungus."

Kareem scurried up to them, chocolate covering half his face. His puppy was flopped under the table at Tani and Sonya's feet, worn out, but the child looked nowhere near ready to call it quits from the party. "Uncle Jackson, Auntie Ariel is here." He pointed to a handsome red-haired woman bearing down on them.

Jackson straightened, then looked over his shoulder. "Good job, Kareem. Did you do what I asked?"

"Yup." Kareem ran away, hailed by some of his cousins.

Eve eyed Jackson curiously, but he was busy with his business partner and manager. Eve shook off his odd behavior and smiled, greeting Ariel warmly.

The redhead wore a chic strapless emerald dress that set her coloring off to perfection. "What a lovely wedding," Ariel said to Eve, her British accent softened from years of travel. "The bride and groom look resplendent and this home is gorgeous. The surrounding land reminds me of home. Thank you so much for inviting me."

"Uh-huh." Jackson checked over his shoulder again.

Eve cleared her throat. "Did you get a chance to look at the gardens?"

"I did, yes, before the ceremony. I was hoping to take a closer look at the roses."

"There's a path out to that section of the garden, if you'd like me to show you."

"No! Not yet. Stay here."

She and Ariel stared at Jackson, who scowled at them. The man's scowl instantly cleared when he looked over Ariel's shoulder. "Aunt Maile."

Maile joined them and gave her nephew a quizzical look. While Tani had chosen a conservative gray mother-of-the-bride ensemble, Maile wore bright red, an off-the-shoulder gown that showcased her powerful and statuesque figure. "Kareem said you were looking for me?"

"Yes." Jackson drew his aunt closer and then

turned to his business partner. "Ariel, this is my aunt Maile."

Ariel's eyes had widened. Her fingers fluttered to the base of her throat. "Oh, hello."

Maile blinked, and then blinked again. She rallied quickly, holding out her hand. "It's a pleasure to meet you finally. I've heard so many good things about you."

Ariel's smile started slow, but spread over her entire face. "And I, you."

Jackson cleared his throat. "Aunt Maile is single. Ariel is widowed. You should both go dance. Maybe later you can go look at the roses."

Eve coughed, but luckily both Maile and Ariel were too caught up with one another to pay attention to Jackson's heavy-handed matchmaking. "I do love this song," Ariel said softly. "Would you like to . . . ?"

Maile shoved the glass of wine she was holding blindly at them, and Eve took it. The two moved away, speaking low.

Eve glanced at Jackson. "How long have you been planning that?"

Jackson shrugged. "Years. I knew they'd be perfect together."

"Do you have a sixth sense when it comes to matchmaking?"

"No. I just watch people."

"Ah."

"I know you and Gabe would be good together, for instance."

She flushed. Did everyone know the two of

them were sleeping together? So much for her ability to keep secrets. "Livvy said something to you?"

"She didn't have to. It's pretty apparent."

"He doesn't do relationships."

"And what do you do?"

Agitated, Eve took a gulp of her wine. "I honestly don't know."

"Well, maybe you should think about that." He gestured to Gabe, who was busy speaking with his sister. "I wish I'd been able to introduce Maile and Ariel years ago. Even if they share nothing more than a single dance, that's worth it. If there's one thing I've learned, it's that you shouldn't waste time not being with people who bring you joy."

"If you want to ask her to dance, do it."

Gabe scowled at Rhiannon. "If you don't stop teasing me, I'm gonna tell Mom."

Rhi rolled her eyes. She'd kept her promise to their mother and hadn't worn her hoodie. Her feminine-cut black tux had only made Sonya huff and puff a little. "I'm just saying. You're mooning over her. Go talk to her."

"I am not mooning over her." Still, he glanced at Eve, deep in conversation with Jackson.

"You like her."

"Of course I like her. I like everyone I sleep with." Their voices were hushed whispers. "I don't know why you're pushing this. You were the one who told me not to get involved with her, that it would be messy."

"I did say that, yes."

"So why now? Since I'm such a serial several-night-stand guy?"

"Did you ever think that maybe you're a several-night-stand guy because intimacy is hard when you don't tell your partner the basic things about your background and origin? When you're keeping secrets?"

He shuffled his feet, the truth of those words stinging. "Mom may have said something similar."

"I talked to Eve. She's a good kid. Sorry, woman. I skimmed her business plan too."

He ignored the pang of hurt that Eve hadn't told him about her business. "I bet it's solid."

"It is. She's going to put other ride-sharing services out of business, if she can follow through on her plans."

It was a ride-sharing service that Eve was launching? He wanted to focus on that, because it felt important, but Rhi was demanding his attention.

"It means something you told this girl things you've never told anyone else. About your dad. And your birth mom too, I'm guessing."

"Yeah." He turned slightly away from Rhi, so she wouldn't be able to tell how much sharing that had affected him, though she probably knew.

They stood next to the entrance to the ballroom. A table held the guest book, and Livvy and Nicholas had peppered it with photos of them and their families. At least two had him and Rhi in them.

Family.

He touched one frame that held a photo of a teenaged Eve. She was a little chubbier, and her sober round face made him smile. She wore an absurdly high-necked shirt, and a plaid skirt. A school uniform, perhaps. He was about to turn back to Rhi when a flash of gold on her wrist made him stop.

He narrowed his gaze at that bracelet. No.

Wait. It couldn't be. Lots of women must have that same gold bracelet. He picked up the frame.

"Gabe?"

"Huh?"

"Uh, if you're trying to sell how disinterested you are in the Baby Chandler, fondling her photo is probably not the way to do it."

He placed the frame down, but his mind was racing. He quickly scanned the other photos, and he found one taken of her and Nicholas, not too long ago. They were at a gala, and she wore a sedate and demure navy blue gown. The same gold bracelet winked on her wrist.

Anne was Eve?

He thought of the conversations they'd had, the way Anne's voice had sounded vaguely familiar. The out-of-season hood pulled up over her face. The sense of déjà vu when he'd lain on top of Eve.

The fact that he'd been attracted to Anne because she'd reminded him of Eve. Which would make sense and would make him not a terrible person . . . if she was Eve.

Eve, who wanted to start a ride-sharing service. There were too many coincidences.

"Gabe!"

"Uh-huh."

"Gabe?"

He shook his head and looked down at Rhi. "Sorry, Rhi. Uh, I have to go . . . do something." He glanced around, but Eve was nowhere in sight.

He'd find her, though. He knew where her room was.

He needed to have a talk with Evangeline Chandler.

Chapter 30

Guests were still dancing below her feet, but the party was over.

Eve eyed the connecting door between her and Gabe's room. She wanted, so badly, to open that door, though Gabe's side would be closed. They hadn't danced together once during the evening, though she'd been hoping he would ask.

She removed her earrings sedately and placed them carefully in her jewelry box. This was not a fairy tale. It was reality. In reality, she'd like to leave their affair on as good terms as possible.

What do you want?

She hesitated, and ran her fingers over the diamonds in her necklace, the cool rocks grounding her. Finally, she placed the jewelry on the table and drifted to the door. With a gusty breath, she opened it.

Gabe's side wasn't closed.

In fact, it was wide open, and his massive shoulders filled the doorway. He still wore his tux, though his bow tie had been undone. He looked as surprised as she felt. "I was about to knock," he explained, and lowered his fist.

"Oh."

"Hey," he said quietly.

Her hands shook, and she had to battle back the surge of excitement and hope she felt. This meant nothing, she told herself sternly. This meant nothing. "Hey."

He walked in, crowding her. She took a step backward, but he countered, so they were standing incredibly close. "You lost something. I wanted to return it to you."

Return . . .

Uh-oh.

Sure enough, he dangled her bracelet in front of her eyes.

She bit her lip. "Okay. So. You're mad, and that's fair."

"Not mad. Confused. Very, very confused."

"Also fair."

"You're Anne."

"Yes."

"The Anne who's been driving me around for months."

"Correct."

"You talked to me. You told me things. Hell, I told you things."

"I know." She'd told him more things as Eve, actually. "I know."

He braced his fists on his hips. "Did it ever occur to you that you should come clean about that?

Maybe when we slept together the first time? Or the second time?"

"Yes." She winced. "I mean, it did occur to me."

"So . . ."

When she was silent, his nostrils flared. "Eve, I need you to start talking."

Be honest. With yourself and him. She finally found her voice. "I liked you."

He froze. "What?"

"I liked you. I've always liked you." His silence, oddly enough, made her brave. She took a step toward him. "It was a childish crush at first, yes. You don't remember, but when I was in college I—" She blushed. It had only been a few years ago, but she felt incredibly young and foolish now, even remembering it. "I tried to kiss you."

His face was blank. She lifted her chin. "I didn't mean to hide who I was when I first started driving you. It happened. And I realized my crush on you wasn't childish anymore. It was a full-blown adult crush, and I didn't want it to stop. I liked talking to you. I liked being with you." Now that she'd started being honest, she couldn't shut up, even knowing how much pain and awkwardness was going to come when he gently rebuffed her.

That was okay, though. She could handle rejection. If she had to crawl into her shell for a bit in order to handle it, that was fine too. She'd live, and that was what was important. "I know you don't feel about me the way that I feel about you, and that's okay. I'm sorry for not telling you." She subsided, waiting.

He didn't speak for one beat, two. Finally she grimaced. "I'll go. I—" She stopped when he grabbed her arms.

"You're not going anywhere."

The gravelly words made her shiver, and she grasped for the most reasonable, pragmatic, nonromantic interpretation of those words that she possibly could.

She wasn't going anywhere . . . because he was justifiably angry at her?

She wasn't going anywhere . . . because it was really late at night?

She wasn't going anywhere . . . because this was technically her room?

His fingers turned caressing, and his gaze did too. "Eve, I'm too old for you."

"So you've said." He wasn't. Not in the slightest.

"Our families—"

"The relationships make things complicated," she said, her voice flat. She didn't need to hear any of this again.

"Yeah. Plus—"

"You're not looking for a relationship. You don't even know if you'd be good at it." She shivered. She should have changed. Her beloved dress shouldn't have to witness this. "It's fine. I got it."

"I'm glad you get it. Those are important things, and I want you fully aware of what you're getting into."

Wait. Getting into? She straightened, her heart beating faster.

"I . . . I may have kind of had a crush on you for a while too. I mean, since I met you as an adult."

"Wow."

Very carefully, Gabe placed her bracelet on her wrist, then raised her hand to his mouth and kissed it. "That dress was worth every penny you paid for it."

She rested her fingers on the low neckline. "Thank you. You look very handsome too."

His lips kicked up. He cupped her face and tilted it up to his. "Of course I remember the time you tried to kiss me when you were in college."

"You do?"

"You were a kid." He lifted a shoulder. "I mean, you were cute, but you were really young. Of course I didn't return your feelings then. It would have been inappropriate. And I never brought it up again because I didn't want to embarrass you if you didn't remember."

"I see."

"But then I met you a month ago, and I've been obsessed."

"Obsessed." Obsessed sounded not terrible. It sounded great, in fact.

"Yeah. Do you know how much I kicked myself for wanting Anne because she reminded me of you?" He raised his eyebrows. "God, Eve. I felt like an asshole."

She thrilled and winced at the same time. "Sorry."

His nostrils pinched as he inhaled. "Rhi pointed out maybe the reason I don't know how to have a relationship is because I don't normally share much of myself with other people." He focused on her bracelet, turning it this way and that. "I grew up knowing I had to keep a part of me a lie. Everything depended on that. My family's well-being, my dad loving me. I had to be funny and charming and . . . and I had to drink those damn milk shakes at the ice cream place whenever Robert took me into town, even though I hated sweets, because I wanted to spend every possible second I could with him."

"You hate sweets?" Such a silly thing to focus on, but she frowned. "You came to a cake tasting with me."

He gave a short laugh. "Yeah, I did. 'Cause I wanted to spend time with you."

She shook her head, still not processing everything he was saying. "Why?"

He gave her a slight shake. "Because I like you too. And for the first time, I wanted you more than I wanted to keep my secrets. I told you things . . . I've never told anyone else. You know everything, Eve." He lifted his shoulders. "And that's scary as fuck. Because what if you hate what's under that mask? I barely know what's under there."

She searched for the right words. This felt important and momentous, and she didn't want to screw it up. Carefully, she placed her palms on his face so she could look directly into his eyes. "Do you know what I think I've learned?"

"What?"

"Lots of people have masks. And it's not necessarily a bad thing to have those masks. Sometimes they can keep us safe." She laid her hand on his chest. "I like your mask. I like what's under it. I'd like to see more. Because I like you."

He closed his eyes, as if he were pained. "Eve," he said hoarsely.

"Yes."

He opened his eyes. "Do you know what I want to do to you?"

She trembled. "No. You should, um, tell me."

"No. Let me show you." His hand went around to the back of her collar and unhooked the button there that kept her bodice up, then drew the zipper down. Her breasts lifted with her quickened breathing, especially when he lowered the bodice and discovered the contraption that had kept her boobs lifted and separated. "This is handy," he murmured, and lifted her breasts out of each cup, one at a time, until they were raised for his mouth.

He pushed the dress down, then came to his knees in front of her. "Let me play with these for a while," he murmured, and then she stopped being able to think, because his mouth was on her flesh.

He spent long, slow moments sampling her. When she was whimpering and shifting restlessly on her feet, he finally directed her to lie on the bed, stripping her panties and the dress off as he moved lower. His mouth on her pussy made her clutch and grab at the sheets, her body tightening and releasing in waves of pleasure.

He raised his head when she came, and stood, stripping his tux off. He climbed on top of her and claimed her, his body driving into hers again and again.

When it was over, he pressed his face against her neck and licked her. She waited for him to rush off of her and away, but instead he pulled out and arranged her so she lay on top of him. "I decided what tattoo I want," she whispered. "I want you to design it for me."

"Yeah?"

"A turtle."

"Why?"

She stacked her hands and peered down at him. "I know it's not the most elegant creature, but sometimes I think of myself as a turtle. Sticking my neck out. Hiding in my shell."

He ran his fingers up her spine. "You don't think of yourself as a butterfly? Free from your cocoon?"

"No. Once a butterfly is out of its cocoon, it doesn't go back in. I'll probably use my shell. It's a part of me. Not a bad part."

"Like a mask."

She smiled, happy he understood. "Yes."

"I can design you the prettiest, tiniest turtle you've ever seen."

"Good." She moved to rest her head against him again, but he hauled her up so they were nose to nose.

"Eve?"

"Yes?"

"No more secrets. You really like me?"

Her smile grew. "Yes."

"I like you too. I like your masks, and what's under them. I like your smile when you just turn up the corners of your lips." He kissed each corner of her mouth, then right in the center. "And I like when you grin with your teeth and eyes. So I need to ask you something. I already asked Anne."

She inhaled. Oh no. This couldn't be happening. It was romantic and perfect and the way he was looking at her, like she'd hung the moon for him.

And maybe she could do just that. Maybe she could do anything and everything. Maybe she could have everything she'd ever wanted.

Maybe she didn't have to be so afraid, because sometimes, every once in a while, when the stars aligned . . . things worked out as they should.

He brushed her hair away from her face. His smile was perfect and beautiful. "Anne, Eve . . . will you go out with me?"

Epilogue

One year later

Tani Oka-Kane was happy.

Happiness was rarely guaranteed for her. It came when she least expected it, and she savored it like other people savored fine wines.

She sat cross-legged on a blanket, spread out in front of a small pond between the Chandlers' mansion and what had once been her home.

Tani looked down at the infant in her lap. The little girl's mouth was pursed into a rosebud, her lashes resting on her cheeks as she snoozed. The hair on her head was dark, her skin a lovely toasty brown. It was too soon to tell who she would take after, Nicholas or Livvy, but at five months old, Samantha Maria Chandler had already established her loud and demanding personality. Livvy and Nicholas both claimed it came from the other person.

Tani smoothed her hand over the baby's head. Her hip would protest when she had to get up, but, yes. She was happy. It was frightening, how content she felt.

Which was why she wasn't surprised when a

dark shadow fell over her and the baby. Darkness often lurked at the edges of happiness.

She tucked Sammy closer to her. "You aren't supposed to be here."

Brendan squatted next to her, his attention on the baby. He was dressed in a suit, though he had no job to go to.

At least, not at Chandler's. He'd left town after selling his half—originally her half—of the company. After Nicholas had bought his father out, with Jackson's and Eve's and Rhiannon's financial assistance, he and John had restructured the stock to ensure Livvy, Jackson, Eve, Gabe, and Kareem held equity. Nicholas and John maintained controlling interest, but the Oka-Kanes were represented in the company again. They had asked Tani if she wished to have a voice in business decisions, but she'd demurred.

The company had never been her interest. It only reminded her of her father and her husband, and the ache of those losses were still as fresh as they'd been years ago. She was happy helping Maile run her knitting business. She'd started painting again. She was busy enough.

"Did you hear me?" she asked when Brendan showed no signs of budging. "No one wants you here."

"I'm not here to cause trouble," Brendan said, and Tani had to stroke Sammy's head again to calm her worry.

"I don't believe you."

His eye twitched. She had grown up with those

eyes. At one point, she'd even thought she'd loved them. "You know I'm not a monster, Tani."

"I know you're capable of monstrous things."

"You know exactly why I did some of those things." There was a scar on his lip that hadn't been there before. Part of her wanted to ask him where he'd been and what he'd been doing for the past year, but it was a very small part.

She adjusted the blanket around her sleeping granddaughter. She had her cell phone, and could easily go back to the house, but she didn't feel fear. Only pity and resentment. "I am aware of why you think you did them."

"I loved you," Brendan said in a low voice. "I loved you for so long."

Tani looked out at the pond. Over a dozen years ago, not far from where she sat, Nicholas and Livvy had carved their initials into the bark of a tree. She'd melted when she'd seen it back then and had stopped coming to this spot, leaving it to young love. "I thought I loved you, but then I met Robert, and I knew I didn't feel even an inkling for you that I felt for him."

He inhaled. She'd been kinder when she'd broken up with him decades ago.

No one had known when they'd started seeing each other. Brendan had been so annoyed at his father's desire to join the two families, he hadn't wanted to give John the satisfaction, and she'd played along.

A small blessing. Because the second Robert had served her a cup of coffee and their fingers brushed, Tani had known who she was meant to be with.

"Regardless of how I felt, though, your love doesn't excuse how you treated Maria. It doesn't excuse how you treated your own children. Or your father." Tani thought of how exhausted and heartsick she'd been in the days after Robert's death and the fire that had taken the store. Never had she felt such despair and loneliness. "And . . . and it doesn't excuse how you treated me and my children." She hadn't wanted the store anymore, that was true, but she could have held out for more money. She could have made sure Paul was taken care of. Brendan had preyed on her when she was at her weakest. After growing up with her, he'd known exactly what buttons to press. "That wasn't love. Love is . . ." She struggled to put it into words. "When you cause pain to someone you love, it should hurt you a million times more. You never cared you were hurting me."

A muscle in his jaw twitched. "I'm starting to see I may have made some mistakes."

"Well. That's good. But it's a bit late." She smiled sadly at his stunned look. "Did you think you could come here and everything would be okay? That you could take your place in the family? You can't."

His nod was slow. "You look nice."

She pleated the skirt of the lavender silk dress she wore, carefully arranged so it wouldn't get dirty. An unusually bright color for her, but Maile had liked it. "Thank you."

"There's a wedding at the house today, isn't there?"

"Yes." She'd taken Sammy out so Livvy could get dressed. She'd have to be back soon, or everyone would start to worry.

"I would have heard if it was Eve's."

Ah. That somewhat explained his presence here. She dipped her head. "You probably would have." Perhaps it was cruel not to tell him for sure, but he wasn't her priority. "Eve definitely doesn't want to see you." Tani wanted this very clear. She didn't want that poor girl to be bothered by this man. Eve had flourished over the past year, free from his presence.

"So she's said." He reached inside his coat pocket and he pulled out a velvet box. "Can you give this to her? You don't have to say it's from me. I found it recently. It was her mother's. I thought . . . well. I don't know what I thought."

Tani's first instinct was to reject the gift, but Sammy stirred in her lap, and she softened. Eve had other jewelry from her mother, but she should have every single item under the sun to remind her she had been loved, and loved deeply. Tani accepted the box.

Brendan's gaze dipped down to the little girl. Tani didn't expect him to ask her name or to hold her and he didn't. What he did do was pull out another item, an envelope with Tani's name on it, and hand it to her. Then he stood and started to walk away.

Curious, she opened the envelope. It took her a

second to realize what she was holding, and she gasped. "How did you get this?"

He stopped but didn't turn around. "I've owned it for years. As my father would say, that's what Chandlers do, right? We look out for Okas."

She smoothed the deed, stunned. It could be fake, but it looked official enough. It listed her, Tani Oka-Kane, as the property holder on record of the house that was right next door to the property she was currently sitting on.

She looked off into the forest surrounding her, in the direction of that house. It was the house she'd grown up in. The house she'd been married in. The house her children had been born and raised in.

And the house where she'd suffered a heartbreak so intense sometimes she still woke up at night with tears on her face. "I don't want to live there. That's why I sold it."

"You have a few kids. I'm sure one of them might like the idea of living in their childhood home again."

Not Jackson, though he would visit. Gabe wouldn't accept it, though his paternity was public knowledge now.

Olivia, though. Tani imagined how her daughter would squeal in delight. Probably run right over and try to slide down the banister again, though she was a mother now herself. Tani bit her lip and folded the deed up. "I don't understand why you did this."

"No thanks necessary."

"I didn't thank you. This doesn't redeem you, you know. You can't buy redemption."

He shrugged and continued walking. She hesitated, but before he was out of earshot, she spoke. "Brendan. You may have held on to some property for me, but I'm holding on to your family. Evangeline, Nicholas. They are mine now, as much as Jackson and Livvy and Gabe. Do not dare hurt my children ever again, or I swear to God, you will see a side of me no one has ever seen."

He didn't stop or acknowledge her words. But maybe he knew: there was no need for a response to a promise.

EVE FIXED Maile's veil and smiled at her in the mirror. Mr. Perez had designed the perfect wedding gown for Maile, a glamorous confection of cream lace and satin, with a fitted skirt and a low-cut bodice that showed off her curves.

"You doing okay?" Livvy asked. Her hair was a light pink, dyed for the first time since her daughter was born, and arranged on her head in an elaborate cascade of curls.

Maile exhaled. "Yup. A little nervous about standing in front of people."

"I was too mad to be nervous on my wedding day," Livvy said fondly.

"I was worried about Kareem not being able to control R2 at our ceremony," Sadia chimed in. She was sitting at the small table in the bedroom, going over a list in her journal, trying to make sure she'd taken care of all the details for the reception following the wedding. R2, bigger but still very much a puppy, lay at her feet and wagged his tail at his name. She and Jackson had had a small wedding ceremony only a couple months after Livvy and Nicholas's.

"Gawd, all this marriage in the air." Madison checked her reflection in the mirror and puckered her lips. She wasn't part of the wedding party—Livvy, Eve, and Gabe were standing up for Maile, with Jackson in the kitchen where he was happiest—but she'd become good friends with everyone in the room, as well as Sadia's younger sisters. "No one breathe on me. Eve can go and get hitched but I am way too young for this."

"Gabe and I haven't even talked about that." Which was okay. They were both so happy and in love, Eve almost didn't want to rock the boat by thinking too hard about the future. She grinned at her best friend. "Reese *has* been looking at you kind of intensely while we've been wedding planning."

"Shut. Up."

The door opened and Tani slipped in, cradling a swaddled baby in her arms. Livvy's eyes softened as she accepted the infant. "There you are. I was wondering where you disappeared to."

"Apologies, I lost track of time on the walk." She shook out her dress, which was a slightly darker shade of purple than Livvy and Eve's.

"Sammy can make you do that," Livvy cooed. "Thanks for taking her," she said to her mother.

Their relationship had greatly improved with the buffer of a child between them.

Tani placed the diaper bag on the floor and sought out Maile, who had stood upon her entrance. "Well." She walked over and rested her hands over the other woman's arms. Slowly, Maile leaned down and pressed her forehead against Tani's. They were silent, and the rest of the room fell quiet as well, R2 curling into a tight ball.

"Thank you for being my maid-of-honor," Maile whispered.

"You were mine." Tani patted her friend. "You don't thank family."

Eve glanced at the other women in the room. Family was what they were, by blood or by choice. A messy, loud, complicated family.

Sadia cleared her throat. "Okay. It's go time."

Gabe was already downstairs, leaning against the door leading to the backyard, tall and handsome in a black suit with a lavender waistcoat. He smiled at all of them, but his eyes softened when they landed on Eve. She knew she was here to celebrate another couple's wedding, but her own love was so overwhelming she wanted to weep sometimes.

After they'd gotten over the initial bumps, life with Gabe had become blessedly easy. She never had to wonder what he was thinking or whether he wanted her. He made it clear in a billion verbal and nonverbal ways.

It wasn't a fairy tale, it was her fairy tale. Feeling was still hard, and occasionally she had to hide from all those sharp winds assaulting her from every direction. But always, when she poked her head out, Gabe was there, checking in to see if she was steady.

Like now, as he took a giant stride toward her and wrapped his arms around her waist. "You look beautiful."

She carefully pecked his lips, conscious of her makeup. "So do you."

Eve reared back as Sadia snapped her fingers between them. "Don't mean to interrupt you love-birds, but we have a wedding to pull off right now. Canoodle later."

Gabe grinned and pulled away. "Don't worry. Eve and I have this wedding party thing down to a science."

He wasn't exaggerating. This was their third trip down the aisle.

Gabe peered around her. "Aunt Maile, you're stunning. So calm too."

"Thank you, dear. I had some nerves up in the room, but they've settled. There's no reason not to be calm. I have my family and the future." Maile squared her shoulders, and Eve wondered if she was thinking about the moments ahead of her, and the moments that would come after that. They would be filled with pain, possibly, but also with joy and happiness. "I'm ready."

Gabe offered his arm to Eve. "Shall we?"

She accepted it and beamed unselfconsciously up at him. Hiding her emotions around Gabe rarely occurred to her any longer. He was so careful with them, she felt no fear. "Absolutely."

GABE WALKED past the library and glanced in, coming to a stop when he noticed John sitting by himself in front of the fire, head tipped back, forehead creased. The reception had ended an hour ago, but the house was still filled with Kanes and Chandlers, many of them staying the night. Including him.

Concerned, he knocked lightly on the door. John roused and smiled at Gabe. "Come in, come in."

Gabe hid his frown. John's arthritis was getting worse every day, limiting his mobility. Though he didn't complain to any of them, his increased pain was apparent, especially after a busy day like today.

Gabe came to crouch next to John's chair and held out his hand, palm-up. After a second of hesitation, John placed his hands in Gabe's, and Gabe gently rubbed them. John closed his eyes and released a deep sigh of relief.

They were silent for a long while, the fire crackling. "It's good to have happy occasions in this house again."

Gabe nodded, continuing his massage. "I'm sure it is."

John looked up at the photo on the mantel. It was a picture of him and Sam Oka when they were boys growing up in California, taken before Tani's father had been sent to an internment camp in Central Utah. The boys were smiling, arms flung around each other's shoulders. Nicholas had recently made sure the photo was reinstated into a place of honor in every Chandler's store across the country.

Gabe loved that photo. He could see Paul in the shape of Sam's eyes, his lips. His grief over his late best friend still ached, but like a healed wound, not a fresh one. Talking about the man regularly with the other Kanes had helped more than anything.

"Do you know what Sam says?"

Lately, every conversation with John had turned to Sam or his late wife, the older man occasionally talking about them in the present tense. Eve and Nicholas were worried, but Gabe understood. John hurt, and his memories of the people he'd loved dearly brought him comfort. Pretending they were still around wasn't harming anyone. "Nothing's over 'til you quit."

John's smile was faint. "Yes. He also says happiness isn't something you should take for granted. It should be savored, because you don't know what tomorrow will bring."

"That's a wise thing to say." Gabe worked up the man's hands, massaging his forearms.

"You could move in here with Eve, if you like."

Gabe raised an eyebrow. Eve had moved into the mansion a month ago, concerned for her grandfather. "What?"

"If you want, I would not object. You don't have to be married or anything. I understand you kids now. You love her, and she loves you." John's smile was tinged with exhaustion. "I'm going to ask

Tani to come live here, too, since Maile and Ariel will probably be traveling a great deal. The house is so large, we may never run into each other, but we could still be a family."

He released John's hands. He loved his tidy little home, with the lawn he mowed himself. Buying it had been so satisfying. The thought of leaving it shouldn't be easy.

However, this proposal, a chance to live with Eve, was so tempting he barely suppressed the urge to accept the offer on the spot.

With all the weddings lately, of course he'd thought about the future, but something stopped him from bringing up any discussion about formalizing their relationship with Eve. She was younger than him. What if she didn't want to be tied down yet?

"Think about it. Talk to Eve. You have my blessing, not that you need it." John's gaze went to the door and he smiled. "Hello, Tani."

Tani wheeled a tea cart into the room. She'd changed from her maid-of-honor dress into a plain button-down shirt and slacks. "Shall I come back later?" she asked politely.

"No, I was heading up." Gabe squeezed John's hands and stood. As he passed Tani, she stopped him with a hand on his arm, and held out a velvet box.

"Can you give this to Eve? It's her mother's. I haven't had the chance today, and it might be better coming from you."

He accepted the box, his mind still mostly on his conversation with John. "Sure."

Tani patted his cheek. She wasn't a demonstrative woman, but she did that now, occasionally touching him as if he were Jackson or Livvy. He had a mother, and it didn't mean he loved Sonya any less, but it was kind of nice to have another maternal figure in his life.

He shut the door behind him, but not before he caught a glimpse of Tani settling into the arm chair next to John. An Oka and a Chandler, under that photo. They looked right together.

Happiness isn't something you should take for granted.

He took the stairs two at a time, barely waiting for Eve to summon him in before entering her bedroom. She was sitting at her desk, tapping away at her computer. She worked a lot lately, which he didn't mind. A fledgling business needed lots of energy, and he appreciated every second they did spend together.

She glanced up, revealing her straight white teeth. She smiled like that more now, but he loved her face whether she was grinning or not. He loved everything about her. She was perfect to him.

"There you are. I was wondering where you went." She stood and closed her laptop. She was already dressed for bed in a silky nightgown, face washed, hair neatly braided. "I thought maybe you got caught up with Livvy and Jackson. You know, I met a guy at the reception tonight who remembered you from—"

He couldn't focus on what she was saying as she moved to the bed and turned back the covers. He rubbed the velvet on the jewelry box he held.

"Anyway . . ." Eve turned to him and froze. Her eyes grew wide. "G-Gabe?"

Oh. Look at that. He was on his knees.

It felt right. He swallowed. Finding the right words now was both difficult and vital. "I know we haven't really talked about the future. We don't have to get married right away. We can move in together, not move in together, have a long engagement, whatever you'd like. Evangeline Lea Chandler, I love you, though, like I've never loved anyone else in the world. I want to spend the rest of my life with you."

She gaped at him for so long he grew worried. "Eve, say something."

She snapped out of whatever spell she was under, shaking her head. "This is the most romantic thing." She came to him, her nightgown fluttering behind her. She dropped to her knees and grasped his face. "You're asking me to marry you?"

"Yes." He gestured at the floor they were both kneeling on. "Sorry. I thought that was clear."

Her smile was wavery. "Gabriel Reginald Kane Hunter, I love you too. I'd like to be with you forever."

His shoulders relaxed. He hadn't really thought she would spurn him, but it was nice to have confirmation they were on the same page. He held out the jewelry box. "I'll get you a proper ring later," he said, hastily. "This is your mother's. Tani asked me to give it to you."

Eve brushed her tears away and snapped open the box. She looked down at it for a long moment and then started laughing. When she showed him the contents, he understood the reason for her amusement.

He grinned and picked up the gold bracelet, a matching pair to the one she already wore. The one "Anne" had left in his bed. "I didn't plan this, but it seems appropriate."

"Fate," she agreed.

He placed it on her wrist, stroked her luminous skin, then dragged her close for a long kiss. His contentment overwhelmed him. With a whoop, he launched to his feet and picked her up, spinning her around as she laughed. "Thank you for sticking your neck out for me. I'm so glad you did," he whispered in her ear.

Eve wrapped her arms tight around his neck. "Me too. You're my home."

Those simple words burrowed into his soul. He thought of his family, family by blood and by chance and by choice, which was growing every day. He tightened his arms around Eve, this woman he adored. He was home.

They were all home.